THE WANTON REDHEAD

When her selfish, flighty sister leaves home following a false promise of becoming the wife of a wealthy sugar plantation owner, Alyssa becomes solely responsible for her poor, deranged mother as well as Thea's bastard son. Viciously raped, then thrown out of the family home, the girl goes on the run, fleeing her cruel rapist. Alyssa's journey takes her far from the Black Country to the wild shores of the Caribbean and puts her in the path of evil men determined to despoil the young girl. For the palm-fringed island of Jamaica is home to a pernicious trade: white slavery...

THE WANTON REDHEAD

THE WANTON REDHEAD

by

Meg Hutchinson

Magna Large Print Books
Long Preston, North Yorkshire,
BD23 4ND, England.

British Library Cataloguing in Publication Data.

Hutchinson, Meg
    The wanton redhead.

    A catalogue record of this book is
    available from the British Library

    ISBN   978-0-7505-2692-0

First published in Great Britain in 2006 by Hodder & Stoughton
A division of Hodder Headline

Published in Large Print 2007 by arrangement with
Hodder & Stoughton Ltd.

Magna Large Print is an imprint of Library Magna Books Ltd.

Printed and bound in Great Britain by
T.J. (International) Ltd., Cornwall, PL28 8RW

For Joe, a much-loved and sadly missed friend.
For the happy times we shared.
God bless.

Prologue

She had to do it!

This was a chance that would never come again! Auburn hair streaming in a breeze that pressed a thin cotton dress against long colt-like legs, the slight figure ran across the open heath.

But if she could not make it happen!

If she were saddled with a child!

Thoughts clanged like the passing bell, the impact of them bringing the flying figure to an abrupt halt.

That would mean the end of everything. If this one opportunity were lost, this one straw Fate was holding out to her was allowed to pass her by, would be to condemn her to a life of misery, a life such as her mother had lived in a poky terraced house back to back with faceless rows of the same.

To live a lifetime as she lived now, sharing a yard with eight other houses, the families of four of them using the same wash-house, the same water pump ... the one privy...

Looking to where the winding wheel of Spindrift Colliery rose black against the vermilion of a cloudless sky, Thea Maybury's pretty young face twisted with repugnance.

That wheel rode the sky like the chariot of death and that was what it brought to many of the people living in its shadow; death to men choking

11

their days away in the black bowels of that coal mine, children sleeping top to toe in beds shoved into rooms whose very air was laden with the dust of the coal they were forced to help drag from the earth, children who coughed with the sickness of the lungs that digging also brought. A life of torment and grime was what she would have, a life many women of Darlaston lived working until they dropped, then every night asking the Lord to keep them from falling with yet another child.

Breath catching in her throat, Thea's nerves tightened. Spindrift Colliery! It was aptly named. Every dream dreamed by men who passed within its black mouth, every dream of women who toiled pulling coal-laden bogeys from the pithead soon spun away; drifting mists of dead hopes.

That was what the child would bring to her.

Staring at the spirals of smoke rising from the chimneys of the houses built simply to serve that colliery, Thea Maybury anxiously twisted the cloth of her cheap skirt.

It would ruin everything, bring an end to her own dreams; they too would be lost like spindrift melting in the first rays of a summer sun, taking with them all she had longed for every day of living in that hovel of a house, what she had prayed for every night – and now that prayer had been answered, the chance she yearned for was offered and to let it pass…!

Disturbed by her presence a bird flew up from among the rough tussocks of grass, its song spreading over the quiet evening as it rose to meet the sky. Watching it glide effortlessly, graceful wings etched dark against the brilliance of a setting sun, Thea felt her heart lift. Fate which had offered the dream now offered the solution.

Thea watched the bird, its wings feathering the air holding it where it wanted to be. As she must hold to what she wanted.

To let it pass... She smiled beginning to walk on. No, she would not let it pass, she would not lose the dream ... not even if it meant dropping the child down a mineshaft!

'You've got to help me, 'Lyssa, you are the only one I can turn to.'

Thea Maybury watched incomprehension become disbelief on the face of the young woman sat on the edge of a narrow iron-framed bed.

'You've got to, you do see that, don't you, it's the only way.'

Stomach nerves taut, Thea broke her pretence of a sob, threading the void of silence. 'Lyssa was not going to agree ... she would not ... but she had to be made to agree!

Beneath the cover of another sob Thea Maybury's mind worked like quicksilver. The offer which had been made to her had come like a gift from heaven; it was all she had ever wanted, a new life in a new country. She would no longer live in near-poverty, no longer skivvy carrying things to market, making do with the cheapest of clothes. She would have her own fine house and all that went with it... Thea Maybury would live like a lady.

'No one will ever know.' Allowing yet another false sob she crossed to a corner of the tiny room where she rested her hand on a chest of drawers

13

before proceeding. 'Nobody will think twice, it won't matter for you, after all it's not like you have...'

Not like you have anyone interested in you. Alyssa Maybury finished the sentence in her mind. Alyssa the older sister, Alyssa the dowdy sister, Alyssa the girl a man never looked at once he had seen the pretty Thea.

'You must see,' Thea persisted, paying no mind to the hurt she saw before those other eyes were lowered, 'this is the only way, the best way.'

Best for all of them or best for Thea? Alyssa could not prevent the thought rising beneath the hurt. Her sister had always been self-centred, the world must not simply revolve around Thea, it must revolve *for* Thea.

'This way I can help more with Mother than I can by taking stuff into town.'

Stuff! Alyssa's fingers clutched the bed's cold iron frame. That was all it was to her sister. Not for Thea the stitching which helped keep a roof over their heads, not for her the back-breaking hours of tending vegetables they sold to the kitchens of Darlaston's wealthy, and certainly not for her to assist in the caring of a sick mother.

Across the narrow space dividing the bed from the chest of drawers Thea felt the weight of hesitation. Alyssa had not answered, she hadn't uttered a single word ... and when she did would that word be 'no'? But it couldn't be ... she would not let it be; there were ways and there were means and if one failed then the other must be tried.

'Don't say no, 'Lyssa, please...'

14

Breaking long enough to force a fresh sob, she pleaded. 'This is what I've hoped and prayed for, you can't let me lose it now, you can't!'

You can't! Refusing to be held back thoughts ran wild in Alyssa's mind. This was the way it had ever been between them, Thea doing exactly as she wished, the blame for any mischief it might cause being left to lie heavily on her sister's shoulders. Always the responsibility had been placed with her. 'You should have watched her' ... 'You should have taken more care of her.' That had been the way of their mother; she could never bring herself to accept there was any fault in her youngest child. But then Thea had always come first in their mother's affections; the delicate, pretty red-gold-haired Thea must have the new dress, Thea lifted to a mother's knee each evening, Thea who must not be burdened with any but the very lightest of chores, Thea who could do no wrong.

But Thea had done wrong and now in typical fashion looked to her older sister to take the blame, to carry the guilt. This though was too much. Alyssa's fingers clutched even tighter against the cold iron. She could not do what her sister was asking. It was morally wrong, a sin against a child and a sin against God; she would not help, not this time.

'No.' Looking to where the slight figure waited, Alyssa shook her head briefly. 'No, Thea, I can't...'

The scarlet-gold of the dying sun filtering through the small square window caught the blue lightning flash of Thea's eyes, her answer spitting the flame of anger.

15

'Can't!' she snapped. 'Can't or won't! Oh, I see why you refuse ... you haven't been offered the chance so why should I have it! That's the truth of it, isn't it? Oh yes, that's the truth all right, you are jealous, you have always been jealous of me, admit it, Alyssa, you have always been jealous!'

Had she always been envious of her sister? Alyssa felt the mental slump as she acknowledged the grain of truth the answer to that accusation must contain. Yes, childhood had been a time of envy and so many times a sadness. Not so much an envy of the lovely red-gold curls and pretty face, not even of the new dresses with their ribbons and bows their mother had sewed. That she had learned to deal with but the sadness of not being shown that same love, that special love which had always been Thea's. Yes, it was the love their mother had lavished on her younger daughter which the plain Alyssa had longed to experience; her mother's love she had wept for in the dark hours of night, prayed for the length of each day, but when evening came it was Thea lifted to their mother's lap, Thea held close to have her head stroked, hers the face receiving the last gentle kiss when put to bed: it was that, only that...

'Admit it!' Anger bruised the silence. 'Admit it, Alyssa, give the devil his freedom!'

Sharp as a blast of cold wind stripping trees of the last of their leaves the outburst blew away the shadows of guilt and for the first time Alyssa faced that which she had known for so long, known yet refused to know: for Thea it was Thea, it would always be Thea and nobody but Thea; in her sister's eyes only self was of any consequence.

16

'Give the devil his freedom.' Calm despite the emotions churning her mind, Alyssa looked at her sister, at the pretty face twisted now with temper and frustration. Always in childhood and even to this very evening she had drawn back from that look, allowed Thea her own way, but now all of that was gone. Thea must face her problems, own to her responsibility, accept the results of her actions. 'Give the devil his freedom,' she repeated quietly, 'that is what you have always done, that is what you did a year ago...'

'That's not true, I was forced...'

'No.' Alyssa shook her head again. 'Mother may have believed your story but I never have. You behaved then as you have behaved all of your life. You fulfilled your own desires, took what you wanted, gave freedom to the devil that sits inside you, the devil of selfishness; but you forgot that demon gives his own rewards and he has given you yours. You knew what you were doing that day just as you know what you are about now, what you are always about, Thea, getting your own way, making things suit you ... but not this time. Yours was the sin and yours must be the carrying of it.'

Across the room a slant of sunset touched red-gold hair lending a halo of flame.

That was how saints had been portrayed in those pictures which as children she and Thea had been shown at Sunday school, holy men and women their heads crowned with haloes of gold.

For the briefest of moments Alyssa was back in the small rectory room of St Lawrence Church gazing in wide-eyed awe at the paintings of

17

people spoken of as the Blessed Apostles, of Saint Anne and her daughter the Virgin Mother of Christ, their calm serene faces captivating her young mind.

'I should have known that would be your answer...'

A toss of bright head threw a thousand gold-tipped slivers of light showering the gathering shadows like tinder sparks. The accusation snapped harshly in the gentle quiet broke Alyssa's reverie and once again it was her sister she watched. No face of gentle saint, no tender loving smile painted those delicate features, they were the look of anger that part of aggravation which, from their earliest years, heralded a fit of the sulks should Thea be opposed in anything. Then as quickly as the storm of temper had threatened so it cleared.

But Alyssa had seen this same swift cessation of anger many times and always it had proved a prelude to another of her sister's wiles. This was not an end of demanding; it was not in Thea's nature to give up before gaining the last little bit of what she had set her mind to.

Across from Alyssa a fresh cascading of light danced like fireflies in the tiny room, a last gift of the disappearing sun touching a blessing to her sister's head. Watching her now, the delicate features no longer wearing the mutinous look of aggravation, the tightness of temper no longer pulling at the pretty mouth, Alyssa thought again of the painted saints. Yes, her sister was beautiful but there was a saying about beauty being skin deep...

Alyssa caught the thought before it could go any further but she could not prevent the sudden rush of feeling in her heart, a feeling of pity. Why? She tried to reason the emotion; surely her sister, the strong-minded, beautiful Thea, needed no one's pity?

'I should have known...' Fireflies fluttered with Thea's brief shake of her head. 'I should have known what you would say but despite your reason being pure jealousy, of your wishing to see my life ruined, of wanting me to lead the same life you will always lead, a soul-destroying poverty-ruled existence, I realise that ... yes, it is best I clear this matter myself.'

Lowering her hand to a half-opened drawer of the chest Thea looked at the sister she had always been able to manipulate. The hair was the same, maybe a shade or two darker, the gold glinting among the rich heavy folds forever dragged back from the face which though not as pretty as her own, yet held a certain attractive quality; but it was the eyes, those dusky winter-violet eyes that had the real beauty, a beauty compelling enough to ensnare any man should her sister but try. But 'Lyssa did not try. 'Lyssa was not given to slipping away at every opportunity and she, Thea, had never encouraged her to. It served very well having her stay at home. Getting on with the business of earning their living meant no encumbrance on herself, instead it allowed that liberty which had ever been indulged to its fullest. In the softening shadows of approaching night the tightening of Thea's mouth remained imperceptible. Liberty! That was the one thing she craved over all else, release from the yoke of living hand to mouth, to escape the smoke and dirt of Darlaston ... of the new fetters threatening to bind her! Her hand closing on the edge of the drawer, she breathed the sharp breath of resolution. She would never wear those chains ... never!

Alyssa had watched ... was watching. Deep inside Thea laughed. The sister she had always so easily twisted round her finger would do her bidding yet again.

'Thea!'

Edged with concern, the call merely had Thea's inner smile deepen, yes, 'Lyssa would do as demanded.

'Thea, what are you going to do?'

Lifting a blanket-wrapped bundle from the open drawer, Thea faced her sister and now that inward smiled etched her lips. The battle was almost won!

Eyes brilliant as the minute lances of light sparkling in her hair, Thea shook her head in affected sadness. 'Do?' she echoed. 'Exactly as you said I should, face up to my responsibility.'

Concern becoming a needle-sharp prick of anxiety, Alyssa watched the smile, the cold glitter of eyes fastened on her own. This was a Thea she had not known before. A girl who had never accepted the results of her foolhardiness was now accepting consequence? No! A trip of nerves told Alyssa there was something else behind this sudden acquiescence, something infinitely alarming. Her sister had never tolerated denial and instinct warned she would not do so now.

'But you of all people, 'Lyssa, should know

what I am *not* going to do!'

The very quietness with which it was said, the calm, even tone smooth as frozen ice added frissons of fear to Alyssa's tense nerves as she glanced at the bundle held in her sister's arms then at the face which gleamed an awful triumph.

'I am not going to allow this...' Thea gave a shake to the bundle, '...this mistake to ruin my life, so I shall get rid of it. You have no need to worry, no one will ever find it ... but should you find yourself thinking in those hours when sleep refuses to come, then remember I told you... I told you nothing would take this chance from me. Remember also that you were as responsible as I, for you sat there knowing all the time I would throw this ... this nuisance ... down the first pit shaft I came to.'

1

'*This nuisance down the first pit shaft I came to...*'

There had been no hint of subterfuge, no attempt at deception, only that ice-bound hardness of the eyes, the look that had said I will do it.

Standing in that same bedroom Alyssa Maybury looked back as she had so many times on the happenings of that night three years ago, the night her sister had vowed to kill her own child rather than forgo the offer of a life of ease and luxury.

'...*the first pit shaft...*'

Those words had rung with an undeniable truth, a truth she had not dared reject and one Thea had taken advantage of. She had simply placed the six-month-old baby back into its bed of a pillow laid in the drawer of the chest and walked from the room. With no other word, no kiss for the child, no goodbye to their mother, she had abandoned her son, turned her back on her family and left to join her new-found benefactor.

How could she have done such a thing! Deep in her secret heart Alyssa felt the bite of contempt she tried so hard to fight against. It was more charitable to ask how could Thea *not* have done as she had? Indulged by a mother, smiled on by a father too workworn and weary after hours of slaving underground at the coalface for twelve hours at a stretch to do anything else, she had come to expect her slightest whim must be fulfilled, using a sister to cover misdeeds that occurred more and more often as they progressed through childhood. But no sister could cover that misdeed which had left Thea pregnant.

Braiding her thick auburn hair Alyssa stared at her reflection in the aging mirror hung on the wall above a rickety washstand, a reflection which as she watched seemed to change, to become the face of a younger girl; vital and alive it glowed with pleasure.

'*I can't describe the feelings...*'

Thea's mouth laughed from the mirror, Thea's eyes sparkled.

'*You don't know what it's like having a man hold you in his arms, to feel the warmth of him...*'

A flush of heat accompanying the memory of those laughing words burned scarlet on Alyssa's cheeks. How could Thea even think such things? But Thea had not only thought, wrong as such thinking was, she had spoken them and those words had lived on, they still came in the night whispering in the darkness, drifted in with the dawn, came with every unguarded moment of the day, reminding, embarrassing ... shaming.

Yes, she felt shame ... shame at having listened to those words and shame for the sister who had gloried in what they had conveyed.

'...it was wonderful...'

Try as she did Alyssa could not fight off the onslaught. Fingers trembling she let the braid of her hair fall to her shoulder, her gaze fastened mesmerically on the face laughing back from the speckled mirror.

'I can't tell you how wonderful, 'Lyssa, the touch of his naked body on mine, the thrill of his manhood entering me, there can't be anything ... not anything ... to compare with what we both felt.'

'But it is wrong, Thea, it is sinful–'

'No ... no it isn't!' Thea's answer had cut away the reproof. 'It is a delight, a rapture which sings in every vein; there is nothing more desirable than lying with the man who loves you.'

'How can you be sure ... how can you know he is not just–?'

'Playing with me?'

Electric-blue eyes flashed confidence.

'I feel it in his touch, in his kiss, I see it in his every look. There is no pretence, how could there be when we both feel the same pleasure? He loves me, 'Lyssa.'

'Thea, please...'

Spoken aloud the half-sobbed words fractured the image and Alyssa once more stared at her own face.

She had been so sure. Braiding left unfinished, Alyssa turned to her bed. Her sister had been so certain, so trusting. But the man who had given so much of himself to Thea, given the pleasure she had said was so ecstatic had not given her his name; no marriage had followed their enjoyment of each other.

Cool against her flushed skin the worn cotton sheet provided some comfort but in her mind thoughts burned like braziers.

It had to be admitted as truth her sister may have thought her lover would marry her, had genuinely believed he would make her his wife, but the weeks had gone by with no mention of marriage.

Oh, why had Thea been such a fool! Alyssa's fingers tightened on the sheet. Why could she not have seen that had marriage been his intention they would have wed in Darlaston, taken their sacred vows in the Church of St Lawrence with her mother and sister present to witness them? But he had insisted they wait and Thea had not questioned, blinded by the promise of a new life, a life which held the fulfilment of all her dreams. But had it? Or was the same thing happening again?

A little while longer, just two more rows of potatoes to hoe and she would rest. Head throbbing from yet one more sleepless night, her bones aching from hours of digging and planting vegetables, Alyssa wiped the back of her hand across her brow, brushing unruly curls from her eyes.

Life had been so different before...

Straightening she looked to where the huge winding wheel of Spindrift Colliery shadowed the huddle of houses.

Her father and brothers had worked there and though it was hard, demanding labour they had done it without complaint and the wage they brought home, though small, had been enough. Her mother had smiled in those days, had sung quietly as she went about her chores; they had been happy.

Then came the disaster.

Eyes half closed against the daylight, Alyssa looked again at the past, heard the cries of women, her mother among them, as they ran to the pit gates.

There had been an explosion deep underground. Standing beside her mother, twelve-year-old Alyssa had heard the terrified catch of breath, seen the blanching of the frightened faces as the news was broken to the waiting women.

Subterranean gas had been ignited, possibly by a spark from a pickaxe striking at the coal seam, and the subsequent explosion had caused some of the coalface to fall. But, 'how much had fallen and whether any of the men were injured could not yet be ascertained'.

The explanation given by the colliery manager had sounded so impersonal, almost uncaring. Only years later had she come to recognise that calmness at that moment had been essential if the women were not to panic. And they had not panicked but had stood quietly, lips moving on silent prayer. Through the night and on into the day they waited, her mother telling her she must care for Thea until the rescue was completed and her father and brothers were home.

And they had come home.

In the near-distance the wheel began to turn. That was how it had turned that day.

So alive was the picture formed in her mind Alyssa felt again the fear which had vibrated throughout every household.

The wheel had turned all of that day bringing up fallen coal that must be cleared so survivors could be reached. Then men had been brought to the surface. Blackened head to foot, coal dust dried onto congealed blood, men and boys had stood in the iron cage with broken limbs. Cageload after cageload and finally her father and brothers.

They had come home.

Watching the great iron wheel slowly notate, Alyssa remembered.

First her father. He had led his sons home as he had led them to work but this journey was different. There was no banter, no joking, no talking of the hoped-for favourite meal of faggots and peas; just a silence. Silence which followed along the street and into the house. On doors hurriedly taken from their hinges to act as stretchers, workmates still caked in the debris of that explosion had carried Thomas her father, Mark her eighteen-year-old brother, Luke just sixteen, Benjamin barely fourteen and then James the eldest at twenty. A girl he had hoped to wed had cried out at seeing the crushed figure but their mother had made no sound. Helped by neighbours she had washed broken limbs, sponged caked blood and dirt from each body and dressed it in Sunday clothes before placing pennies on closed eyelids and one more in their hand. For a week the five had lain in the shuttered fireless house, a week in which friends came to pay their last respects, and throughout it all their mother remained locked in her dark world of grief. Only at the graveside had that awful silence been broken, broken by screams as she threw herself at the plain wooden boxes which held her life. They were screams Alyssa could hear still, her mind was filled with them ... but the laughter? There had been no laughter that day of the funeral so why was it here with her memories?

'Stop...'

Had she said that? Was she so tired she didn't know thought from sound? Frowning with confusion Alyssa swept her brow again then her hand dropped to her side as she stared towards the house.

The laughter she had heard was real, the frightened cry had not been her imagination but that of a terrified child. Unable to comprehend the reality of what she was seeing she stood a few moments longer. It couldn't be!

Her mind was playing tricks! But as the second cry rang on the quiet morning air Alyssa realised the truth and with the hoe she had been using gripped tightly in her fingers she began to run.

'It be time to set the water to warming, Thomas and the boys will be wanting their meal when they comes from the pit.'

Oh, not now ... please not now!

Nerves strung so tight they twanged, Alyssa turned from the child she had at last settled to sleep.

'It's all right, Mother, everything is ready.'

But it wasn't all right, things would never be all right again. She must not cry! Fingers clenching 'til pain stung, she swallowed hard on the tears filling her throat. If she allowed them to start they may never stop.

'Thomas be finishing of his wash ... the meal must be set to the table.'

This was how it had been since the explosion at the mine had killed her father and brothers. The shock of it had been too much for her mother to bear and as a result her mind refused to accept the truth; she still lived in yesterday but her daughter lived in today... with all the pain and horror it held.

She must not think ... must not give way!

'The meal is all ready for eating, Mother.' She crossed quickly to the thin worn figure reaching towards the kettle hung above the fire. 'I did exactly as you said, faggots and peas with fresh baked bread.'

'Thomas be coming...'

'Soon, Mother ... he will be home soon.' Softly spoken the lie lay bitter on Alyssa's tongue. But it was the one way she had found to soothe her mother's fragile mind. 'Rest for a while.' She guided the fretful figure upstairs. Undressing her, slipping on her nightgown then settling her mother into bed as she would a child, she could no longer hold back the tears. Why must these things happen? Her mother's mind broken with sorrow, herself...

Choking on the memory rising like a black tide she stumbled to her own room.

David ... it had been David she had heard cry out, his small body huddled into itself as two men on horseback had cracked riding whips above his head. It had been their laughter she had heard, laughter which had rapidly become lewd.

She had run to stand beside the child, one hand holding his face hidden in her skirts, the other trying to ward off those whips with the hoe.

'*Leave him alone,*' she had shouted above the crack of leather, '*he has done nothing to you.*'

They had reined in the horses but a whip sang close against her ear.

'*He doesn't have to do anything!*' One of the men had snarled, shaking the thin plait of leather about the shoulders of the trembling David. '*His presence is enough; in fact it is too much ... such as that should not be allowed to live, they are a blight to the eye, a scum to be got rid of.*'

'*Then get rid of him.*' The second rider had smiled coldly. '*You don't have to put up with anything which displeases you; kill it as you would any vermin, the girl also, the world can only benefit by ridding it of whores.*'

'*I am not a whore!*'

The answer she had hurled had been countered with a sneering reply. '*Not a whore ... you who have a child clinging to your skirts yet no ring on your finger! I say you are a whore and that blind thing holding to you is your bastard.'*

'A whore!' Brown hair glinting in the pale March sunlight the first man had rested his whip hand on the pommel of his saddle, his eyes narrowing as they roved the length of her. *'Now if that isn't just what a man needs.'*

'If you want it then take it.' The cold smile still played about the other man's mouth. *'How could a slut mind, after all you won't be the first to ride her, a whore who takes all-comers will hardly refuse a man of quality.'*

'Well then, we mustn't refuse her, must we?'

Stood in the shadows of her darkened room, Alyssa fought to curb the scene playing so vividly in her mind but still it came. What moments before had been amusing to those men had soon died, the laughter in their hard eyes had vanished leaving in its wake the heat of lust and they had both dismounted ... dismounted and–

Pressing a clenched hand against the scream erupting in her throat she ran from the bedroom, her feet clattering on the bare boards of the narrow staircase, her mind aware only of the nightmare rising from the depths.

One rider, the taller of the two, had thrown aside the short whip reaching towards where she protected the child. *'Go.'* She had pushed the boy from her. *'Go, David.'*

They had made no effort to prevent his stumbling towards the house, but her... Oh God ... her...!

Trembling, each thought a fresh assault, she took the kettle carrying it into the scullery tipping its contents into the tin bath she reached down from the wall. She had washed and washed again, scrubbing her body over and over, the sting of hot water and carbolic soap as nothing against the sting of memory, but for all the scrubbing the horror stayed with her; the smell of sweat in her nostrils, the touch of hands grabbing, kneading her breasts, the red-hot pain of hard flesh thrust deep into her.

The brown-haired man had caught her by the shoulder, his free hand knocking away the hoe then as she struggled he had hit her hard across the temple. Half unconscious from the blow she had fallen to the ground, her senses only fully returning as he had thrust himself into her.

Great sobs rising from her stomach, Alyssa rubbed the kitchen scrubbing brush between her legs, wincing at the bite of coarse bristle against lacerated flesh.

He had raped her

Breath caught by choking sobs coughed back across the quiet night-bound scullery.

The brown-haired, hard-eyed man had raped her then had invited his companion to do the same. She had cried out, tried to rise but the brown-haired man's boot had caught her on the chest, knocking her once more on to her back, a second kick at her ankles pushing her legs apart.

He had come to stand over her...

Eyelids pressed hard down Alyssa tried to shut out the picture.

Not as tall as his companion, his hair once dark was greying like mist over newly turned earth, but it was the eyes ... they had not been filled

31

with the carnal heat, the lust she had seen in the eyes of the first man; those of the second rider so dark they were almost black had glittered an insensibility, a cold, unemotional disregard of any suffering he was about to impose; his was a look of passionless cold-blooded cruelty.

They had stared down at her those cruel, inhuman eyes, stared as he had reached down to grab one breast, squeezing it until she had cried with pain, then one boot lashing into her side had turned her facedown, his companion laughingly urging him to enter her. Then she had felt the touch of him, of that same hard flesh being brushed back and forth across her buttocks. He would have raped her, brutalised her a second time had not a shout echoed over the stretch of open land.

Disturbed at their pleasure they had sworn loudly but had ridden away ... ridden away leaving her to lie in their filth.

It had to wash away!

Sobs raking the silence, Alyssa dragged the stiff brush across her stomach and breasts, pressing it deep into raw bleeding flesh as if she would scrub her very mind clean of all memory of what she had been subjected to.

It had to wash away!

But she knew it would never wash away. What one man had done to her and that which a second man had intended would remain with her all of her days, a brand burned so deep nothing would even erase it.

The thought hitting her like a stone, Alyssa's trembling legs gave way and she slumped to her knees, water splashing over the sides of the bath to settle in puddles on the quarry-tiled floor.

'A man of quality!'

He had said it as though rape by such a man was a mark of honour. But from this day Alyssa Maybury would be shown no honour, no respect. The shout which had driven those men from her had come from someone who, while she had run into the house locking the door behind her and therefore avoiding any meeting, had obviously witnessed her rape.

But was that how it would be reported in the town? Would the people of Darlaston believe instead that she had been a willing partner?

A whore!

Both hands covering her face, her body folding tight into itself, Alyssa gave way to the desperation inside her.

2

She had to go, she had to deliver the vegetables if they were to have money to buy milk and bread. But having to face the people of the town, people who might already have been told, who might think her a whore. Alyssa looked at the small cart her brother James had made so many years before, a cart made for his sisters to play at horse and carriage. But as with all things with Thea it was she had done the riding while others of the family – mostly her sister – did the work of the horse.

Why had there been no word from Thea, no letter to say she was safe, she was happy? These questions and many more had plagued in the weeks following Thea's departure, weeks of wondering. Could the absence of any letter be the result of her sister being so full of happiness, of discovering the benefits and delight of life as the wife of a wealthy sugar-plantation owner be so time-consuming she had not yet found a moment to spend on writing to ask of their mother ... of her son?

Or maybe there was some other cause. Alyssa piled potatoes she had dug and washed clean onto the cart. Had Thea been taken ill during the voyage to that new country and so needed time in which to recuperate? But then could not the man responsible for taking her away from Darlaston have written or even paid someone else to write? But there had been nothing. Thank God their mother did not know of her younger daughter's abandonment of the family which had loved her.

Alyssa's fingers stilled on the last potato. She had never thought to be grateful for the terrible affliction which had taken the mind of Hannah Maybury, thankful that every day took her further and further from reality; but now, knowing what she did, Alyssa repeated in her heart those silent words of thanks.

But the condition of the mind brought on by the accident which had taken the lives of husband and four sons had gradually worsened, bringing a need for almost constant attention, a need only attended to by one daughter. It had not been so bad those first years. Their mother had been able mostly to cope with life but then despair had taken its toll until sadness had become depression and then an instability of the mind for which the doctor had said there was no cure. Yet their mother's sickness had no effect upon Thea. The remaining years of childhood had been spent like all of her years, doing exactly as she pleased; then reaching teenhood, the time when understanding was expected Thea had not changed. She had refused to help with the caring of their mother saying she could not stand any sort of sickness. But that was not all she had refused. She had talked less and less with the mother who had so loved her, had eventually flatly rejected Alyssa's requests she spend some time with her until finally not speaking with their mother at all.

Yet that evening some three years ago she had gone into that room. Was it Thea had thought words would somehow penetrate the veil lowered over her mother's mind; had it been she thought that way to alleviate the guilt her own reck-lessness had brought?

'*It wasn't my fault, Mother...*'

Cart and vegetables momentarily forgotten, Alyssa watched the mental image memory was casting over her mind, heard the confession wept by a girl knelt beside a bed, a confession so different to the one told her sister.

'*It wasn't my fault, honest it wasn't...*'

Caught by a scene alive only in her mind Alyssa's eyes remained unseeing of the cart.

'*...he forced himself on me...*'

The vivid red-gold hair had dropped hiding the

pretty face in the bedcover.

'...*Believe me, Mother, I am telling the truth ... only the truth, honest...*'

Honest! Alyssa swallowed as she had swallowed while watching her sister, while listening to words she knew held no truth. There had been no honesty in Thea, not that evening nor at any other time.

'...*he forced himself on me...*'

Soundlessly the repeated words ran on as echoes in Alyssa's mind.

'...*He said he would kill me if I screamed, that if I wished to live I must do as he said. Oh, Mother, you know I would never lie to you.*'

That had been the biggest lie of all. Alyssa seemed to see the slender figure emerge from that bedroom, the pretty face wreathed in the triumphant smile her sister had so often worn when the shifting of blame from herself to someone else had met with success, and with the image came the feeling, the mixture of sympathy and contempt that memory always aroused; sympathy for a mother who no longer possessed full power of the mind and contempt for the confession she knew to be a lie.

Of course their mother would have believed, just as she would have believed the man said to have raped her younger daughter was a stranger, a man Thea's confession held to say could only have been passing through the town because though she had searched for him, wanting him made to acknowledge his action, he could not be found.

Bending to take the handles of the cart, Alyssa stared across heathland cringing beneath a heavy threatening sky.

A stranger! A man Thea could not find! That too had been lies. Her sister had not been raped. The man responsible for her pregnancy had been no stranger.

The breeze playing loose strands of hair across her face seemed to hold within it the sounds of laughter; Thea's laughter when later she had once more told the nearer version of truth in the bedroom they had shared, telling without trace of shame how she and her lover had lain together not once but many times, how they had shared the pleasures which should only be shared between man and wife, how they had both revelled in the game they played.

'...I can't describe the pleasure...'

Lying on the bed her arms raised above her head, Thea had gloried in her sin.

'...I can't tell you the thrill his naked body gives me, the feel of him, that need which becomes a fever in the blood, a rapture which steals the mind, an all-encompassing passion only the thrust of his hard flesh can assuage; there is nothing to compare with the desire of it and it is a desire we shall satisfy so many more times when we are married.'

But the game they had so enjoyed, the rapture they had shared, had ended abruptly. There had been no marriage for Thea; the man who had made her pregnant had disappeared leaving the child he had fathered to be born a bastard, a child she had left without a qualm when opportunity had beckoned. The son she had claimed belonged to her sister.

And what if there should be another bastard

child? Alyssa's grip tightened painfully on the handles of the small cart.

She had not been a willing partner, she had enjoyed no rapture and the fever in her blood had been that of fear. So different an experience to that of Thea, but like her there would be no marriage, no man to own to his responsibility ... only one more fatherless child.

'I'm sorry, Alyssa wench, but that be the way of it. Word come from the owner this mornin' and I has to abide by it.'

Weary from delivering fresh vegetables to Deepmoor House, a round trip of some four miles and then delivering to Miss Harriet Nichols' gown shop in Horton Street a blouse she had sat long into the night to have finished for today, Alyssa looked at the man standing in her mother's living room. He had been known to the family since her birth; he had been one of the men caked in blood and dirt who had helped bring her father and brothers from the bowels of the earth when ignited gas had brought the coal seam crashing in on them, then had helped carry their broken bodies home. Now he was here to tell her she and her mother must leave.

'I don't understand, Mister Richardson.' She frowned, her mind still not having taken in what he had said. 'We have paid the rent regularly ... we do not owe the colliery a penny.'

'I knows that, wench, but it ain't a matter of money ... well, not money as be owed.'

'Then what!' Tiredness had Alyssa snap the question.

'Seems the owner been 'aving hisself a mite o' thinkin' and has come to the conclusion it don't be of benefit to the pit having folk as don't be a'workin' there livin' in houses belongin' of it.'

'But my father and brothers worked there...'

Elijah Richardson accepted the offered tea, sitting with it at a table he knew was scrubbed white beneath a threadbare chenille cloth. 'That be well known, Alyssa wench.'

'...And Mister Marshall said after the accident that we would have this house for the rest of our lives ... you know that also, Mister Richardson, you heard him say it and so did half of Booth Street.'

'I 'eard it.' Elijah Richardson nodded.

He knew the promise. Elijah sipped the tea. It had been given to each of the families of the men injured or killed in that disaster.

'It has been eight years since my father and brothers died, eight years and never once has there been mention of us having to leave this house, so why now?' Still bemused Alyssa shook her head. 'Why has Mister Marshall changed his mind now?'

It was hard for him being the one to bring this news to the family of a man he himself had grown alongside, a man he had ever respected but he too had a family to keep and to have refused the task would see him with his tin in his hand and also out of a home.

'Why is Mister Marshall doing this?'

The question again. It was one he must answer. Setting his cup aside Elijah Richardson shook his head. 'Ain't Mister Marshall as made that

39

promise be the one who now be a'breaking of it, that be down to his nephew, him bein' the heir ... you knows the old master died a week back...'

'But his promise didn't die!'

He could see fatigue in the young face, the weariness of being responsible for a mother whose mind was failing and of caring for a young child her flighty sister had rejected; but worse than tiredness was the fear shining brilliant in tear-threatened eyes, the fear of being turned onto the streets. But behind that another deeper fear ... Alyssa Maybury seemed afraid of something more.

'There 'as been more'n a few changes along of the pit,' he answered, his voice low with sympathy. 'More put out of their jobs by reason of bein' thought too old to swing a pick, an' that meanin' they, like yourself, be out of house an' home; the Turners along of Beard Street be already gone into the Poor House an' it don't need no guessing that there'll be more a'followin'.'

John Turner, a man who had lost a leg in that mine explosion! His wife Mary who had scrubbed and cleaned for the Marshalls until rheumatism had her limbs so painful she could scarcely walk! The Poor House... Alyssa felt her heart twist. A place where man and wife were separated, not allowed even to sit together ... it would be a sentence of doom for them.

'How can Missis Marshall allow such a thing to happen, how can she be so heartless!'

'We can't go a blamin' of her.' Elijah answered what he knew was a cry as much of fear for her own family as pity for the Turners. 'What be

40

'appening don't be none of the mistress's doing; Spindrift Colliery an' all that goes along of it be the property of her husband's nephew and it be his deciding as to the runnin' of it, he it be who says who will work or won't work, him who says who will stay on in a house or who—'

'Who will go into the Workhouse!'

Rising to his feet Elijah Richardson took the dust-laden flat cap he had thrust into the pocket of his jacket before entering the house, using it as a means of not meeting eyes he had seen sparkling with fear. The wench had more than enough to try her without this new burden being laid on her shoulders. He had tried telling Marshall's nephew of the promise made by his uncle, tried also to explain that folk such as the Turners had no place other than the Poor House to turn to, but the answer had been 'those who could not work would go ... and any who questioned the word of the new master would also go'. That had been the end of asking for leniency; friends, even life-long friends, had to look to their own family first. That was what he had been forced to do though the hurt of it stuck like a rock in his throat.

'Like I said...'

'I know, Mister Richardson.' Alyssa answered quickly, the hands twisting the cap telling her the turmoil of feeling in the man. 'You have to abide by that man's decision as we all must. I bear you no hard feeling and I know my mother would say the same if ... when I tell her.'

That were a blind, a cover to mask her mother's illness. Hannah Maybury's mind were too far gone to reason who or why; but it were loyal of

41

this wench to include her as though naught were wrong. It were a pity Thomas Maybury hadn't fathered two the same instead of one who had run off with the first man who didn't know her for what she was.

It was no more than thought yet the gist of it showed in the look lifting to Alyssa.

'You 'ave ever been a good daughter to your mother.' Elijah Richardson's answer was gruff with emotion. 'I knows your father would 'ave been proud of you. That be all I can offer you, Alyssa wench, that an' the asked-for blessin' of the Lord, may He do for you what I cannot.'

'*May He do for you what I cannot.*'

Alyssa stared at the empty space where her visitor had stood.

Had the Lord seen fit to restore her mother's mind? Had He answered those prayers which begged sight be given to the eyes of a child born blind? Had He turned a man from rape?

A sob rattling from the deepest reaches of her stomach, Alyssa covered her face with her hands.

She had believed so implicitly... had put all of her faith, all of her trust in the teachings of Church and Sunday school which had said heaven listened to prayers of the heart.

Painted pictures and plaster saints! That was all they were, all that heaven had ever been for Alyssa Maybury.

'*May He do for you what I cannot.*'

The echo of Elijah Richardson's parting words had Alyssa drop her hands, her teeth clenching against a fresh sob.

There would be no help for Alyssa Maybury!

3

It was over. Her life here in Darlaston was done. Alyssa watched the last contents of her home loaded on to a low-backed cart.

She had spent a week asking in every place in the town for work and every place had given the same reply. There was no work that carried a place to live; no house, not even one room.

Securing a chair, knotting a length of rope to hold it fast, a stockily built man paused to look at the young woman watching from the open door of the house he had emptied of every last article. 'That be the lot, you be sure now there be no piece you wants the keepin' of?'

That had been her father's chair. Alyssa stared at the cart. That of all it held was the one thing she would have kept, the chair she would kneel by when fetching pipe and tobacco for her father, kneel there with his hand resting on her head. Had he known her unhappiness? Her feelings of never being so loved by her mother as Thea had been?

'If there be summat you wishes teken off, summat you wants to 'ave along of you for memory's sake, then point it out an' I'll tek it from the cart.'

'No...' Alyssa blinked away the pictures rising in her mind. 'No thank you, there is nothing I wish to keep.'

'You be sure now? It'll be too late once I be gone.'

'I am sure, but it is kind of you to ask.'

'Don't cost naught to ask.' The man shrugged. 'But folk usually teks a thing or two just as a reminder of the past...'

She would need no reminding of what had happened here in Darlaston; how could it ever be the past when it would live with her every day?

Seeing the involuntary shake of her head and taking it as a final refusal the man finished knotting the rope then climbed aboard the cart calling, 'Then I'll be a wishin' you good day.'

Twenty-one years of life gone in less than half a day! Alyssa watched the laden cart rumble away. It held every part of her existence, every part except memories and they would be with her forever.

'You mind me now, Benjamin, stay close to your father.'

How was she to manage? The sound of her mother's call to a son alive only in her own tortured brain had Alyssa draw a long helpless breath. A three-year-old child who was blind and a mother whose mind was more lost every day! David she had been able to keep with her having him sit in the cart or on the grass near by while she worked the vegetable plot, but a fully grown woman could not be held to one spot, and that meant returning to the house more and more during the working day to ensure her mother's safety ... and more often in these last weeks she had found her gone from the house wandering the streets, 'a fetchin' o' the boys' dinner'.

Releasing a trembling breath Alyssa stared at the piece of ground in which vegetables still awaited harvesting. This had been their living. Difficult as it had been to manage digging and planting whilst caring for David and her mother she had managed, but like the contents of the house the vegetable plot could not be taken with them. It would have to be replaced ... but with what?

'Ride in the cart ... me ride in the cart.'

Lost in her own misery she had not heard the small figure come to stand beside her in the doorway but with the tug at her skirts she swept the boy into her arms. Soon he would outgrow the cart, she would be unable to leave him playing on the grass; and her mother...?

Arms tight about the child she loved so dearly, Alyssa fought tears lurking near the surface.

How would she find work when it was no longer possible to leave her mother even for a few hours?

'Each of the houses are now available for occupancy by new tenants?'

'All of 'em, sir ... just as you ordered...' Elijah Richardson bit hard on the rest of what he wanted to say: that he had followed the orders of a heartless bastard who he hoped would rot in hell for his cruelty. Instead he asked, 'Will you be wantin' the properties painted afore folk moves in?'

'Painted?'

'Ar, sir. Mister Marshall he always had the practice of seein' every wall an' ceilin' of a house were given a fresh coat of whitewash afore any new tenant were allowed in, said it med the place fresher like.'

'Let us get things clear, Richardson.' Cain Lindell looked up from a paper he had been studying. 'I am not Mister Marshall, that man is dead and so are his practices. *I* own Spindrift Colliery and all the properties pertaining to it and I say if a tenant wants walls and ceiling whitewashed then, so long as he does the work himself and buys whitewash with his own money, he can paint as many as he wishes. Now, reallocations...'

He hadn't so much as mentioned any of the folk he had ordered put from their homes. Elijah Richardson watched his new employer run a finger over the list of properties recently vacated. It didn't matter to this man that old couples had been put into the Poor House, that they would live apart the rest of life left to them, that others too crippled to work would be left to beg; to Cain Lindell nothing mattered but money.

'This one...'

Having dealt with each property in turn, giving tenancy to those families with the most members of working age, making it a clause of that tenancy that any over the age of sixteen years would carry extra payment of rent, Cain Lindell tapped a finger against the paper.

'This one, number forty-one Booth Street, it also is vacated?'

'As you said, the folk be gone.'

'Hmmm.' Cain Lindell's lips pursed as though he thought deeply. 'My aunt tells me the father was killed in an explosion at the mine some years back...'

Him an' a few others. Elijah's reply was silent.

'She also tells me there is a young child, a blind boy...'

He must not seem over-interested, this man might have the appearance of a clod but a sharp brain lay beneath that cap. Lindell kept his glance on the paper.

'She says also there are no menfolk to support the family, is that correct?'

Elijah knew he must answer. 'Was four lads. They all worked the main seam, all of 'em were at the face when that explosion 'appened.'

'Were they all killed?'

He was goin' all around the Wrekin askin' that which without a doubt he'd asked already. If his aunt 'ad told him anything at all her would 'ave told him that! Thoughts becoming needle pricks of suspicion Elijah nodded.

'All of 'em, I helped carry 'em home.'

'The widow...? I am presuming there was a widow.'

'Hannah.' Elijah nodded again.

This was like extracting winkles with a pin! Cain Lindell's patience began to wane.

'This ... Hannah,' he snapped, 'was she also employed at the Spindrift?'

Why 'adn't his aunt given him answer to that one! Elijah met the sharp gaze lifting from the paper, his reply a flat 'no'.

'Was there any reason for the woman not being employed there?'

Why the interrogation? There had been not one enquiry concerning the other folk been thrown from their homes so why the interest in these? Unless...! A worm of anger began to wriggle in Elijah's stomach.

'Hannah sewed linen for Deepmoor; I would

47

'ave thought Missis Marshall to 'ave med mention o' that when tellin' the rest.' It was a barb he could not resist throwing and the look flashing in cold black eyes said it had struck home. Good! Elijah smiled to himself. Let the smart-arsed bugger think on that!

He could dismiss this man on the spot, take away his living, his home, destroy his life with a word and very probably would ... but first the answers to his questions. Cain Lindell masked a now rapidly rising irritation.

'Sewed?' He asked instead. 'Does that imply she is no longer in service there?'

'Hannah were not rightly in service, her sewed for other houses as well as Deepmoor, her were helped in that by her two daughters.'

'The young woman with the auburn hair. Yes, come to think of it my aunt did mention them, she said how satisfied she is with the mother's needlework and asked they be allowed to stay on in Booth Street. I have no wish to deny my aunt so you may tell the woman she and her daughters can return to the house.'

Cap set firmly on his head Elijah strode across the colliery yard towards a line of bogeys ready to offload their tons of coal into the barges waiting at the canal running alongside the Spindrift.

'...*no wish to deny my aunt*...'

The words had almost had him laugh in the man's face. Were the Holy Virgin Mary herself Cain Lindell's aunt he would still deny her anything which wasn't to his liking ... and the new master of Spindrift Colliery had liking only for money; money and–!

48

He had not been mistaken in his beliefs. The worm of anger rose to Elijah's throat. He had not been wrong in thinking Cain Lindell to have been one of the men he had watched ride away from that vegetable patch and now Lindell had certified that suspicion as fact. He had been a mite too smart! Had Missis Marshall said anything at all about Hannah Maybury then it would have been to say the woman's mind had failed following the loss of her husband and sons … also that only one daughter remained to care for her, the other having run off leaving her sister to care for a child with no father to own it. Money! No, that were not all Cain Lindell had a liking for, he had a liking for rape and it could be that liking were thinking to be indulged again!

'Tell the woman she and her daughters can return to the house.'

Entering the winding shed Elijah paused but his mind ran busily answering thought with thought.

All of those questions, why? The answer were there for the seeing and it were no clearer than it were in Lindell's final words. That bastard had no concern for Hannah Maybury, his only reason for saying her could return lay with the daughter who would be returning along of her. Lindell's so-called wish to please his aunt were naught but a blind! But Elijah Richardson wasn't blind, nor were he fooled.

Lifting his cap Elijah ran the fingers of one hand through his hair, a gesture he did when perplexed.

The men he had seen, the one who had risen to his feet as the shout had echoed over the heath, had that one also raped Alyssa Maybury...? Had

49

he already carried out that vile act or had he just been about to do so? Whichever way it seemed the swine had intention of repeating it.

'*...tell the woman she and her daughters can return to the house.*'

Replacing his cap, Elijah's mouth firmed.

That was something he would never do!

4

'You knows what this be saying?'

Alyssa glanced at the sheet of paper being waved at her then at the man who held it.

Slightly stooped shoulders and hair peppered with grey evidenced he was no longer young but that was the only deferment he made to the advance of years. Hands, though workworn, looked strong and the eyes which watched her were clear and penetrating.

'The envelope was sealed when it was given me and you saw that seal was unbroken when I handed it to you. Should you think I am lying you have only to ask Mister Richardson.'

'You claims you don't have the knowing of what this be about yet clearly you knows the sender.'

'*Me dad says should you be goin' by way of Wednesbury would you tek this along forrim.*'

They had left Booth Street coming almost to Catherine's Cross when Elijah Richardson's young son had come running up to them panting the words Alyssa now heard in her mind. The distance they had walked was not great, her mother's constant stopping to call to her dead husband and sons, to call for Thea, the daughter she imagined to be at her side, was already having a tiring effect and Alyssa had accepted the letter thrust at her without question; only later deciding the town of Wednesbury would be as good as any to search for somewhere to live. But the few miles separating it from Darlaston had taken nearly the whole day. Urging her mother to walk on, and carrying David who, unusually fretful, refused to ride in the small cart, had combined with the worry of finding shelter for the three of them taking its toll of her strength until now, faced with this man's ingratitude and scepticism as to her honesty, the fragile thread of patience broke and tired eyes flashed their anger. 'I know it was Mister Richardson's son asked me to bring that letter to this house; as for the sender I can only rely on your testimony that the signature is that of Elijah Richardson. I have done what a good friend of my family asked and now–'

'Wait!'

Halted by his call Alyssa saw the man's glance take in the boy now asleep in her arms, the older woman with her waist circled by a cord which in turn was fastened to the wrist of the younger one before his look returned to her face.

'Wait,' he said again, 'Elijah be my brother, he tells of friendship with your father, he also tells you might be a' needing of help finding a place to settle.'

Frustration and weariness had had her take the cord from her petticoat and fasten it about her

51

mother to prevent her wandering away but how long could they remain tied like this? Alyssa glanced at a sky purple with approaching night. And who, seeing them arrive roped together like oxen, would give them lodgings? If indeed Mister Richardson had written what was said then it was no more than the truth, she was in need of help.

'It'll be a task findin' of a place tonight.' The man followed her own glance. 'Another half hour the night will have the streets dark and you being a stranger to the town will mek finding some-wheres other than a hostelry that much harder, and hostelries don't be no place for women on their own.'

Especially one with an ailing mother and a young child. Alyssa's mind supplied the words the man facing her clearly thought yet did not say. But thought was not going to find them a place for the night and neither was this exchange of words with a man she did not know.

'Set the bucket to the fire, the menfolk will be wanting their bath. Thea, my little love, put the plates to the table, you does it so pretty.'

'Don't need no explaining.' Voice soft with sympathy the man glanced at the thin figure pulling against the cord. 'I've seen this sort o' thing more times than man should be med to see it; this town be sister to Darlaston with the coal mining; like that one Wednesbury has its share of disasters an' many a wife an' mother has suffered the loss of husband and sons, that loss tekin' her mind along of it; you mustn't mind my knowin' ... brother talks to brother an' Elijah told me of your father an' brothers being killed in the underground

52

explosion along of Spindrift Colliery.'

And had brother told brother of one daughter's bearing of an illegitimate child ... had he made mention of another seen lying with one man straddled across her while a first fastened his trousers? Had he spoken of a whore!

'Forgive the saying, wench,' the man spoke on, 'but don't seem like them two be up to trekkin' much further and neither does yourself. If it be you trusts the word of Elijah Richardson's brother as to you being safe in this house then you be welcome to rest the night 'neath his roof.'

It had been an offer she could not refuse but the night spent sat before a well-banked fire had not afforded the longed-for rest.

Allowing the delicate cloth she was repairing to lie on her knee Alyssa stared through a small window looking onto the hill upon which stood the time-blackened church of St Bartholomew.

David's fretfulness had worsened until afraid his crying would awaken the man who had given them shelter she had rocked the boy in her arms until daybreak. But dawn had brought no respite; hot and feverish David had tossed and cried, then frighteningly had become still, falling into a deep dreamless sleep. She should have been comforted that at last he slept but instead a worrying fear had settled over her. Had he caught a chill while they were crossing the heath? Was it some sort of fever taken from water they had drunk from a brook? Each thought more frightening than the one before she had held the child close against her breast, only her mother's restless cries having her lay him down for a few minutes at a time.

'You can't go dragging a sick child about the town looking for a place.'

Joseph, Elijah's brother, had argued against her leaving, pointing out that though she had money from the sale of her mother's household effects nevertheless a hotel was no place in which to nurse the boy.

Perhaps she ought not to have listened, ought not to have allowed herself to be persuaded. Her head resting on the back of the chair, Alyssa let her mind carry her back across the months since that day.

She had stayed, grateful for Joseph's assistance in providing cool water and cloths with which she had sponged the small hot body, of his preparing food and cajoling her mother into eating while she herself had held David close, afraid that if she laid him down he might never wake again. But long hour had passed long hour and throughout them all she had murmured to him of rides in the cart, whispered of his stroking the cows they had passed on leaving Darlaston, yet not once had those pale eyelids fluttered. Then as evening had threatened the sky with darkness Joseph had gone for the doctor.

'*How long has the child been ill?*'

Eyes closed, Alyssa listened to words she heard nightly before sleep came.

'*He was fretful yesterday, I thought perhaps he was cutting some back teeth.*'

The doctor had looked up from examining David.

'*Yesterday! Why was I not called then?*'

He had listened to her explanation, making no question of it and asking only had the child suffered this way on any previous occasion.

'*Yes, several times...*' she had answered, watching the hands move gently over the little body.

'*...whenever he has been teething he has been fretful, crying from the pain of it, but that was the natural way so all of the mothers in Booth Street assured me; but none of those times did he fall into such a deep sleep.*'

He had made no response to that, just his gentle fingers lifting pale veined lids to look into eyes of the same deep hyacinth-blue as Thea's.

'*How long has he been blind?*'

The question so quietly spoken had come unexpectedly. How could he know of David's blindness? Unable to see what it had to do with that feverishness and now this deep sleep she had frowned saying he was born sightless.

He had put away the listening tube he had held to David's chest, closing the black leather Gladstone bag he had carried with him into the house shaking his head at her own worried asking was this illness the dreaded measles?

He had not answered immediately, his glance going first to her mother who was calling out to her sons telling them it was time they were off to the pit. When he had returned it to her it was full of sympathy.

'*The boy does not have measles.*'

It had brought a swift surge of relief, the feeling of a weight being lifted from her; she had spent yesterday and all of the night fearing David had caught a chill and today had come the dreaded thought of measles. She had known so many children die from that awful disease and though she had found no trace of the telltale spots behind the ear or elsewhere yet still the fear had throbbed in her: but now it was gone, her beloved nephew was safe, it was as she had guessed, a painful cutting of back teeth. She had fastened David's clothing, wrapping him once more in her own shawl before smiling her relief at the man now risen to his feet.

'It is not measles...'

A shake of the head had interrupted her thanks.

'I am afraid it is far worse than that.'

Hands tightening on the soft cloth, Alyssa's eyes remained shut as if she would blot out the rest, but as always it came whispering into her mind, cutting into her heart.

The deep sleep David had sunk into was termed a coma. The doctor had touched a hand to hers, a look of pity in his grey eyes as he continued to speak.

'The child's blindness is, I believe, the result of a tumour resting on the optic nerves; the intermittent bouts of feverishness are most probably due to the expansion of that tumour touching the brain...'

He had paused as though waiting for her to say something and when she had not he had gone on.

'It is a malignant growth which will continue to enlarge. I am afraid there is no way of preventing that; it will press more and more on the brain...'

He had withdrawn his hand but his kind eyes stayed with her.

'My dear, you must know, the resultant pain also will continue to increase until the child is in agony.'

She had cried out then, bent her head over the boy in her arms as if to shield him from the world, from the pain it would hold for him, the rest of the doctor's words coming as from a great distance.

'...*that is why you must see the infection of the lungs, the pneumonia, as a blessing. The boy is not strong enough to fight it... I'm sorry.*'

The rest had left her in a kind of half world, a place where she could see and hear but was not a part of; a place which threatened to close her away entirely.

'...*as I say, think of it as a blessing. This way your son will not know a pain that would be unbearable.*'

There was no cure, the doctor had explained gently. Though the Lord had given the medical world skills enough to overcome many illnesses He had not as yet seen fit to impart the knowledge and skills needed to remove a tumour from the brain.

'*The Lord had not seen fit.*'

Eyelids lifting, Alyssa stared at the church steeple rising black against a pale sky.

How many times had she heard those words? How often had she listened to women murmur it to others crying against the pain of bereavement, heard it when disease had swept the town leaving so much heartache in its wake?

Beyond the window a puffball of white cloud touched the spire. Watching it drift, Alyssa could not but liken it to her life. Happiness for her had been brief, fleeting moments brushed away by a mother's preference for one daughter over the other, a mother who never seemed to see the hurt in a young girl's eyes, to hear her quiet sobs in the night; joy had been swept away from Alyssa Maybury's life as breeze swept away that cloud.

'*The Lord had not seen fit.*'

Long-held pain rose again.

He had not seen fit to have her mother love two children equally. He had not seen fit to save her father and brothers. He had not seen fit to keep her mother's mind whole... He had not seen fit to allow David life!

'*The Lord had not seen fit.*'

Tears stinging like gall in her throat she took up the cloth jabbing the needle hard into the delicate fabric.

'*...your son...*'

David had not been her son but she could not have loved him more had he been born of her own body, yet she should count his being taken from her a blessing! Where was heaven in all of this, where its mercy?

She stabbed again with the needle, the prick of it against her finger no match for the stab in her heart.

Pictures and Plaster Saints! She would never call upon them again.

5

'I tells you I think it be shameful, how her can show her face among decent folk while her be livin' along of a man old enough to be her father...! It don't be right, it don't be right at all!'

'I knows what you means, Eliza, an' while I don't never speak ill o' nobody I must say I agrees with what you says, a young woman a carryin' on like her be ... her ought to be ashamed.'

'Trollops like her don't know the meanin' o' shame!'

There had been no attempt to lower their voices. Coming from the churchyard where she tended the tiny plot of ground which held the child she had loved as if he had been her own, Alyssa drew her shawl closer about her head. It took no measure of thought to decide who it was those women standing at the church door were talking of, who it was they were condemning; they were speaking of her. But wasn't that often the way of things, people arriving at conclusions without asking any questions, determining the character of a person they had not even spoken with.

Shawl drawn tight beneath her breasts Alyssa tried not to look at the two women staring in her direction. It had not been the first time she had heard such words but each time the vilification grew worse.

She should have left this town immediately after the burying of David but it had seemed that by doing that she was leaving him alone and three months ago the pain of that had been too raw.

'It shouldn't be allowed!'

A few yards from the graceful sandstone doorway a thin woman dressed in black bombazine coat, its folds spreading over black skirts which brushed the ground stepped in front of Alyssa. Sharp blackbird eyes glaring from behind a fine black gauze veil attached to a bonnet perched atop grey hair.

'...nor will it be for very much longer.'

'Sayin' be one thing, Eliza, but doin' be summat different altogether; I mean we can't just order ... an' if it be as her mother be sick...'

'That be no more than a tale put about to cover them carryin's on!'

As thin and sharp as the figure they came from, the words rang on the mild spring evening.

'...a tale her and Joseph Richardson thinks will put folk off suspecting the truth ... that her be his whore!'

Whore! Alyssa stopped in her tracks. Had that word been used of her in Darlaston? Had it followed her here?

'I says that be what her be, why else would a man share his home with a woman this town ain't never seen afore? Well, I tells you this...'

The vehemence of her words cut into Alyssa sharp as a sword slash.

'...I tells you it won't go on for I intends to mek it my business to see trollops like you an' the one you reckons be mother to you be sent packin'. Wednesbury wants none o' your sort, you be an insult to decent women.'

'That be true, Eliza, Wednesbury don't be wantin' the likes o' them, but you knows Joseph Richardson same as I does, he won't go tekin' notice of what we says.' Dressed as severely as her companion, a woman of slightly stouter stature clutched a Bible in black-gloved hands.

'Mebbes he won't.' Behind the flimsy gauze Eliza's almost non-existent lips tightened into a vicious line clamping on every word, but that did not restrict a spite which flowed like a stream. 'But he will listen to Amelia Bancroft. Once her be informed as to what be tekin' place beneath her very nose, that this here trollop an' the one not daring to show herself be livin' in property belonging of the Hall then both them dirty no-goods will be havin' to find somewheres else to play their sinful games ... and so will Joseph Richardson should he try arguin' with Bancrofts.'

'...*the world can only benefit by ridding it of whores...*'

Suddenly he was there again, his dark cruel eyes burning into hers, his black hair overlain with grey, his hard malicious mouth swirling that same evil non-smile, the man who had been about to brutalise her that second time. Fear of that day still so vitally alive in her, Alyssa gasped, then turned to run down the path leading from the church, the bite of stones through the worn soles of her boots lost amid the deeper pain of those remembered words pounding her brain.

Whore...! Whore...!

Each syllable like a physical blow it slammed in her mind. That was what those men had thought her, what those women thought her. It was what the whole world would think her when her child was born– the child!

Halted as if caught by some unseen hand, Alyssa stared out over the stretch of open land fronting the house in which she and her mother had found refuge.

Joseph! She frowned as for the first time she realised the situation his kindness had placed Joseph Richardson in. The child she was carrying, the child of her rape, it would certainly be thought the child of Joseph Richardson.

She could not let that happen, she must not let him carry the blame of another man's actions. They had to leave now, tonight, she and her mother, that way the mistress of Bancroft Hall must believe Joseph had simply offered a sick woman a place to rest and with she and her daughter gone would not penalise Joseph by evicting him.

On the rim of the sky the last rays of the sun spread streams of scarlet-gold edged with purple and grey. In another hour it would be night ... where in so short a time would she find a roof for her mother to lie under?

Cain Lindell held one hand to his brow to shield his eyes from a sky filled with the flames of a setting sun. He had thought of her several times during his stay at Deepmoor House. She had a compelling something ... beauty? Yes, but not the artificial paint-pot variety he was used to; that girl he had been about to rape, hers was a freshness, an innocence not simply of the body but of the mind, it had shone from those eyes. Dusky violet eyes, red-gold hair, and had she been a virgin! That would have brought a small fortune, it was a pity she was not ... but then even damaged goods found a market and that girl most certainly would.

It was quite a comfortable living he had carved out for himself and so long as he was careful to offer employment and living accommodation only to girls whose families were so poor they would thank God for the opportunity offered, and would not think twice as to why it should be offered to a daughter of theirs. and with a letter signed with her name being sent home occasionally then why would they question?

Yes. He lowered his hand. He had himself a very lucrative lifestyle ... one which this addition would bolster very nicely.

But would she be willing to leave her bastard behind? But then what did that matter? He smiled, touching a heel to his horse. Bastards, like worn-out whores, were easily got rid of.

The smile still touching his mouth he rode into the yard of Spindrift Colliery. It had been fortunate for him Laban Marshall had fathered no child of his own, and even more fortunate he had died when he had.

Dismounting he ignored the boy running quickly to take the animal's rein and lead it towards a brick building across the yard from the winding shed, Marshall's stable ... except it no longer belonged to Laban Marshall, neither did a stick or stone to be seen for miles in any direction, nor that which lay below sight beneath the ground. Coal! The smile deepened. Black gold was a name often given to those lumps prised from the belly of the earth and that dragged from Darlaston would bring him the wealth if not of a king then certainly that of a lord; and Cain Lindell would live like a lord.

'You be doing what?'

'Leaving, Joseph, we are leaving Wednesbury.' Alyssa turned to help her mother, tying the corners of a woollen shawl about the thin shoulders.

She had walked away from that church with the words of those women ringing in her mind. That was how she was thought of here, how she would always be thought ... a whore.

She had not returned directly to this house but had gone instead to the pawnshop she had noticed on visits to the town to buy sewing threads, and there had purchased the shawl, a skirt and a warm coat for her mother. The pawnbroker had not sold cheaply but even so she had had to buy that clothing; she could not risk her mother getting that same infection of the lungs which had taken David.

'So where is it you be havin' a mind to go?'

The shawl tied, Alyssa reached for her own. She had known he would ask and all the way back from that shop she had tried to think of an answer but none had come, nothing but those spiteful words.

Trollops like her don't know the meanin' o' shame.

Loud as the bells of the church beneath whose porch they were spat they had kept all else from her mind, all else except for the realisation she and her mother must no longer remain in this house, they must not jeopardise the living of a man who had shown them both nothing but kindness.

'I asked where is it you be having a mind to go?'

He would not be put off. One thing she had learned from their first meeting, Joseph Richardson was a man unworthy of deception and she would not lie to him now. Resigned to the truth Alyssa held the shawl in her hands.

'I...' She hesitated, 'I don't know.'

'Then if you can't tell me that p'raps you'll tell me this ... how?'

'How?' Perplexed she repeated his word.

'Ar ... how?' He said again. 'How be you going to get your mother any place ... be you going to carry her? 'Tis certain her won't be able to walk many miles and that that there cart of your'n don't be big enough for her to ride in, so then, how be you thinking her to manage?'

She hadn't! She had not thought of anything other than taking them both away, of removing any further embarrassment from Joseph.

'There be no chance for you to go answering for I can see for meself you have no answer.'

'See you washes all over, you hear me, Benjamin, don't go thinking to get away with a cat lick ... James, there be a clean shirt ironed and airing here afore the fire...'

'There be your answer should it be you still haven't thought.' Joseph lowered her back to the one armchair the room boasted, then looked again to Alyssa. 'Ain't just a place to live you'll need look for, but employment along of it ... and the sort which will enable you to stay by your mother's side a' caring of her. While you be doing of that, work might not be easy come by.'

'The meal be to your liking, Thomas?' Hannah smiled at the man only she could see. 'I made the faggots fresh this morning and there be a basin of pig's chawl set in the larder along of taking to the pit tomorrow, I knows how you likes a bit of pressed chawl with new baked bread along of midday.'

'You sees what I mean?' Joseph touched the

65

older woman gently on the shoulder. 'You couldn't go leaving her by herself.'

No she couldn't ... but neither could they stay here. Oh, why had Elijah sent his son to chase after her, why had he asked she bring a letter here to Hall End? But that was one question that need never torment by having no answer. Elijah Richardson had acted from friendship, as his brother had acted from kindness.

'Tek your mother to her bed.' Joseph eased the shawl from Alyssa's fingers. 'There be time to talk of leaving come morning.'

Time to talk come morning. Stirring the sleeping fire with an iron poker, Joseph stared into its heart. And time for him to find out what it was brought the heartache he so often caught in that girl's eyes. A lost child, a mother whose mind was gone? That were enough to cause anyone heartache, yet deep inside he knew there was something more, something set to drive this girl away.

'I have a secret, something my pretty little girl doesn't know...'

Hannah had stood smiling to herself while Alyssa had dressed her for bed and now she smiled again looking into the mirror as her hair was braided.

'...it be a secret will bring a smile, but then your little face be ever wearing of a smile, that lovely angel face.'

'Tomorrow, Mother, you can tell your secret tomorrow.'

Tying off the long grey-threaded braid, Alyssa took her mother's arm guiding her to the bed they shared but as she made to settle the bed-clothes over her they were pushed aside.

'Fetch the pot which be alongside the candles in the scullery.' Hannah laughed softly, the imagined pot twisted and turned in empty hands. 'I've been a saving of this … see it, my little love…'

She had seen this same thing so many times before. Alyssa watched the hand stroke a head which she knew was not hers, watched the smile she knew was not directed at her. It was Thea her mother spoke to, Thea that smile was given to.

'See…'

Hannah laughed again, a soft laugh full of love, a laugh which stabbed Alyssa's heart with the sharpness of a blade. Even now, in those moments where her mother spoke to her daughter, that daughter was Thea.

'I've saved this, 'tis to buy the cloth for a new dress, cloth the colour of those lovely eyes … my darling will go to the Goose Fair looking as pretty as a princess.'

They had both been taken to the annual Goose Fair and both had worn new dresses. Her mother now sleeping quietly, Alyssa began her own preparations for bed. Their father would not have one daughter dressed with new and not the other … but he could not make a mother's love for her daughters equally deep.

She had tried so hard, tried to hide the pain, to tell herself her mother was not being unkind … that Thea being the youngest of her children was the reason she was cosseted, but none of that reasoning had stemmed the tears inside, none had taken away the hurt.

James had seen, James who had made that cart; had there been something in his early years had him know the same hurt, had he experienced that same withdrawal of love? Was it with his growing he had learned to live with it, to not let it hurt and so expected it would be the same way with her?

She had lived with it.

Heavy folds of hair partly plaited, Alyssa's fingers stilled.

'I learned to live with it, James,' she whispered, 'but I don't know how to stop it hurting.'

6

She had not thought him to be away so long.

Alyssa looked at the parcel she had wrapped neatly in tissue paper. She had hoped to deliver the pretty lace-trimmed organdie dress on her way out of Wednesbury ... to have gone to say goodbye to David. That would be the hardest, leaving him to lie in a town where no one knew him, where no one cared; but she could not take him with her except in her heart and there he would always be, always loved.

She had held him the night through, held him as the last tiny breath had ended, held him until the touch of death had the little limbs stiff and the face pale as marble. She had not wanted to let him go; it seemed if she held him, sang softly to him, the life would return to that small cold body; it was only when Joseph had gently asked might he hold the boy she had released him.

How had she lived through it? How had she stood the pain which had ripped her very soul? Yet she had stood it.

Joseph had helped with advice but kind as he had been he could not carry out the process of registering the death.

Remembering it now Alyssa saw again the look of distaste on the face of the registrar when she had said David's father was not known, the look of disbelief when she had said the child was not her son but her nephew. The man had sniffed through pinched nostrils, his quill pen scratching at the certificate he wrote before pushing it at her then snatching the money it required.

That had been another two shillings and sixpence from the money left from the sale of every stick and piece of her mother's furniture, of crockery and linen.

'I be flooded wi' stuff...'

The words of the dealer in second-hand goods sounded once more in her mind.

'...be a good few folk wantin' to be rid o' furniture an' the like. I'll 'ave a job sellin' o' this like as not, so fifty shillin' be the all of what I can offer; I can't go a tanner above that ... tek it or not as it suits.'

Two pounds ten shillings! Alyssa stared at the tissue-wrapped parcel. The cloth and lace it held would account for more than that, yet two pounds ten shillings accounted for all her parents had ever possessed ... accounted for their lives!

It had had to suit. They could not leave Darlaston with no money at all. But those shillings had dwindled so quickly.

There had been the doctor's fee of five shillings, another twelve for the small coffin. She could have a cheaper one, Mr Webb the undertaker had talked kindly with her. A plain coffin without lining or brass plate would not be so expensive. Maybe it had been guilt had her spend so much, guilt for being unable to provide the child much of anything except love. David had known nothing of worth, no real comfort in his brief life but he could lie on padded satin for eternity. So she had thanked the undertaker then asked for the costlier version.

Then there had been payment for the church. She no longer had the faith of her childhood, heaven had turned its back on Alyssa Maybury and she would not call upon it; but was it fair of her to impose the same upon a child who as yet had no understanding? A child far too young to make his own decisions? She had wrestled with the problem coming at last to the decision she must not deprive David because of her own feelings.

So she had taken him to that church.

Her glance going to the window she stared at the mass of the building blackened with age and with the soot of iron and steel factories, of houses jammed hard around them, all with chimneys belching smoke.

There had been no house-to-house collection, no neighbours putting their penny or tuppence into a man's cap then given to offset the cost of a funeral as had ever been the practice among the folk of Booth Street; no one come to pay respect, no children bringing posies of wild flowers they had picked themselves nor any family but herself to walk with that tiny boy to his last resting place, no male next of kin to wheel the coffin along the streets then carry it into the church.

'Let me do it, wench, let me carry the little lad.'

It seemed she heard Joseph's quietly spoken words again and quieter still beneath them the ones which had immediately whispered in her mind.

Perhaps subconsciously she had known then the effect Joseph's accompanying her to the church might have upon his reputation among the people of the town, perhaps even then she had wanted to protect him from slander; so she had gone alone.

'...me ride in the cart, 'Lyssy, me ride in the cart.'

That had been the silent whisper, the words which had followed Joseph's. They had brushed against her heart, reached into her soul, a request she could not deny. David had loved to ride in the cart while alive ... he would ride in it one last time.

She had gone to the rectory, spoken with the Parish priest. He had listened patiently, his eyes as they watched her showing none of the condemnation those of the registrar had shown. He understood her wish not to have the kindness of Joseph Richardson imposed upon a moment longer than absolutely necessary, therefore he would conduct the service that same evening.

She and her mother had gone to the heath together.

Alyssa's glance reached past the church to rest on the open land which was covered with a carpet of scarlet poppies, foxgloves and deep cornflowers spreading out from Hall End Cottage.

She had hurried back from her meeting with the priest. Thanking Joseph who had spent his afternoon break sitting with Hannah, she had taken her mother with her to the heath. David's grandmother would have a part in his burying. Hannah had not known the reason of that collecting of wild flowers. Lost in her unseen world she had talked with her dead husband and sons, whispered to her 'pretty little angel', her hand moving as though stroking a head. The memory a knife thrust, Alyssa's breath caught on the sob she choked back. Her mother was lost to her as David was.

It had been a mild day, the cold winds of March relenting in their usual wildness. The heath had not boasted the brilliant grandeur she saw now, the almost regal splendour of scarlet poppies, tall mauve foxgloves, the pale blue of hare-bell and deeper cobalt of cornflowers interspersed with the brilliant yellow of dandelion and buttercup. Yet spread with the paler colours of spring it had held a quieter beauty, a gentle grace which in her years of growing had always pleased her the most; and that day it had given freely of that beauty.

She had gathered as many flowers as she could carry taking them back to Joseph's house and there had woven them into sheaths. Violas the colour of the spring sky had peeped between those of palest lavender; tiny yellow primroses half hidden shyly among wallflowers of purple and gold, their delicate heads cushioned with the dark green fluted leaves of groundsel. But of all the flowers she had picked there was one she had not used in posy or sheaf.

The memory a great swell sweeping from

stomach to throat, Alyssa pressed her eyelids down hard in an effort to hold the emotions stirred yet again.

It had been almost time to go, to take David to the place she must leave him, a lonely heart-breaking place.

'Will you be wanting to see the lad afore...?'

Joseph had broken his question abruptly and though the room had been shadowed by the approach of evening she had seen the tears glistening in his eyes.

She had not spoken. Tears blocking her own throat she had taken the sprig from where she had set it aside. White and delicate, their petals standing proud of green-toothed leaves, the lovely little flowers had proclaimed their name, Honesty.

She had looked one last time on that beloved face, kissed the brow now cold as marble then put the sprig of flowers in the small hand.

'...you could not see them...'

She had whispered against the little face. *'...you did not know their name, but God will know. He will know you go to him with nothing but honesty on your tongue and in your heart ... go to Him now, my precious one ... go to Him who loves you as I do.'*

She had stood then while Joseph had fastened the lid on the coffin, stood while the one person who had truly loved her was taken from her sight.

Joseph had carried the small box from the house, laying it in the cart as tenderly as he might his own son and she had placed the flowers all around.

It had looked so pretty, a bed of beautiful flowers, but their beauty masked a heart scream-ing its agony as she had pushed it to the church, a

73

church where only she was present to hear the priest exhort the mercy of heaven for David.

Mercy! She had swallowed hard on hearing that word, clamped her lips firm together to prevent the cry which rose from her heart leaving them. There had been no mercy for David ... a little boy, who had never seen flowers growing wild on the heath, never seen it covered with a blanket of snow so white you had to shield your sight against the glare; he had not seen raindrops glistening on leaves of trees, or the clouds white against the blue of the sky. Heaven itself had been blind to all it had denied him.

She had stood staring at that dank opening dug in the earth, stared until night shadows came to take it into themselves, hiding it away among their blackness; only then had she turned away.

Every step back to Hall End Cottage had been a nightmare, every step accompanied by a frightened voice calling her name.

''Lyssy.'

It had sounded so real, so afraid; like the times he woke in the night after having a bad dream. She had taken him in her arms murmuring away his fears on each of those nights, holding him until he slept. But she could not hold him that evening, could not stop the cries heard only in her heart.

Opening her eyes, Alyssa looked again to where the church stood high on the hill below which the town lay.

David was asleep now, a sleep no nightmare could invade; but it was one from which she could never wake him.

White with suppressed anger, Cain Lindell's thin lips firmed tightly. He had told the man to return that family to their home, to bring the girl back, only to be told that order had not been carried out.

'Why have they refused?'

Cap in hand Elijah Richardson regarded the man he had come to dislike intensely. Cain Lindell had stripped away men's livelihoods, given them their tin without thought of how they would fare without work or home; was he also thinking of stripping away a young woman's life ... of treating her like some woman of the streets, use her for his own amusement then when he tired throw her aside as he had thrown men from the Spindrift.

'Well, man ... I asked you why have that family refused the offer to return?'

Just like the traps set to catch rats! Elijah watched the lips snap together then answered, 'D'ain't refuse.'

There was no respect in the answer. No deferential 'sir'. Cain Lindell's dark eyes flashed their chagrin. Maybe he could not command respect but he could certainly command fear.

'Richardson!' Like the fracturing of icicles it cracked over the sounds of the colliery yard seeping through the heavy glass of the office windows. 'When I give a man an order I expect ... no, I *demand* ... that order be obeyed; you, it seems, are incapable of doing that ... and where I find a man to be incapable then I no longer employ him.'

Hadn't he already shown that? Showed the sort of man he really was, one with no thought of any but himself!

'I done like you said, but the family were gone an' seems nobody knowed where.' Elijah held to the dark stare. 'I asked all around ... Queen Street, Perry Street ... even so far as Beard Street but not a soul 'ad the knowin'; but then there 'ave been so many folk a'leavin' of their homes these past weeks that one more brought no interest.'

Then neither would another! About to say as much, to tell the man stood facing him that he, like the 'so many' he had referred to, was also out of a job and out of a home, Cain Lindell bit back the words. To sack Richardson would mean employing another in his place and being so recently come to Darlaston he did not yet know any other of the hands well enough to judge them capable of running the colliery ... and he certainly did not have that knowledge himself. But that situation would not last long ... and neither would Elijah Richardson's employment! Holding this thought to himself Lindell forced his reply to come calmly.

'So the offer was not refused?'

'Folk can't refuse what they don't be asked, and they can't be asked when they don't be found.'

No, it could not be asked when that family had not been found. But Elijah Richardson's not finding them did not mean that was the end. Cain Lindell watched the figure stride away across the yard replacing his cap as he went. What Cain Lindell wanted was what he got ... and he wanted that girl!

'You be certain sure of what you be doing?'

The parcel in her hands Alyssa looked at the man who had helped her through the trauma of losing the child she loved. Joseph had given them a place to stay. Joseph had fetched the doctor, advised with church and burial, Joseph had stayed with her mother that evening and now ... but this time she could not accept his help, this time she and her mother must leave.

'I won't be asking where it is you be going, 'cos you don't know that y'self, but I do be asking why... why do you feel you have to leave?'

'...*trollops like her...*'

The woman had spat the words like poison from her tongue. Alyssa felt again the hurt she had felt then. It was almost like the woman hated her, but how could you hate someone you had never before spoken with?

'...*put folk off suspecting the truth ... that her be his whore...*'

That was what was thought of her here. Painful as that was she might have lived with it for her mother's sake, but they could not remain in this house; they must not repay kindness and friendship by being the cause of this man's eviction from his home.

'Do I be getting answer to my asking on do you be leaving with a quiet tongue?'

Alyssa's fingers tightened about the package. Where else had she found the kindness they had found here, what person other than Joseph Richardson had offered herself, her mother and David a home? He deserved the respect of a reply.

'Joseph...'

She swallowed on the word, struggling with the

emotions bubbling inside.

'Joseph, it ... it is as you said, I don't know where my mother and I will go but you have my promise I will write from wherever it is we make a home.'

'That be no more than I knows but it don't go being any answer. I asks again, why do you feel you have to go leaving Hall End?'

She could not tell him, could not repeat the words of those women. Joseph Richardson must never hear them, not from her and not from any other. He was a good man whose name was being slurred because of her and that she could not live with.

Watching the drawn face, the nuances of misery flicking like shadows in eyes turned quickly away from him, Joseph Richardson felt a pain he had hoped one day would go from him, yet each day the stab of it was as sharp and agonising as the one which had gone before. Now it would be added to again.

7

'Inheriting your uncle's estate will, I hope, mean we can look forward to the pleasure of your company more often here at Bancroft.'

There was a hollowness in the proposal, a lack of sincerity he would need to be blind and deaf not to have observed and one which once would have aroused Cain Lindell's anger but now aroused a deep satisfaction. Amelia Bancroft was old money married to new and the resentment of it showed clear in the eyes that rested on his. Her father had been one of England's privileged, a baronet with house and lands to match his title but without money enough to pay the debts his gambling had accrued. Marrying his daughter to an industrialist, a man whose wealth was built on commerce, had solved his problems although it had meant Amelia, his sacrificial lamb, being denied the promise her youth had held out, a marriage within the aristocracy ... and that she had never forgiven. The aspect of this Black Country town with its perpetual pall of smoke rising from a myriad of chimneys was a far cry from the pretty Worcestershire countryside, and elegant as Bancroft Hall undoubtedly was, it did not have the grace or beauty of Whitchurch Priory. But the Priory was the all of what she had left behind.

Cain Lindell took the hand held out to him, the smile touching his mouth hidden as he bent over the slender fingers. The arrogant hauteur of the woman was as strong in her now as it ever must have been and the distaste of history repeating itself, of having a son marry for money while he, Cain Lindell, a nobody with a nothing background, had become a man of considerable means was acid in her throat.

'That was my sincere hope also.' He straightened, no trace of smile marking his mouth as he released the hand his lips had not touched. 'But alas I fear it a pleasure I must forgo for some months. I must return to Jamaica. Like yourself and your son, Lady Bancroft, my living is dependent upon the welfare of my business.'

79

It had gone deep! Clearing the long avenue of birch trees lining the approach to Bancroft Hall, Cain Lindell reined in his horse. The arrogant sow had been hard pressed to contain the anger his reply had obviously aroused in her. The Honourable Lady Amelia! He laughed softly; she had not liked being reminded of her own dependence upon commerce; but he had liked the saying of it, he had liked it very much ... and he would give himself an even deeper gratification of rubbing that arrogant nose in the dirt. Yes, he would enjoy that pleasure very soon.

Touching a heel to the stallion, set it to a trot, he held the thought, savouring its taste. The plantation in Jamaica ... like the colliery it had come to him so easily... and so would the next! Marlow Bancroft was the gambler his grandfather had been. He spent sovereigns as if they grew wild in the fields ... he spent what he did not have!

Reaching the beginning of rough heath marking the boundary of Bancroft Hall estate he reined in once more, turning the horse about to look the way he had ridden.

A year or two at most! A year or two and Marlow Bancroft would have frittered away every penny of the fortune left by his father... and Cain Lindell knew just how close that was. Marlow in his cups let his tongue run away from his brain; not that Marlow Bancroft's brain was much good to him, the way he ran that sugar plantation; bad management resulting in dwindling profits year upon year vouched for that. But Cain Lindell would be the last man to advise a mending of the ways, why would he when Bancroft's IOUs were amassing in his safe? So why go on lending the fellow money while debts were outstanding? Why provide the means for the man to satisfy his craving for cards and women?

Shading his eyes, Lindell stared back towards Bancroft Hall. Its sandstone walls gleaming dusky red, the glint of the brilliant sun sparkling like diamonds on the glass of its mullioned windows. That was the reason he financed the man's ventures, loaned what he needed to go on gambling, and when the last card was played there would be just one winner ... and a new master at Bancroft Hall.

He had not thought to care so deeply for people ever again, never wanted the closeness of friendship. Joseph Richardson stared out from the window of Hall End Cottage, his mind registering nothing of the beauty of the heath adorned now with the peacock colours of summer nor the grace of the ancient church looking down on it, the scarlet flames of impending sunset softening the blackness of its stones, spreading over them until they gleamed dark red.

Red ... the colour of blood ... their blood!

Fingers rolled into hard balls, teeth clenched against teeth, Joseph Richardson fought the anguish rolling up from his stomach to grip his throat with the savage pincers of memory.

A dark stain on grey clay soil!

Breath shivered on memories he could not repulse.

It was spread like a shawl, threads of it veining from its edges like fringing, the earth drinking it

81

in, swallowing greedily until it was gone ... the lifeblood of his loved ones was gone!

It would be the last visit for some weeks. Ruth had protested when he said she should not make the journey to Darlaston; Adam so enjoyed the outing, the playing with his cousins, being fussed over by his grandmother, and anyway the walk would be good for them.

Why had he relented, why had he agreed to her going?

Sobs caught by fast-held breath fluttered in his chest like the wings of trapped birds.

Twinges of concern had worried at him the whole of that day causing him to speak sharply to the men who worked alongside him at Bancroft Hall; concern which on returning home to find the cottage empty had rapidly deepened. Had Ruth's time come sooner than expected? She had said there was two weeks yet before the child she carried would make its way into the world ... but how could she be sure? Nature had her own way, was what Ruth had said when telling him she was pregnant with their second child, but Nature could be precocious, she could turn her face from you with the blink of an eye.

But maybe it was Adam ... the boy might be taken with an illness!

The thought had been a straw too many. Fear weighing cold and hard inside he had left the house. There had been no figures coming towards him on the heath, no child shouting a greeting.

Oblivious to soft sounds in the room, Joseph stared at the pictures in his mind, at a heath overlain with a veil of mauve, the first messenger of evening, and felt again that same quickening of nerves, heard the very air whisper to him urging him to hurry, heard the gathering shadows call as they had seemed to call him then.

What had turned him from the track worn across the heath? What had caused him to leave its path?

'Oh God... Oh God!'

The anguished words ripped from his lips, the pain of remembering arching his head back on his neck, but still the pictures came.

He had struck out across the tussocky ground, running as if led by some unseen hand. Then he had seen them, Ruth and Adam, his wife and son ... he had seen them lying together, Ruth's body half covering the boy.

Colly's Bloomers! Two gin pits lying close beside each other, both abandoned when the coal thought to lie beneath the stretch of ground had proved non-existent, had been nicknamed Colly's Bloomers by locals who had advised a Mr Colly that no coal would be found where he dug.

He had stood the briefest moment of time staring into the opening dropping away at his feet, at the crumpled figures, then a shout of agony sent him hurtling down its steep sides.

He had held them in his arms, cradled them close against his heart. All that night he had held them; whispering his love was the only thing that had kept him sane. Then in the first hours of morning men crossing the heath to their place of work had helped him to take his family home. Ruth he had carried himself, her skirts crimson with the blood of her lost child clinging to her stiffened limbs. He had refused all help, wanting only to be close to her as long as he could, wanting every precious one of those last moments, holding her as he had held her living body, with a tender, gentle love.

A shudder rippling through him dissolved the images in his mind and at their going Joseph became aware of the spire of St Bartholomew church rising tall against the sky.

They lay there now, his wife and the son born of their love, and with Ruth the child which had known no birth; his world, his life, his heart lay there in the grounds of the church which had seen their marrying, where their son had received baptism – beside them a small boy whose blind eyes had never witnessed the face of the woman who had loved him as Ruth loved their child.

'I asked he be laid next to you, my dearest love...' Joseph's whisper hung in the quiet room, intimate words of a man almost lost in grief. '...I knowed you would not refuse comfort to a child, I knowed you would tek 'im to you in heaven where, God willing, we will one day be together. I love you, Ruth ... I love you...'

Emotion choking the last word in his throat he stared at the church then reached for his jacket. He had one more business there.

'Will you be tekin' your mother that walk to Bancroft Hall?'

Returning along a broad avenue bordered by birch trees their leaves glistening silver as a light breeze rippled through them, Alyssa was grateful

84

Joseph had argued against her mother being made to accompany her to Bancroft Hall.

She had not wanted they stay, the longer she put off their going the more danger of Joseph being turned from his home. That thought in mind she had ushered her mother only a few yards from the house before she had almost collapsed to the ground.

A few yards! Alyssa felt the worry of it. How could her mother walk to some other town when a few steps had her exhausted?

'Wait here...' Joseph had said. 'Let your mother rest in her bed; one more day won't see the fox have the chickens.'

One more day! Joseph had no way of knowing the distress that extra day would lay on her shoulders, but she had been forced to admit her mother was in no state to walk.

She had been even more fretful than usual. Alyssa hurried her steps wanting to be back with her mother as soon as she could. Nearly all day she had called, first to her husband, then to her sons. They must be away to the pit ... the tin bath was filled and waiting in the scullery ... no catlick, Benjamin or I'll come and wash you meself like you was a babby... Thea, come try your new dress, Thea, see the pretty ribbons for your hair...

Thea ... it always came back to Thea. Her feet moving quickly, Alyssa tried to stem her thoughts.

Joseph had heard some of the mumblings and he must have caught that sadness she could not always keep from showing on her face but he had passed no comment, saying only he would be working in his vegetable plot should she have need of him.

Should she have need! How would she manage without him, without the kindness he had showed? But she had to manage and tomorrow they would go.

Across the distance the sound of bells rang soft on the evening and for a moment Alyssa was back in childhood holding her father's hand as the family walked together to Sunday evening service.

So far away it seemed now a world of make-believe. She swallowed hard, her fingers holding tight to the shawl draped about her shoulders. It had not been a world filled with magic, or blessed with the same love given a sister; her childhood had known heartache and tears shed in the darkness of night; her world had been so different to that enjoyed by the reckless Thea, and now it was even more so.

So much worry! It folded in on her, dragging at her, holding her in depths she felt she must drown in ... but day followed on day and she lived ... she lived a life which was no life.

Thea knew nothing of that life, nothing of the legacy of grief she had left behind. Gone with her new love she had experienced nothing of the stress of nursing a mother whose mental capacity grew less seemingly by the hour or of the caring for a blind child. Sweet, darling David. He had not been strong enough to fight the infection in his lungs, the fever which had raged so suddenly in his small body, the pneumonia which had claimed the tiny life.

She had buried him there in that churchyard. Her glance lifted to follow the rise of ground that was Church Hill. He lay there alone. Pain she had striven to hold when seeing that small white coffin being lowered into the ground, pain which had been so strong, so powerful, it seemed nothing she might ever feel in the future would hurt as that did, shot its stab wound through her heart.

But the future had been closer than could have been imagined, and the pain ... the pain was overwhelming.

Already so advanced into the terrible illness of the mind the doctor had termed dementia, her mother had not attended that funeral. Often in the long hours of nights thinking of the child growing in her womb, of what would happen when the child came ... the days following when she could not look to her mother ... trying to calm those endless calls to a family Hannah no longer had, Alyssa had pondered the wiseness of the decision she had made. Had it been right not to have her mother present? Ought she have attended? But what purpose would it have served taking a mentally ill woman to that church, to have her stand beside an open grave, to listen to words intoned over a small white coffin while all the time she had no knowledge of where she was or why she was there.

What purpose would it have served?

She had asked the question of herself so many times since that day, tried to find an answer. Struggling to come to terms with the death of a child she could not have loved more had she given him birth, to face the recognition of a woman too ill to follow a grandson to his burial, a grandmother who would never know she had a grandchild.

Yes, she had asked those questions many times. The last peal of bells hovering on silence, Alyssa realised at last the conclusion. Any answer would serve no purpose at all!

8

'You'll be wanting to say a last goodbye to that little 'un along of the graveyard?'

She had wanted to visit there on the way back from Bancroft Hall but the church bells ringing for Evensong had told of the time she had already taken delivering the garment she had sewn for the mistress there, more time than she had anticipated, so she had continued on to the cottage.

'No.' Alyssa shook her head. 'I have taken too much of your Sunday already. I will just get Mother and we will be away.'

'You'll travel a heath you don't know, and that travelling done by night!' Joseph's reply was almost a rebuke. 'I gave you credit for having more sense than that, wench. How far d'you reckon on getting afore Hannah collapses on you? To my way of thinking it won't be many more yards than her got this morning.'

She had no argument against the common-sense of that, but then again she had none that would counter the threats of those women, threats which would not only blacken Joseph's name in the town but would lose him his home.

'Your mother don't be well enough to go walking along of the daytime much less at night...'

'I know!' Alyssa gripped tight fingers in the fold of her shawl. 'I know my mother is weak but don't you see–!'

'I sees a lot more'n you thinks I see.' Joseph cut through her words. 'You thinks I don't understand your need to be gone from Hall End, you fears what folk might get to thinking.'

They had already passed the stage of thinking, they were talking and loudly! Alyssa averted her gaze.

'Do you be thinking the same? That Joseph Richardson be a man would offer a woman a home just so he could tek her to his bed?'

'No!' Violet eyes darkened with worry and fatigue, glistening with the moisture of swift tears, lifted the gaze she had deliberately averted, meeting the clear one regarding her with quiet deliberation. 'Joseph, I would never think that but others–' She stopped in mid-sentence but the look coming to that kind face said the rest was not necessary.

'But others be saying so; that be it, don't it?'

There was nothing to be gained by denying it.

Alyssa held the calm stare for a moment then, unable to bear the question repeated silently by those brown eyes, turned her face away.

'Think you I d'ain't know?' Behind her Joseph's voice was gentle. 'And think you that you and Hannah would have spent more than an hour under my roof had I thought you were that which dirty-minded folk might say? The letter you brought from Elijah told what had gone before, of that little lad being a child of your sister; he spoke high of your character but I speak even higher: you be a wench any man would be proud to think his daughter ... and that be the way Joseph Richardson thinks of you. You and Hannah be welcome to bide here for as long as you wishes.'

Throat tight with tears she knew must fall should she try to speak, Alyssa turned away.

So he had been correct in his surmising! Joseph watched the girl he had befriended, saw the tension holding the slight form rigid. There had been talk in the town ... but how much slime had been thrown in this young girl's face? What filth had she been accused of?

Suppressed anger lending an edge to his voice he said, 'There be tea fresh made, get y'self a cup,' then reaching his jacket from the wooden peg set into the door added, 'I'll be gone for a few minutes, meantime look you to Hannah and bear in mind my words, you be welcome in this house for the time you wishes.'

Everything was done. Alyssa looked about the room she had tidied. Everything was as clean and shining as she could make it. Hall End Cottage had been a refuge, a place where her mother and she had found kindness, but it was not their home. It was Joseph Richardson's home and if he were to remain in it then they must not.

They had risen earlier than usual. Her mother's restless cries having her fearful of Joseph's rest being disturbed, she had helped her into her clothes and down the narrow stairs intending to be gone before Joseph was awake.

But he had been there in the living room knelt before the grate feeding the small fire with fresh coals. He had said nothing when she had returned upstairs to fetch the few belongings she had wrapped in her own shawl but just carried the coal bucket to the yard to refill it before washing his hands at the pump.

She had tried to thank him again for all he had done for them but he had cut her short saying her mother and she should have breakfast then allow the day time to air before setting off. Then he had left for his work.

'Mind you remembers, Thomas, you tell Elijah we all be goin' to the Mayday picnic ... don't want to ride in different carts...'

Sat beside the table Hannah's fingers wrapped imagined sandwiches then placed them in some unseen basket.

'Thea, my lovely, you watch that pretty new dress now, don't go gettin' it spotted afore ever we sets off.'

Thea! Alyssa felt the tug at her heart. Would it ever be Alyssa? Had her mother forgotten totally her first daughter? But then, hadn't these last months proved that to be so!

Pushing the thought aside she helped Hannah rise from the chair then stood as a knock sounded loud on the door.

Immersed in hot soapy water, long legs draped over the curved edge of the bath dripping spots onto wooden floorboards, Marlow Bancroft let his head loll back onto the white porcelain rim.

91

He had been so damn sure! So confident the cards he held could not be beaten. So sure he had raised the stakes to five thousand.

'Christ Almighty!'

Eyes closed, he breathed the words aloud. 'Five thousand … five thousand pounds! Why the hell did I do that?'

'*You are sure … sure you want to borrow so much?*'

Cain Lindell's question flicked the edge of a mind still not clear of the effects of brandy.

Had he been sure? Marlow stared at the ceiling. So sure he would have signed more than Cain Lindell's marker … he would have signed away his soul.

Three queens and a jack. Nobody at the table held a hand as good as his. The blood in his veins had raced. This was his chance to wipe out all of his debts, to pay Lindell and take back every last one of those bloody IOUs. So he had pushed up the stakes until all but one player threw in their hands. It had been too rich for them, the gamble too high; but not for Marlow Bancroft, he had ridden the horse of fortune, flogged it on to pass the finish … but the man he raced against had crossed before him.

Three queens and a jack! Above his head steam curled against the ceiling, swirls resembling drifts of cigar smoke which had lain over the card room of the George Hotel.

He had splayed the cards, their colours bright against the green baize the smile he directed at his opponent as bright with triumph; but the smile had died when that opponent's hand was spread like his own.

Three aces and a King! Christ, how was it he hadn't seen that coming! But he hadn't ... he had been so positive when one queen followed another he had failed to take sufficient account of the cards being discarded, placed in the centre of the table, failed to notice just one of those cards had been an ace. Those others, the men who had withdrawn from the game, they must have taken note, deduced what another of the players must hold and judged the risk too high to take.

But he had taken it and now was in debt for another five thousand. How in God's name did he find cash enough to pay a sum like that?

Lindell had said there was no immediate hurry. Drawing his legs in, he stood sharply sending surges of water splashing in puddles beside the bath. But immediate or not, the day would come when demand of settlement was made.

The plantation in Jamaica? Drying his body, donning the clothes laid out for him in his dressing room, he went through the options he had gone through so many times. A sugar plantation was good for a couple of thousand ... at least that was the sum the bank had lent as security on it. The Brunswick and Monway collieries...? They had both been lost to the cards as had his shares in the LMS and GWR railways.

Bancroft Hall! Dressed in scarlet split-tailed coat, a white silk cravat expertly tied at his throat, knee-length leather riding boots, complementing tailored breeches, Marlow surveyed himself in a tall mahogany-framed Cheval mirror.

Master of Bancroft Hall!

Reaching for pigskin gloves he looked again at

the reflection, an almost regretful smile tracing the corners of the mouth.

Master!

For a moment the smile rested, then old arrogance returned blazing in the grey eyes. Slapping the gloves against his thigh he strode from the room.

Minutes later, astride a chestnut stallion, hounds racing away in front, Marlow Bancroft drew his mount to a halt to gaze back to the large house standing proud among cultured grounds.

Bancroft Hall, his father's pride, his mother's humiliation. He laughed, a quiet mirthless sound which barely left his throat. His mother ... daughter of the aristocracy in every sense of the word! Coming to Bancroft had been odium for her, a degradation she had never got over, a shameful fall from her high estate! What degradation would she feel if even this house should be taken from her?

Master of Bancroft Hall!

The laugh already cold and dead in his chest he played a glance over tall chimneys and high gabled roof. That was what he was, but for how much longer?

Lindell had been present that evening at the Hotel. Sensible Cain Lindell. He had declined the invitation to join the card table simply observing the game as he always did.

They had played into the early hours, himself and James Knowles his host, the stakes getting ever higher while each game fell to him. Luck had sat on his shoulder, he could feel her soft hand, smell her sweet breath. This was his night, he could not lose! Then Knowles, sweating profusely at his continued losses, had bet Beechcroft, his home, together with his Vulcan Ironworks, against a last turn of the cards.

Morning sun glistened on glass, bright and dazzling as the gem Knowles had dangled beneath his nose.

The magnet had proved too strong. He had accepted the bet matching it with money he did not have ... and Lady Luck...? She had taken it with her to sit on James Knowles' shoulder!

Lindell had not had sufficient funds to cover the note written for Knowles yet the debt had had to be paid if Marlow Bancroft was not to be branded a liar, a man not good for his word. So it had been the house, given as collateral against yet one more loan from the bank.

Master of Bancroft?

Hand tightening on leather he snatched the stallion's head up, a jab of his heel against the flank sending the animal galloping hard after the hounds.

Only if he found means to repay that loan!

The mistress of Bancroft Hall wished to see her. Alyssa watched the man walk away from the cottage.

She had sent a messenger to Hall End with the request Alyssa call that day.

Was that request an outcome of that scene last night? Of course, it had to be, why else would the woman want to see her?

Thin as a shadow, nevertheless her mother hung heavily on Alyssa's arm making each step a burden.

She could have refused what to others of this town would come as a command, she owed nothing to Amelia Bancroft, she was not dependent upon that house for her living. Pride had brought that answer swiftly to her lips and pride had held it unsaid. To refuse, to leave Wednesbury without answering what she knew would be accusation, would serve to compound the slander those women had hurled at her, to confirm what they said about Joseph, that she was his whore. So she had thanked the man and asked the reply be given his mistress. Alyssa Maybury would call at Bancroft.

She had said it with head held high yet fear for what Joseph might suffer on her behalf sat like a stone in her stomach.

He had left the house last night the ringing of Sunday church bells still resonating on the evening air. Gone just a few minutes he had returned with the daughter of a friend, the girl given her parents' permission to miss church service if it meant being of help to Joseph.

Sunday evening was the time he visited the churchyard to tend the grave of the family he had told her of that night before David had been laid beside them. His voice had become no more than a whisper, the light of the lamp reflecting in eyes dark with grief as he spoke of finding them fallen into a shallow pit. Heaven had turned its back on him as it had on her ... yet Joseph did not have it so, he still spoke of God's mercy, of His love which one day would heal all hurt.

All hurt? Alyssa's arm tightened round the thin figure as her mother's foot caught in a tussock. The hurt of a child feeling unloved and unwanted by a mother? The hurt of another yet to be born when it came to know it was a bastard, the child of rape...

He was going to the cemetery and she should go also. Joseph had brooked no argument. She must take this last chance to say goodbye to David for tomorrow neither he nor the girl would be available to sit with Hannah.

Pausing to allow her mother a moment of rest, Alyssa glanced behind. It looked so peaceful now, the church seeming to float against a sky of cloudless blue ... so different from last evening.

Evensong had ended but she lingered where Joseph had left her beside that sad little plot graced with a handful of wild flowers placed in a chipped jar which had once held potted meat. Having no wish to meet with any of the parishioners she had remained where she stood; but on hearing a voice she recognised as Joseph's, a voice raised in anger, she had gone quickly to the front of the church.

He had been standing just beyond the lych gate. Alyssa felt the same tug of anxiety pull at her stomach as had pulled at that moment, at seeing who his anger was directed at ... the two women who had said such dreadful things to her the Sunday before.

'*You have a wicked tongue, Eliza Tonks...*'

Memory brought the scene to vivid life in her mind and it seemed the words rang now across the deserted stretch of empty heathland.

Severe black bombazine had rustled, the thin figure it covered drawing sharply to a halt as Joseph stepped closer and blocked the exit from the gate.

'*...you be a woman filled with spite and that spite you throws at any you knows won't answer back ... well I be here to answer so throw your lies at me.*'

'*Lies!*'

The black gauze veil had fluttered on the breathy laugh.

'*Lies you calls it, Joe Richardson ... but then I don't expect to 'ear no differed from you, but I says...*'

'*Tek care, Eliza...!*'

Joseph's eyes had flashed a warning, furrows of anger deep as plough lines on the fields creasing across his brow.

'*...Tek care your spite don't come home to roost!*'

'*Tek care, you says ... care be the reason you be 'ere now, care your carryin's on don't be told of...*'

Topped by its black bonnet the woman's head had turned towards the church door, her words held back as though awaiting the arrival of someone, then when the priest in white cassock had led the mistress of Bancroft from the church she had turned back to Joseph, her deliberately raised voice carrying across the quiet churchyard.

'*...but I says they should be told of ... I says them women you've taken 'neath your roof be naught but whores!*'

White cassock fluttering, the priest had rushed to where, separated by the space of the lych gate, the two faced each other.

'*Please...*' he had urged softly, fingers twitching like sparrows fighting over a perch, '*please, you are distressing Lady Amelia.*'

'*I 'pologises for that...*'

Black skirts brushed the path Eliza bobbing a

short curtsy towards the woman stood at the church door.

'...*but what I says be only truth an' truth should be said whoever has the hearin' of it, an' truth be Joe Richardson be consortin' along of no goods ... that the women he's teken into that cottage belongin' of the Hall be no better than they should ... and her standin' so brazen over there be naught but a whore! A trollop of the worst kind, a wanton, a redheaded wanton an' that be the truth of it.*'

Maybe she should have been less hurt by the woman's malice, by words which had been said before but the shock and hurt of hearing them again had cut as deeply. Pushing at the thoughts, wanting them gone from her mind, Alyssa spoke gently to her mother, urging her on but memory refused to be dismissed.

'*A whore you says...*'

Joseph's voice sounded clear in her head, each word chipped and hard.

'...*but then you knows all about whores don't you, Eliza? Yes, you knows all about that...*'

'Please, Mister Richardson!'

The priest had tried to intervene but Joseph had brushed him aside.

'*No, Vicar! Eliza Tonks said truth should be told and that is what I aims to tell though I be willing to hold my tongue long enough for the mistress to go beyond the hearing of it.*'

The mistress of Bancroft Hall had looked directly at Joseph, her unveiled face showing no emotion and she had made no move to leave.

'*This don't be the place for bickerin'...*'

'*But it be the place for lies, don't it, Sadie Platt! Lies*

99

spread by you and Eliza Tonks!'

Joseph's ice-cold accusation halted the plump figure dressed head to foot in black, her face also covered by black gauze but her words seemed to shoot forward.

'I don't speak ill o' nobody...'

'Nor no good of 'em neither!'

Unleashed, Joseph's anger snarled. *'You be two forra pair with your spite and your backbiting!'*

'I don't be going to stand listenin' to you, Joe Richardson...!'

'Oh yes you be, Sadie Platt, you and Eliza Tonks both, and if any man be of a mind to tell me otherwise then he best do it now!'

At her side Hannah mumbled, calling out at intervals for her husband, to her children, but Alyssa heard only the voices in her head.

Joseph had waited a full minute for any man of the assembled crowd to act on his challenge but when not one came forward he had continued.

'You wants that truth be told ... then here it is! I said as you, Eliza Tonks, be familiar with the ways of whores and that be no lie for you offered yourself to me, you stripped yourself stark naked in one of the barns belonging to the Hall, you lay in the hay and spread your legs wide, then when I refused to lie with you, you vowed vengeance. That vow lived with you, it rooted deep and though you went on spreading your legs for others even long after Edward Tonks wed you cos he thought the babe in your belly was put there by him, you nurtured that vengeance, waiting for the chance to strike me.'

'Mister Richardson, please ... there are people listening.'

100

'*There was people listening when this pair slandered an innocent wench, when they pointed the finger at a woman robbed of 'er mind!*'

Joseph had cut off the priest's protestation, his next words scything the air.

'*An eye for an eye, that be what the Good Book says, don't it, Vicar, an eye for an eye?*'

Beside a sobbing Eliza, Sadie Platt's plump hands had lifted the Bible she carried, her own words scorching through her dark veil.

'*The Lord put His curse on you, Joe Richardson.*'

'*And what curse would you have the Almighty lay?*' Joseph had thrown a scathing glance at the plump figure. '*The same pox you passed to Daniel Platt, the pox you caught from lying with a pedlar along of the Goose Fair ... the pox forra ribbon! Be that the root of your spite, Sadie Platt?*'

Across the distance the barking of hounds penetrated the curtain cloaking Alyssa's mind from the present and her glance followed the sound ... followed to where a rider on a chestnut horse watched her.

9

'Let her bide there while you be along o' the mistress.' Bleached twill apron scratched over dark skirts, their wearer nodding towards a chair set beside a door opened to the warm air of late morning.

'Thank you...' Alyssa answered the round-faced

woman stood smiling at her, '...but my mother...'

'No buts, wench, seems your mother could be doin' wi' a bit of a sit down, an' p'raps a cup o' tea wouldn't come amiss.'

'That is very kind.'

'T'cha, wench, t'aint kind but selfish.' The round face creased in a smile. 'I be wantin' of a reason for to tek a cup meself. Now you go along, mistress don't tek kind to bein' kept waitin'.'

Following behind the trim figure of the lady's maid sent to bring her to the mistress of Bancroft Hall, Alyssa held shawl and skirts close to her body afraid they might brush against a beautiful chair, touch a brocaded sofa or shining cabinet filled with delicate china. The outside of Bancroft Hall had overawed her, but the inside took her breath away.

Keeping pace with the quick footsteps of the maid Alyssa felt the weight of wealth press in upon her. Never could she have imagined, even in her dreams, never have conceived of a house as grand as this one was; but then how could she when the house she had lived her life in would be lost in a corner of the scullery where her mother had been given a chair.

'In here.' The maid paused before a closed door, her hushed tone almost reverent. 'This is her Ladyship's private sitting room, not many folk get to be invited into this part of the house... I wonder could it be...?'

The tinkling of a bell cutting off any further conversation, the maid tapped once on the door then entered, her deep blue skirts rippling against a sea of cream-coloured carpet as she dropped a curtsy towards a seated figure etched sharply against sunlight flooding in from tall windows.

'Miss Maybury, ma'am.'

A whiff of toilet water followed the maid's exit, a regal flip of the seated figure's hand dismissing her. It must be wonderful to dress in clothes such as she wore, to smell of violet and lavender instead of scrubbing soap.

'Come closer!'

Imperious in tone as well as command the words snatched away Alyssa's conjecture. She had lacked manners. Colour warm in her cheeks, she dropped her own curtsy.

'You asked to see me, ma'am.' Quiet as her movement the words hung for seconds in the beautiful room before the answer came.

'Indeed I did.'

Had her needlework proved unsatisfactory? Had closer inspection of the garment she had delivered yesterday revealed some fault? Alyssa's throat contracted beneath the high collar of her cotton blouse. The money she had received for the making of that gown would have to be repaid, but how? She had left almost all of it behind, only by leaving it there at the cottage without word or explanation as to her reasons would Joseph Richardson take the keeping of it; even then it could come nowhere near showing the appreciation of all he had done for her mother and herself, nowhere near displaying the affection she felt for him. Affection! Thought snapped to a halt.

Centred on an ornate stone fireplace a gilded clock ticked on silence. Was it right she should feel this way towards Joseph? Was it respectful? Worry

103

she might in some way have embarrassed a man who had shown her only civility and friendship tracing shadows across her face she was unaware of the scrutiny of the seated woman.

The girl was pale and drawn, too much work and too little rest. Amelia Bancroft's sharp eyes inspected the young woman stood before her. Thin ... yes, but not from lack of food, hers was a thinness caused of worry, but no, not worry.. Amelia's glance took in the lovely haunted eyes. Not worry, more than that. Somewhere in this girl's background lurked heartbreak.

'I said come closer, girl, are you deaf or so ignorant you do not answer when your betters address you?' She had spoken sharply, her words deliberately belittling; now Amelia Bancroft carefully watched the reaction, watched the thin figure straighten, the head lift and the deep violet eyes suddenly spark with life. Hands folding into her shawl Alyssa drew a short breath, her glance firm on the haughty face regarding her while it seemed the world waited to hear her reply. Then, soft as the question had been sharp, it came.

'No, ma'am, I am not deaf nor do I feel I have shown ignorance; as for my betters, you are that, in wealth though not in civility...'

A swift intake of breath caught like a cough in the other woman's chest but Alyssa went on.

'...the gown I delivered to this house yesterday is obviously not of the standard you require, for that I offer my apology and will return the money which was paid. I wish you good day.'

How! Alyssa's nerves jarred as she turned for the door. It was one thing to tell this woman her

104

money would be repaid but quite another to do it.

Still seated Amelia Bancroft watched the girl she had ordered come to Bancroft Hall. Ordered? A tiny frown accompanied the thought remaining to nestle between brows which might have been carved from stone. The girl's whole body refuted that. Instead it showed a simple defiance. This young woman had spirit, it was clear in the proud lift of the head, in the cool regard of the steady gaze. The game of life! Amelia Bancroft felt the stab of bitterness deep inside herself. The girl standing in her sitting room was little more than a pauper yet she had a richness of dignity and an honesty of self, qualities lacking in the son of Saul and Amelia Bancroft. The game of life! Bitterness stabbed again... it was a game Amelia Bancroft had lost!

'Wait!' She half raised a hand as Alyssa moved towards the door. 'I did not ask you here to discuss the satisfaction of a gown ... that would have been made for my daughter-in-law...'

Not the gown! Relief swept a warm hand over Alyssa.

'...I wished to speak with you regarding the disturbance outside the church following yesterday's Evensong.'

Relief cooled with a swiftness that had Alyssa's veins throb. She had heard ... she had heard the accusation of those women, heard Joseph's response; now she was to deliver her own.

'Ma'am,' she turned to face again the seated figure, 'Joseph Richardson offered my mother and myself shelter out of a goodness of heart, he has acted towards us both with kindness and never once asked anything in return; if there is blame then it is mine, I should not have stayed at Hall End Cottage ... please, I ask you, do not take Joseph's home away from him.'

'Take his home away!' The frown resting between Amelia Bancroft's brows deepened slightly. 'Why would I do that?'

She knew why. Alyssa stared into eyes which held challenge more than they held question. She knew very well why but she would have it said again nevertheless. Chin lifting slightly, fingers laced into the frayed edges of her shawl, Alyssa answered firmly, 'Because you believe me a whore!'

There it was again, dignity, honesty and yes ... courage, it took more than a mite of that to answer the mistress of Bancroft Hall in that fashion. Despite herself Amelia felt the warmth of appreciation. If only her son had proved of such vintage. Unable quite to push the thought away she answered. 'What I do or do not believe of you is of no consequence, what I believe of Joseph Richardson however is very much of consequence.'

'As it is with me!' Alyssa cut in sharply. 'What those women said of him–'

'Is again of no consequence to me!' Amelia Bancroft's intervention was equally acute. 'I make my own decisions of people and the one I made long ago concerning the character of Joseph Richardson remains the same today. He is loyal and dependable, with an honesty which has never been brought into question. Of all the men in Wednesbury he is the one I trust to speak neither flattery nor falsehood but only truth; it was that truth he told weeks ago when he informed me of his taking a sick woman and her daughter beneath his roof.'

Joseph had told her! He must already have asked this woman not to turn him from his home yet he had said nothing.

'No, he did not come to me in order to beg not to be evicted.' Amelia Bancroft's sharp scrutiny caught the bewilderment flash across the deep violet eyes and guessed the cause. 'It was politeness and good manners brought him to this house, to tell me of his action; manners not readily possessed of every man I know. He felt it proper to explain the reason for his giving you lodging though he had no need to do so. I appreciated that.'

'Then you will not turn him out?'

Sunlight sparked on silver streaking carefully coiffured brown hair and somewhere deep in hazel eyes a faint smile lurked as Amelia Bancroft shook her head.

'Not even if I could. Joseph Richardson it seems has kept his own counsel regarding his home but this is one time I shall not. That cottage and its acre of ground does not form part of the Bancroft estate. It was sold to Joseph Richardson by my husband many years ago, hence the name Hall End; Joseph was making it plain where his property and that of the Bancrofts became separate. Yes, I could have had my son dismiss him of his employment had I so wished...'

'Had who dismissed from his employment, Mother?'

Intent on what the other woman had been saying Alyssa was unaware the door to the room had opened but at the sound of that voice, of the hard laugh following the words, her stomach lurched.

'*A whore...*'

It rang in her brain as that whip had rung close against her ear.

'*...now if that isn't just what a man needs...*'

'Well, Mother, who is it you would have dismissed from his employment?'

Alyssa's hand caught at her throat as if to hold the sickness flooding into it. She could not be mistaken, she heard that voice every night keeping her from sleep, heard that hard, cruel laugh each time she scrubbed her body trying to wash away the still vivid memory of hands kneading at her breasts, of the breath snatching, the pain of hard flesh driving brutally into her ... the laugh of the man who had raped her.

10

She had seen the colour drain from that young woman's face, seen the revulsion flood into her eyes just as she had seen the shock come to Marlow's face, the flick of fear whip across his eyes. Sat alone in her private sitting room Amelia Bancroft relived a yesterday long gone.

She had prayed she might never again see that look on her son's face, prayed that that which had happened once would never be repeated.

Glancing beyond the window her eyes rested on a rose bed, the colours mingling like the complementary chords of a beautiful soundless melody, while the rapid beat of her heart told her it had been a futile prayer.

Marlow had come to stand beside her and as he had looked at the girl his face had said it all.

Two faces saying the same thing!

It had been only too clear, so clear it brooked no question. Revulsion on the part of the girl, shock followed by fear in the eyes of the man.

Eyelids pressing hard down Amelia tried to clear the image from her mind, to tell herself what she thought to have seen was nothing other than imagination, but still the pictures danced.

Two faces saying the same thing – *rape!*

Never easily conforming either to school or to the running of the collieries, business his father had built, held no interest for Marlow, he had wanted no part of them. It had often led to words between father and son.

Flower heads bobbed in a slight breeze, their colourful petals shimmering like butterflies, but lost in her dark world of memory Amelia Bancroft saw none of their beauty.

Words! It seemed even now they rang in her ears.

Saul had been so angry. Yet another gambling debt. But he would pay no more, Marlow must face his responsibilities like any other man, he must work for what he wanted.

'*Like your father...*' Marlow had retorted, '*...like you have worked for what you have ... and what is that? What do you have other than a wife who despises*

109

what you brought her to? What do you have but a life empty of pleasure? Well, that is not for me, I–'

Marlow had got no further. Saul had risen from the luncheon table, his face tight with the anger he was fighting to suppress.

'That is not for you...'

He had spoken quietly while across the table Marlow had emptied a glass of wine with one gulp.

'...you want no part of the business I have built, that is your choice and I will honour it. From this day I will pressure you no more; but I also have choice and now I make it. You will receive no further allowance from me, neither will I pay your gambling bills nor any other debt you may incur!'

Saul had walked stiffly from the dining room and Marlow had followed up the withdrawal by smashing his wine glass against the opposite wall before he too had left the room.

To retire to his bedroom to think on his father's words? That had been her hope but it had proved futile as those later prayers.

Marlow had not gone to his room.

Caught in the nightmare she knew was reality Amelia's fingers dug convulsively into the soft flesh of her palms but she was oblivious to the pain, alive only to the pictures racing across her mind.

It appeared he had stormed across to the stable, thrown himself onto his horse and galloped off.

If only that had been the all of what he had done.

Warm tears blurred the flower bed to a confusion of colour.

It had been evening when he returned. He had

been drinking, that much was obvious ... so too had been something else. Watching him during dinner she had seen it ... worry at his father's decision not to finance his easy lifestyle? No... her heart as well as her eyes had told her that was not the cause of Marlow's sullen silence just as her senses warned it was something far more. But not in a thousand years could she have divined what that something turned out to be.

Saul had been called from the dining room then minutes later had sent a manservant to request his son's presence in the library. What had passed in that room had been kept from her until five years later Saul had told her from his deathbed.

Marlow had spent the rest of the day in some tavern. On his way home he had seen a young girl crossing the heath. She had been pretty and had waved a hand as he rode past. But Marlow had not ridden far. He had turned about, bringing the horse alongside the girl. They had laughed and talked, she smiling up at him; then he had offered her money to lie with him. The girl had refused and ran away but he had ridden after her using the animal to knock her off her feet, then before she could recover he had leapt to the ground and there he had raped her.

Rape! God, if only that had been enough!

Tears ran unchecked.

But it had not been enough, not for Marlow. The girl's sobs and vows to tell her father what had been done to her was too much of a threat. He had snatched her to her feet then wrapping the riding whip about her wrists had dragged her behind his horse, dragged her until they came to an open mineshaft and there had thrown her in.

He had raped what had proved little more than a child … raped then murdered her!

Her spine ramrod straight, her body still as stone, Amelia Bancroft stared at the ruin her life had become from that night.

The awful realisation of committing such an act should have sobered Marlow, instead it had simply added to the false elation afforded by drink. He had forced himself on a girl but who was to know? Who was to say he was guilty? Hadn't he destroyed any source of accusation?

She had not wanted to listen to any more, not wanted to hear more defamation of her son but Saul had insisted she know it all.

Filled with self-congratulation Marlow had resumed his journey. He had heard the chimes of the church clock ring over the quiet heath, chimes which mingled with the laughter of a child, a child skipping a few yards in front of a woman. He had watched them come towards him, she with a basket on her arm calling to the small boy not to venture too near to the horse and as he watched the devil of lust had risen once more.

There had been no need to offer her money, no need to proposition; what he had taken once he could take again: but more aware than the young girl had been, this woman had grabbed the boy and run with him, but with every few yards Marlow had followed cutting off her path, using the animal to turn and return the woman, chasing her until she would fall exhausted at his feet. And at last she had fallen, though not at Marlow's feet. She and the boy had tipped over the edge of an open cast mine, tumbling to the bottom.

It had been the next day she had heard the news, news of Joseph Richardson's wife and son being found dead at a place called Colly's Bloomers!

Loyal ... dependable ... one I trust to speak neither flattery nor falsehood but only truth.

Those were the words she had used a few minutes since, words spoken of Joseph Richardson. But what could be said of Amelia Bancroft? She was a woman who had hidden the truth, carried the secret of her son being a rapist and murderer deep inside, but how else to protect her only child, to protect the name of Bancroft?

Saul too had protected name and son. The night he had been called from the dinner table, it had been to speak with a man claiming to have witnessed a man hurl a girl into a mine shaft, a man mounted on a horse, a man he said was Marlow Bancroft. Saul had sent for their son who at the man's repeated accusation had laughed and called him a liar.

But the man had not been a liar. The look which had haunted Marlow for days afterward had said as much.

She should have known then ... or had she known but refused to accept?

Saul had agreed to pay the man one hundred pounds. The price of silence! Amelia's fingers bit deeper.

But Saul had paid a higher price, one which had brought him to an early death. Lying on his bed, worn to a shadow by the worry of it all, he had confessed. He had felt instinctively that the man who professed to have been asleep behind a

113

rock only to be awakened by the cries of a girl and the shouts and laughter of a man, who then had watched unseen as the same man threw the girl down a mineshaft could not be trusted to hold his tongue. So he had met with him, offered him the wad of banknotes, then, as the man took them, had struck him over the head with his walking cane before rolling his unconscious body into the waters of a canal.

'I had to do it.'

Saul had fought for breath enough to say the words. 'When news of Richardson's wife and son was brought ... how long before the two happenings would be linked ... should it be known Marlow had raped a child then thrown her alive into a mine-shaft it would be a short step to link him with the death of Richardson's family, and even if not proven the stain would remain forever on the name of Bancroft.'

A month later Marlow had been dispatched to the Sugar Islands to manage a plantation bought by Saul.

Husband and son, one guilty of rape, both guilty of murder! Amelia drew in a shuddering breath. Five years she had lived with that terrible knowledge and every day of those years she had prayed such evil might never come again; but the look which had come to Alyssa Maybury's face and that quick flare of alarm she had seen flash across Marlow's eyes as he glanced at the girl told it already had.

It was him! Body and mind had told her so even before she had looked into the face of Amelia Bancroft's son.

Sickness rolling in her throat, stomach turning like leaves in the wind, Alyssa followed the maid whom a small silver handbell had summoned back to that sitting room.

'You look pale, like you've seen a ghost.' The maid sent a glance to the figure half walking, half stumbling along the deep-carpeted corridor leading to a curved staircase. 'But you shouldn't be scared, ain't no ghosts in Bancroft Hall, or is it the mistress bawled you out? Her can be a right tartar, I know for I've felt the rough edge of that sharp tongue times enough; but if you be coming to work here then you best get used to sharp tongues for cook has one that would slice leather.'

They had reached the kitchen though she had no recollection of coming there. Alyssa stumbled into the large room its air hot and stifling from the huge range stretched along one wall. She remembered only the man, the same man who had played a whip about the shoulders of a trembling, blind little boy ... the man who had then raped her.

'What be wrong wi' you?'

A white apron starched stiff as card reaching to her feet, white cap so starched it stood several inches above faded mouse-coloured hair, a woman turned from basting a large roast.

'Mistress bawled her out,' the maid answered treating Alyssa to a sympathetic glance. 'I told her to take no notice.'

'Oh, you did, did you!' The large bowled spoon dripped hot fat spotting the edge of a thick oven cloth. 'Well, I be tellin' you, me wench, you teks care her upstairs don't go catchin' you tellin' folk

115

so, and tek even more care as to what you be tellin' as to the runnin' of my kitchen for I brooks no backchat as I brooks no idlin', so you be about your work lessen you fancies standin' the line tomorrow!'

A tinge of pink rising to her cheeks the maid glanced once at Alyssa, her expression one of 'what did I tell you?', then she was gone.

'What goin' to be your position then?' The spoon hovered, globules of fat hanging suspended, their droplets cooling and congealing until they looked like pear-shaped blisters. 'I ain't asked for no 'elp in my kitchen an' I ain't 'eard no word of it bein' needed nowheres else in the 'ouse, not lessen it be from that fancy piece the young mistress brought along of 'er; do that be it? You bein' appointed to the young mistress?'

He had recognised her as she had recognised him, the look darting into his eyes as he turned towards her had betrayed the fact. Her mind numbed by the encounter, Alyssa heard none of the cook's words, realisation of where she was impacting upon her brain only with the sharp metallic scrape of the roasting pan and the ring of the heavy cast-iron door of the oven being closed with an unmistakable clang of vexation.

'Mother?' She glanced beyond the kitchen door to the scullery where Hannah had been allowed to sit.

'Hmmph!' Sharp and indignant the sound snapped from the throat of the woman. 'Can't be bothered to answer a civil question ... well you let me tell you, miss 'igh an' mighty, you might 'ave bin teken into the employ of the young mistress

116

but that don't butter no parsnips wi' me... I'll 'ave respect or–'

Alyssa blinked against the nightmare threatening to swallow her. 'I'm sorry, I don't have time...'

Already rosy from the heat of the oven the woman's face flushed an ever deeper carmine and breath snorted through her nostrils as from some enraged bull. 'Time!' she bellowed. 'You don't have time! Well, you best find time enough to look for another position for you won't be gettin' no post along of Bancroft 'All, not once I speaks to Lady Amelia ... once I tells 'er of your uppity ways...'

Senses returning, Alyssa cut through the irascible tirade and crossed the large kitchen, reaching the other side before saying, 'Thank you for allowing my mother to rest here, it was very kind of you.'

The quiet dignity with which it was said had the cook, mouth half open, stare after the figure already at the door of the scullery.

'I give 'er a cup o' tea like I said.' The round face which had beamed kindness as they had come to the scullery door was now creased with uncertainty. 'Her drank it down then said as 'er 'ad to be about fetchin' meat for to cook against 'er 'usband and boys comin' from the pit.'

'How long ... how long has she been gone?'

The quiet dignity was replaced by an anxiety which trembled through the slight figure. The cook stepped closer to the connecting door, her ears trained as a bloodhound's nose, fastening eagerly on every word.

'Almost as long as you been 'ere, swallowed 'er

117

tea right down 'er did then said as 'er 'ad to be leavin'.'

'Did you see which way she went?'

There was real worry in that. The cook's ears honed even sharper. Now why would that be?

'I said for 'er to wait of you but 'er wouldn't 'ave the listenin' of that.' The scullery maid shook her head. 'I said as p'raps 'er should ought to wait of you finishin' wi' the mistress but 'er wouldn't be told, said 'er must 'ave the meal on the table along of her menfolk comin' in. There were no stoppin' 'er short of lockin' 'er in an' I couldn't be a doin' of that—'

'Please!' Alyssa interrupted the part explanation, part apology. 'Please, did you see which way she went?'

Perhaps it was the glint of sunlight playing on a snow-white apron or the scullery maid's instinct telling her she was being watched and listened to by more than the girl whose eyes were now scanning the grounds stretching away beyond the rear of the house. Lifting a corner of her apron she rubbed her hands on the coarse brown-speckled cloth.

'Can't say as I did.' Eyes flicked in the direction of the kitchen accompanied the reply. 'I 'ave me work to see to, don't give me no time to watch folk comin' an' goin'.' Then, voice lowering to a whisper, came an added, 'I be sorry you be given worry, wench, your mother 'er went along the way of the kitchen garden.'

She had thought her mother to remain there in that scullery. Skirts held above her ankles, shawl hanging loose on her arms, Alyssa ran past a high brick wall enclosing the kitchen gardens of Bancroft Hall. *'Almost as long as you been here.'* The words rang in her mind. How long a time had that been, ten minutes ... twenty? Maybe even longer; how far could her mother have walked during those minutes? Not very far, she tired so quickly these days. Hadn't they stopped for her to rest a dozen or more times since leaving Joseph's cottage?

Breath held tight, lips compressed as though allowing any air to escape from her lungs would impede her, every atom of her concentration on the ground stretching away in front, her eyes searching for any sign of her mother, she did not notice the gate set into the wall nor the man coming through it.

'Whoa there...!'

A half-laugh followed and strong hands catching her against a firm body prevented her being knocked to the ground from the impact of the collision.

'Where is the dragon?'

Pent-up breath released by the jolt of being caught, her brain still wrestling with the problem of finding her mother, Alyssa made no answer.

'I asked where is the dragon? I presume there must be one to have you running like a frightened colt.'

Dazed from holding her breath and then bumping into what felt as solid as stone, Alyssa did not register the gentle tease of the question, or the friendliness of the tone – only the fact of being held, of a hard body pressing against her own.

He had left the house ... left it while she was speaking with the cook and then with the scullery maid ... he had recognised her and come to lie in wait...

Thoughts raced one after the other, tumbling through her mind.

She had seen it in his eyes ... the same look she had seen that day ... a hot burning before it was hidden away...

Thoughts whipping with the force of storm winds, dark on dark the black clouds of fear, gathered shutting out the light of reason.

It had been there in those hard eyes, that look of evil ... the glint of lust ... of rape...

'No!' It tore from her, echoing on the sleepy sunlit silence, its sudden sound having a pair of blackbirds cawing resentfully as they took flight.

'Steady ... there is nothing to hurt you.'

Locked in her living nightmare Alyssa was deaf to all but the ferment in her mind, the whirling vortex of fear, the hard grip which held her prisoner; then as that grip fastened firmer still, the pressure of that body becoming more pronounced, the horror clutching her brain broke its bounds. Head snapping back on her neck, eyes blind with horror, she writhed and twisted, feet kicking, hands pushing, revulsion lending strength while dry sobs choked the cries in her throat.

'Not again ... please, not again!'

11

'I tell you it was her! She was there in my mother's private sitting room.'

'So?' Cain Lindell raised a dismissive eyebrow.

'So!' Droplets of wine spattered across Marlow Bancroft's pale yellow waistcoat. 'What the hell does that mean?'

'It means, why worry.'

'Why worry! Why bloody worry?'

'Exactly, why worry?' Cain Lindell sipped at his own glass of claret.

'I don't think you realise what this means.'

Lindell held his drinking glass gazing into the rich depths of the wine. 'I realise this. Unless you wish every man here to know your business you would be well advised to lower your voice. As for the girl, you are certain it was the same one you pleasured yourself with the day we visited the Spindrift Colliery?'

'The same you also intended to take the pleasure of except a man's shout interrupted.' The snide remark lent a source of satisfaction as Marlow raised his empty glass, the movement capturing the eye of an attentive waiter.

'So, you say she had come to speak with your mother.' Glasses replenished and the waiter beyond hearing range, Lindell resumed the conversation.

'Right.'

'So what did she speak about?'

'How the hell should I know?'

Watching his companion toss half the contents of his glass into his mouth, Cain Lindell felt a trickle of warmth not altogether the product of wine. Bancroft depended upon his estate for funds, should that source dry up it was his mother he would turn to. Should she be alienated then Marlow would be forced to look elsewhere for money to save his skin and where else but to Cain Lindell.

'Did you not ask?' He resumed as Marlow half lowered his glass.

'Ask the girl...! Do you take me for a complete fool? That would have been owning to having–'

Wine tossed deep into the throat cut off the reply. Marlow's raised hand beckoning again for it to be replenished holding silence between them until once more the waiter had withdrawn then, 'You did not ask? And the girl?'

'Huh!' Marlow grunted into his glass. 'Took one look and bolted.'

'Your mother, she gave no explanation for the girl's visit?'

'Said something about a scene outside the church the previous evening but that was all, I didn't stay to hear any more.'

'Then if you have heard no more–'

'There is no need to worry!' Marlow interrupted with a coarse laugh. 'You don't know the Lady Amelia! She had caught the look that came to the girl's face when she saw me and I don't doubt that which flashed to my own went entirely unseen. My mother might have enjoyed a sheltered upbringing but she has a mind sharp as a razor's edge; she saw all right, put two and two together and didn't come up with five ... she guessed it was the same as before–'

The same as before! The abruptly broken sentence caused no blank in Cain Lindell's understanding. That girl loading vegetables onto a small cart was not the first Marlow Bancroft had forced himself upon, the question was who, and when? It could only be beneficial to listen more closely to his friend's drunken ramblings in future; a little blackmail could loosen a man's pocket.

'Then there was no question regarding the happenings of that day at Darlaston?'

Tipping off the remnants of claret Marlow rose sharply from his chair, the brush of it as it caught against the wall bringing glances from others taking lunch at the George Hotel.

'There was no question,' he answered thickly, 'but there will be, I know Mother too well to think otherwise; but she will hear no more from Alyssa Maybury ... I'm going to make sure of that right now!'

She had not returned to Hall End Cottage. Alyssa stood in the tiny living room of the house she had left that morning with her mother. She had prayed as she had run from Bancroft Hall, prayed her mother would be here in Joseph's house ... but then what did prayer do for Alyssa Maybury!

The scullery maid had whispered to her to follow the way of the kitchen garden. *He* ... breath ragged and hard caught in her throat but

123

did not stop the rest of the thought ... *he* had been waiting there, waiting for ... her!

She had fought against that same thought, thrown it from her mind again and again as she had run in search of her mother, but now, standing in the silence of the empty house, it refused to be dismissed.

He had recognised her, he knew she was somewhere in the vicinity ... the son of the mistress of Bancroft he would know every nook and cranny of Wednesbury. It would not take long to find her! Thought following a new trend crashed into her brain. Maybe he knew already... had followed her to this house!

Horror following hard on the last slammed like a sledge-hammer, the force of it rocking her mind, churning a whirlpool in her stomach yet it held her limbs as though frozen in ice.

Sound ... quiet sound.

Caught in the web her fear had spun, Alyssa's body obeyed only her own terror.

Once more a sound! At the edge of fear, Alyssa's brain accepted the message of her ears.

It was not in her head, not imagination, it was outside of herself ... outside of this house!

It was him ... the man who had raped her ... he was here!

The rush of it flooded every vein, the heat of panic melting the ice which held her immobile, leaving her trembling.

It must not happen again ... she must not let it happen again! The back way... through the scullery and across the yard, she could be away...

She had already taken a step, made her bid for

escape when the sound came again, a careful furtive sound, a sound she was not meant to hear.

Nerves jarring once again she listened.

'I hoped you would be here.'

Behind her the voice was deep, the voice of a man. One scream erupting from her lips, Alyssa fled from the house.

He had followed her to Joseph's cottage! Followed as she had dreaded he might, as he could be doing even now. The pounding of her heart, the fight for breath saying she must rest or collapse, Alyssa halted. She had run through the scullery. In her mind she heard again the tread of a quiet footfall. It had come from the doorway at the front of the cottage, had been here with her in the living room, only a footfall giving his presence away.

He could have grabbed her. One hand pressed to the throbbing ache in her side, the other supporting her, she rested against an outcrop of rock. In the first seconds of realising someone else was with her in that small room her legs had seemed paralysed, every effort to move blocked by fear.

Those few moments of time, they had held so much danger. He had been close enough for her to hear his breathing, so close he could have knocked her to the ground as he had done before. Had he expected her not to move? Did the son of Bancroft Hall think to take what he wanted, think it should be given without opposition, was that why he had hesitated? But he had hesitated. Leaning against the rock Alyssa dragged air into lungs still threatening to burst. He had hesitated and that had been her salvation; but how certain was salvation?

Hating to look back, afraid of what she might see, Alyssa remained another minute, her whole weight against the pale, almost white mound of rock, a minute in which reason argued against reason.

She could run on ... but should he be close behind then she would be quickly overtaken; she could stay here, hide behind this rock until night ... that would mean searching the heath in pitch darkness and she could not hope to find her mother without light.

That thought ended all others. Her mother was somewhere on her own, without help anything could happen. Drawing a long painful breath Alyssa pushed away from the support of the rock. Using the breath to bolster courage she knew was on the verge of deserting her she forced herself to turn about.

Bare of all but scrub, a few stubby bushes of yellow-flowered broom and lumps of grey-white rock, the heath stretched away in all directions, a circle empty of human life.

She had not been followed. Alyssa released the pent-up breath exchanging it for one of relief, only to snatch a further anxious one. Where exactly was she? She had fled in blind panic taking no note of direction. Think! The mental command steadied senses ready to bolt in the way they had in Joseph's living room. Alyssa took in the emptiness surrounding her. Her mother had said she must go fetch meat to make a meal for her family coming in from their work. Could her mind have directed her to Darlaston, had forgotten memory somehow returned taking her back to the town she had known so well? There was no way of knowing, nor even of knowing whether the direction her own flight had brought her in would lead to Darlaston. How could she tell? She had only ever once crossed this heath and that had been with a heart too heavy to take in her surroundings; so how could she distinguish? Without a landmark she could identify with how could she be sure of heading the way she wished to go?

Confusion attacking the frail discipline she had managed to impress upon her mind, Alyssa felt her brain whirl. Any way she chose to go could be the wrong way; instead of bringing her nearer to her mother it could lead her further away; but which way was the right way ... she didn't know! She didn't know!

Despair rising, Alyssa lifted her hands to her face.

'When things get too 'ard for you to bear alone, should time be when you don't know what be best for you to do then ask heaven, remember, my little babby ... ask heaven.'

The words of her father pressed into her mind, the words he said when longing for a mother's affection had painted unhappiness on a small girl's face. But heaven had long since estranged itself from that same little girl, given no heed to the prayers whispered beneath the sheets and no solace to a breaking heart.

Painted Pictures and Plaster Saints!

Warm tears squeezed between Alyssa's fingers.

She would ask no help of heaven.

Could it be night so soon! Bones aching from repeated bursts of running, walking and running again, feet smarting from the sharp bite of stones penetrating the thin soles of her button boots, Alyssa glanced at the sky. No trace of blue looked down at her and what had been puffballs of white feathery cloud were rolling together to form a dark grey barrier to fight the daylight. She had thought to see some evidence of a town, the rise of smoke stacks, the winding wheel of a colliery, but there had been nothing. Had she perhaps been walking in circles, covering the same ground without realising it? There was no other explanation. Darlaston was not so far distant from Wednesbury she could not reach it in the length of time she had been walking. Then if not towards Darlaston where was she heading?

She glanced again at the sky. Thick and heavy cloud rolled into cloud, spreading, lowering, the heralds of storm. As if in confirmation a brilliant streak of lightning lanced between the banks of sullen grey followed seconds later by a clap of thunder.

Her mother had always feared storms. She would dart quickly from living room to kitchen hiding away cutlery, then upstairs to turn bedroom mirrors to the walls. All shiny objects which might reflect lightning she saw as a means of causing fire so they had to be draped with cloths; but even that had not entirely relieved her mother's stress, nor did the opening of doors to the front and rear of the house thus creating a pathway for a fireball to follow should one fall down the chimney. Electrical storms had been a fear almost as great in her mother as that of the accidents of the mine; and now she was somewhere alone with that fear.

Thunder crashing again, its accompanying vivid flash temporarily blinding her, Alyssa drew her shawl close to hold the corners across her breasts. She had to find her mother ... she had to find her before the storm snatched away whatever senses remained to her.

There was almost no light in the sky, only brilliant flashes where fingers of the storm grabbed at the earth while the fierce onslaught of rain raged its own battle. She had walked those earlier hours in silence afraid that to call to her mother would attract the man she had not so far observed following after her. She could not rule out the possibility of his having done so, of his being within range of her shouts, but now she must break that silence. Regardless of the consequence she must call her mother's name, find her before the final closure of night made search impossible.

'Mother!' It rang across the stretch of land before fading into oblivion. 'Mother, where are you?'

Alyssa listened, straining the silence for the slightest sound, wiping the rain from her eyes to peer out across the rapidly darkening land. It was with another brilliant flash of light that she saw it, a movement in the distance.

'Mother!' She screamed the word into the driving rain, her feet flying over the pitted stony ground, running, running like the devils of the storm were at her heels.

It was not her mother. What she had thought to be a figure hunched against the lash of rain had proved no more than a tree moving in the wind. The hope which had driven her so long, the straw which had kept trust afloat, broke and Alyssa sank to the ground, her whole body quivering with sobs rising from deep inside.

How long had she sat there? Clothes soaked by rain, her limbs stiff from contact with the wet earth, Alyssa pushed to her feet. Dawn? She looked at the sky. No, not dawn, the scarlet and gold came from the lowering sun. It had not been night that had taken the light from the sky but the thickness of cloud, cloud which had now all but disappeared, only their edges tinged with mauve and pearl to say they had ever existed. There was time yet to continue her search.

Lifting the shawl from her shoulders she shook it and as she turned her face from the shower of raindrops it threw, she instinctively stepped backward. A few more yards and she would have been over the lip of ground, into a shallow bank surrounding a pool of black water. A flooded mineshaft! How often had she been warned of such? Hidden by bracken or tall tussocky grass they lay in wait for the unwary. This area, like so much of Darlaston, was likely riddled with these hazards. Not all coal mining had been evidenced by winding wheels standing tall against the sky, her father had told her, it had been practised years before by individuals sinking bell pits into the ground, digging out coal until the roof was in danger of collapse at either side, then they would abandon it and begin again near by. For that reason if for no other the heath became a dangerous place to walk alone, and all the more dangerous walked at night. And soon it truly would be night!

Her glance travelling swiftly over the wide stretch of ground rested briefly on the horizon. So low they seemed to touch the earth beneath, clouds were changing the exquisite brilliance of evening for sombre grey. An hour more and all of sunset's gift of light would have been swallowed. But she had searched so many hours, covered so much ground and found no trace of her mother ... how much more could she do in an hour! It would be sensible to wait until morning, but to leave her mother out here ... try to find a house, someone to help ... where? Hadn't she run all that time and seen not a building, not a single person! Thoughts struggling one with another she wrapped the damp shawl about her head and as she did so her glance returned to the pool of water. Sheened now by the setting sun the waters glistened like liquid bronze while all around rough grass glittered with a million diamond raindrops. So beautiful beneath its canopy of purpling gold the scene drove away all mental problems and Alyssa sat once again with her father and elder brother beside the canal linking Darlaston to Birmingham. She had so loved those Sunday afternoons sitting on her father's jacket spread for her beside the towpath, Mark teasing her with a worm before he fastened it to the hook of his fishing line. It had been a different world, one where unhappiness was forgotten, a beautiful peaceful world of love and laughter.

131

'It's like a green ribbon, a pretty green silk ribbon.'

She had kicked off her boots and removed her stockings, an eagerness to paddle her feet in the inviting water bringing her skipping to its edge.

Still caught by the beauty of the scene spread a little in front of her, Alyssa allowed memory to transport her to that other place.

She had stretched out one foot when her father's hand had snatched her back, pulled her sharply away from that promised delight.

'No, my little wench...!'

His voice had been harsh with what she had thought to be anger at her removing her boots and stockings, that the roughness of his jerking her backwards had been due to the impropriety of behaving that way in public and she had dissolved into tears.

But he had not been angry.

The shawl drawn close about her became those arms holding her, folding her in against her father's chest while the lap of water on the surface of the flooded pit whispered his words.

'Things don't always be what they seems; sometimes beauty masks a danger hidin' it from our eyes, them there waters be such for they be deep ... they don't be for little 'uns to go paddlin' in. Remember, my little love, our minds don't always be a tellin' of the truth ... like that there canal it can deceive.'

He had held her from him then, his eyes filled with love as he looked into her own tear-filled ones.

'...remember, my little wench, truth don't always show its face on the surface.'

It was a phrase he had used once more when he

132

had found a fourteen year old shedding secret tears. She had not given him a reason, but deep within her misery she felt he understood, understood her longing for a mother's love, if she had told him, confided in him, he would ... but that was why she had not spoken of the grief which lived inside her. To have had her mother show her affection only because her father had ordered it so ... that would be harder to bear than the lack of it. So she had kept her silence ... and in a month her father and brothers were dead and with them the only real love she had ever felt.

Overhead a skein of geese passed on their way to night roost, the beat of their wings sounding over the heavy silence and brushing aside the memory.

She would have to go on, she must search

Fingers tying the corners of the shawl suddenly stilled... Limbs chilled by rain froze. Alyssa stared at the shimmering pool.

12

'Mother!'

It was a whisper, a soft breath kissing a newborn breeze, a shadow of sound echoing the movement of lips before Alyssa's hand flew to her mouth.

She had not noticed it there close in under the rim of the bank caught by an overhang of reed and brambles. Now she stared, her glance snared as fast as the floating mass moving gently with the motion of wind-teased water.

It was no more than pieces of broken twig ushered together by the rippling of water. She had thought in that moment of blind horror the dark blotch swaying on the surface of the gold-painted pool to be her mother, but it wasn't ... it wasn't! Her mother had not come this way! Alyssa continued to stare, her only movement that of a fear-driven mind. Her mother had not come this way! She would have seen her!

Yards away, beneath the treacherous lip of ground, the lap of water rocked the dark bundle, lifting and lowering, offering then drawing it back but always leaving it there on the surface, leaving it where frightened eyes could see it.

It was not ... it was not...!

Driven by revulsion Alyssa stepped backwards until a thin spike of broken twig pressing through the worn cloth of her shawl jabbing into her arm, brought her senses flooding back.

It was not a mass of twigs, it was not wind-blown leaves ... rags then ... a collection of rags thrown into the pool perhaps by children larking about at a picnic? But who would bring children to spend a precious day's outing to so desolate a spot!

She should go on, continue to look for her mother before daylight failed completely. Commonsense followed on reasoning but still Alyssa did not move. Held to the spot she watched the gently bobbing shape, a swath of dark on the glittering gold. It could have been a scene of beauty, a dance of shadows, their graceful movements an enchantment as they changed and

134

changed again in rhythm to the tiny surges of water; but it was not beautiful, it was forbidding, repellent; something about it was ugly.

Dropping the hand which pressed against her lips she had half turned when a slightly stronger breeze whipped across the surface of the pool, the surge of it flicking the floating bundle, snapping it free of the anchor of brambles, twisting it over – twisting it to show the face of her mother.

Hair broken loose of pins spread on the water, lappet-like tendrils slithering like grey-white snakes over the face staring up from the pool, sliding in and out of the open mouth, touching eyes which did not blink.

Horror-struck, Alyssa felt the world tilt, her stomach heave into her throat. Then came the screams; soundless, wordless screams filling her head, dragging at her heart, over and over, building and building until her very soul was screaming.

Then she was running, a few steps seeing her trip over the jutting lip of the shallow bank. Feet sliding from under her she tumbled and slid down the rough sides, jagged pieces of razor-sharp rock exposed by weather tearing viciously at her skirts, biting into the flesh of her legs and hands. And then she was in the water. Liquid ice it stung through the miasma holding her brain. Just one more step could take her from the solid ground that circled the pit, hidden beneath the water the mouth of it might be only inches from her feet, a watery hell waiting to suck her in.

From the open heath a gusty breeze whipped

across the pool ruffling the glistening surface, the swell of ripples lifting a black-draped arm, a lifeless hand bending at the wrist, the limp movement rising and falling as if waving goodbye.

'No!'

Every fibre of Alyssa, every nerve, every vein, throbbed in a wild chorus of despair.

This was her mother, the woman she had loved most in all the world.

Stirred by the touch of a promiscuous breeze, tiny waves undulated gliding sinuously forward only to be pulled back, parting then merging like lovers engaged in a sensual dance. Long slender tendrils of weed spread, reaching for the sodden mass, wrapping about the dark-clothed body, twining green fingers among the grey-streaked hair while silently, insidiously, drawing the unresisting body further into itself, carrying its offering to the dark maw of the drowned pit shaft – as it drifted the arm lifted again, the pale hand waving its goodbye.

Not like this...! Not this terrible way...! Her mother must not lie in some black water-filled hole!

Thoughts painful as the cut of a knife drove everything else away and Alyssa reached out both hands, closing her fingers into the slime-covered clothing. Like a live thing deprived of its prey the water, which moments before had appeared tranquil and serene in its mantle of gold, now showed its true self; the body it had nursed to its death belonged only to it. Waves cavorting beneath a freshening wind gathered strength, snatching, dragging, resisting Alyssa's efforts to separate it

136

from its victim.

With its resistance, the force of water churning itself into rage, Alyssa's feet slipped on the treacherous ground.

Loose shale! Nerves stretched to breaking point rocketed again. Small stones and soil loosened by digging was left to lie, miners working gin and bell pits merely moving to fresh locations giving no thought to the dangers they left in their wake. This must be one such pit! A fresh onslaught slammed itself against her thighs rocking her, seeking to throw her off balance ... a few moments and she would be pitched head first into the depths.

Across the space of heath the breeze became a wind, a squall adding force to the churning water, scooping it into billows before hurling them against her. Its mocking, derisive howl ridiculed her efforts to drag the weed-wrapped bundle from the water's grasp.

Swaying from the buffeting, Alyssa's fingers slipped from the sludge-rimed cloth. Instantly caught by wind-tossed water the inert body drifted further away.

'Mother!'

The sobbed cry snatched by the mocking wind was carried into the distance.

She could not reach ... it was too far ... the water had taken her mother too far for her to reach!

'...*remember, my little love, our minds don't always be a' tellin' of the truth...*'

Quietly, across the distance of childhood, the words of her father crept into her mind.

'...*truth don't always show its face on the surface...*'

It was as if he were there beside her, speaking

137

to her as he had beside the canal, his gentle voice calming her fears.

'...*truth don't always show its face on the surface*...'

He was telling her what to do... somehow her father was telling her not to be afraid.

'Help me,' she whispered. 'Help me, Father.'

In that moment a lull in the wind stilled the turbulence to a gentle breath, a breath catching the soaked bundle and drifting it to where her fingers could once again grasp it.

He had not found her! Marlow Bancroft stared into an empty fireplace. He had not found the bitch! What he thought to be easily accomplished had proved a fallacy; she had been nowhere on the road, he had glimpsed no sight of her though he had ridden half across the town ... so where had the slut taken herself? Wherever it was he had to find her, she was a threat, a problem he must rid himself of; and he would, a dead woman could bring no case against him ... and allegations ... who would dare voice them against the Master of Bancroft!

She had called at this house, spoken with his mother who perhaps had enquired as to where her visitor lived ... but to ask would be to arouse curiosity in the Lady Amelia, and that he could do without. But that girl had to be found and dealt with before she could do him any harm. But she was not the only woman who could harm the character of Marlow Bancroft, there was another who could bring him disrepute, criticism which would hound him from society.

A hand resting on the fireplace gripped the

stone. There was another also to be dealt with.

He had discussed the situation with Lindell and his conclusion had been the same as the one he himself had arrived at; the matter had to be dismissed ... finally!

Pay someone to do it for him? Lindell had advised against that, it would like to prove one more thorn in the side should blackmail follow murder. No, Lindell had said, what had to be done was best done with the fewest people knowing of it; in other words...

The hand curled into a fist and hit several times at the stone mantelpiece.

...in other words Marlow Bancroft must do the deed himself.

Amelia Bancroft sat opposite the ornate marble fireplace of her private sitting room looking at his back turned towards her. It could have been the man she had married, the man who had taken her away from Whitchurch Abbey, from the life she had cherished only to bring her here to Wednesbury where coal mines bled their waste like black scabs on the land while the chimney stacks of iron manufacturers hid the huddle of miserable houses beneath a thick pall of smoke. Whitchurch Abbey! Her throat tightened at the memory of the gracious old house that had been her former home, of the rolling downs free of any other building, a sky never darkened by smoke. But this house was not her beloved Abbey and the man standing across from her was not Saul, not her husband but her son.

They were so alike. Her glance played over the

tall figure. The same brown hair, eyes that same shade of grey, shoulders though while not broad topped a firm body. Yes, so alike yet not alike! The similarity between father and son was a superficial one, apparent only in looks. Though she had never loved Saul she had come to recognise the strength of the man, his will to achieve, a strength of character she had never witnessed in her son. Marlow had none of those attributes, his had been a dissolute life, one of gambling and self-satisfaction, one she knew he followed even now, that same disregard for truth and honesty, for the feelings of anyone other than Marlow Bancroft. It had been a lifestyle which had robbed Saul of any pride he might have felt in his son.

Knowing him for a gambler and a liar had been a heavy enough burden for Saul to carry but when those lies had covered rape and murder the burden had become too heavy, the blow too hard. Yet still he had shielded Marlow, protected her from the odium of having her son brought before the courts, kept the name of Bancroft clear of scandal and humiliation by himself committing murder. The stress of having killed a man, of living day to day with the knowledge of his own vileness had eaten away at Saul, corroding the pride he had once had, eroding his self-esteem; shame and guilt combining until they had become a poison in his soul, a canker which had slowly claimed his life.

She swallowed hard freeing her throat of the re-striction of longing for what once had been. Saul had sacrificed everything ... and for what? For a son who had continued a life dedicated to squandering the inheritance his father had worked hard for, a son who had taken everything and given nothing; and she ... what had she given Saul? Not warmth, not appreciation and certainly not love. She also had taken while returning nothing, how then could she judge herself any different to her son? Was she not equally guilty of deceit? Was she not compounding that deceit even now by not admitting her true reason for having Alyssa Maybury come to this house, by not asking the girl the question which had played in her mind since knowing it was Marlow who had caused the death of Ruth Richardson and her child ... by not asking did Joseph Richardson know it also? Often she had watched him from her pew in the church wondering did he know, was he searching for some means of proof, then eased her mind by telling herself no magistrate would accept what he might say, not after so long an elapse of time. Ease of mind? That was also a deceit. Each time she met with Joseph Richardson, each time he doffed his cap in respect she felt her nerves jar, refused to meet his eyes for fear of what she might read there ... no, there had been no ease of mind, no peace of spirit these many years and now a new weight was added to that pressing on her heart.

Her glance still on the figure standing staring down at the empty fire grate, Amelia knew there had been something, some terrible something, between Marlow and the girl who had answered questions while looking her in the eyes. How would Marlow answer?

Drawing in a deep breath, her corseted figure held immobile, hands resting one in the other on her lap, she heard the answer in her mind. He would lie, as always.

'You knew her, didn't you?'

He had been expecting to be asked. Amelia saw the shoulders slump slightly beneath the expensive evening suit; as with every facet of his life Marlow took what pleased rather than what his pocket could match.

'Am I to have an answer?' she asked when he made no move to turn, her own hands closing together as she saw his spine tighten, the shoulders square beneath black Alpaca. Another scene no doubt, but then when did talking with Marlow not develop into a scene.

Worry, that had been his companion since entering his mother's sitting room early in the afternoon, still sitting heavy in his stomach, Marlow tapped an irritable foot against a gleaming brass fire dog.

Lord, this would happen! Why had that slut of a girl decided to show up now just when he needed his mother's co-operation most! Tell her of raping some wench he had come across working a bloody vegetable patch and he could say goodbye to any chance of assistance ... yet she had to help, if she didn't then–! But the outcome need not be thought of, his mother would give what he asked; hadn't she always? Hidden from view his mouth curved in a cynical smile. Whitchurch Abbey! The seat of the De-Thaine family for generations, his mother's precious heritage; that had to be protected from scandal whatever the cost, nothing must cast a slur upon house or name and in that lay his own security. A daughter of the house of

De-Thaine. His smile deepened. It made no difference to his mother that her cherished background held death and destruction, that the buildings and lands she had called home had been given to Roderic De-Thaine as payment for allying himself to the King when England broke from the Roman Church; the fact that her forebear had slaughtered those refusing to leave their homes, that he had driven the monks from the Abbey at the point of a sword! That had never found consequence in the mind of Amelia Harford-De-Thaine. Still staring into the cold grate Marlow's smile vanished. His mother would co-operate. The risk of a blot on that holy escutcheon? That could not be countenanced.

Amelia watched his black patent-leather shoe tap its rhythm against a gleaming brass fire dog, the beat of it echoing the tick of the French singing-bird carriage clock which had been a present from her father on her sixteenth birthday... A birthday at Whitchurch ... it had been another life, a life she yearned still, the years of marriage adding rather than detracting from the misery of losing it. Her father had seen that misery, known her unhappiness at his consenting to a marriage which would take her away from the Abbey. But the inheritance was her brother's, he would have all, therefore a daughter must be matched to money. Sold like a sow at the market! Old bitterness rose warm in Amelia's throat. That had been her lot. But this sow had not produced the expected litter, one child had been pain enough for her to bear; she had provided the Bancroft heir, her husband must find pleasures

143

in some other woman's bed. Sold to the highest bidder! Heat burned in the back of her throat. *It was for her own good, she would have the comfort of a fine home, a husband with wealth enough to ensure she continued to live as she had always lived.* The words of her father matched the quick sounds of the clock as they flitted through her mind. *'I want only what is best for you.'*

Best! Clenched teeth prevented bitterness escaping in a cry. What had her father known of this dark hole of a town? Of what her life would become here? And, had he known, would she still have been given in marriage to an industrialist, to a business man, to a member of the working classes? There could be only one answer ... yes. Yes, her father would have done only what he had done; they were alike, father and daughter, both would sacrifice their very soul for Whitchurch. A sacrifice she must make yet again if the look of fear on Alyssa Maybury's face meant what she feared.

13

Backbone stiff, head held high, Amelia broached the silence.

'You have met the girl you saw here today, met her on a previous occasion, am I not correct?'

'I might have seen her somewhere.' The reply was sullen.

'There is no "might" about it, you recognised that young woman, I saw as much in your face.'

How did he get out of this one! Seeing that girl here in this house, in his mother's most private inner sanctum, had caught him unaware. Marlow Bancroft's nerves sang. It wouldn't do to aggravate his mother, not if he were to have any hope of her complying with the request he had come to make.

'There was something familiar about her.' He answered as nonchalantly as his flicking nerves would allow. 'Is she a daughter come to plead the cause of a father you have dismissed?'

They had played through this charade before. Amelia Bancroft's fingers pressed into the folds of pearl-coloured lace overlying the oyster taffeta of her dinner gown.

'Marlow.' She sighed. 'Let us not pretend. You know the girl you saw here in my room, what I ask is how *well* do you know her?'

Irritation carved a path along Marlow's spine. How long before he was free of this ... free of his mother's sniping and suspicion? One foot kicking against the fire dog, he forced a careless laugh. 'Really, Mother, do you think me to remember every girl I pass in the street!'

In her chair beneath a window now shut away behind blue damascened velvet curtains released from gold tasselled ties, Amelia Bancroft felt her heart skip. It was ever this way. Even from being a young child he had bluffed, pretended innocence of any wrong doing, but she had seen through it all, seen the guilt lying behind the protestation and it was guilt she was seeing now. Every fibre taut against the dread which had remained with her the entire afternoon, her

145

answer came on a note of quiet finality.

'No, Marlow, I do not expect you to remember every girl you pass in the street, but I suspect you did not pass by Alyssa Maybury.'

Alyssa Maybury! He had not asked the name, owned no reason to have done so. She had merely been there, a tool to serve a need, something to take the itch from his loins. But now she was here, here to denounce him a rapist. But that pigeon would not settle to the roost, it would be dispatched and soon.

'You suspect, Mother,' he laughed again, 'but that has ever been your nature.'

'While it has ever been yours to lie!' Amelia's reply snapped.

That bitch of a girl must have told everything! Quick anger flared in Marlow. She must have told of his raping her ... but it need not be called rape! Steeling his mind he let the thought develop.

'Very well.' He turned about, his face displaying none of the anxiety of moments ago. 'I had met that girl before, it was on the heath...'

The heath! Amelia Bancroft's hands pressed harder against the soft yielding cloth of her gown. The heath where he had raped and murdered a child then gone on to cause the death of a woman and her son.

'I was riding here to Bancroft with Cain Lindell. The girl you spoke with earlier today, she called to us, asked were we of a mind to spend a shilling ... don't ask me to enlarge, it would be indelicate. Suffice to say I bought what she offered for sale. Lindell will be here for dinner, if you have doubt as to the truth of what I say then ask him, only be

146

considerate enough to delay putting your questions while my wife is present. Her condition is delicate, I would not have it put under stress by hearing of what was after all simply a moment of foolishness, a moment of which no one takes account but you, Mother.'

A moment of foolishness! Amelia's contempt was almost tangible. That was what Marlow would have her think but the colour draining from that girl's face, the quick uncontrollable flash of consternation racing across his own, had both told a very different story. There could be little doubt Lindell would corroborate what Marlow professed ... but then she had as little faith in Cain Lindell as she had in her own son.

'I prefer not to discuss family business with anyone,' she replied coldly. 'Unlike you, Marlow, I value the name of Bancroft.'

'Value!'

It exploded across the elegant room, resounding from tastefully decorated walls, a shellburst of sound bouncing against graceful furniture.

'Value!' He laughed gratingly. 'Since when did the Lady Amelia ever value the name of Bancroft? I'll tell you ... never! You have never valued anything other than the bloody place you called home, Whitchurch Abbey, a church ripped from the monks by your ancestors; but that did not end its consecration did it, Mother? You, like the rest of your clan, worshipped the place, re-sanctified its walls with your own devil-brewed piety, instilling successive generations with the belief that a power greater than that of the King had given it into their keeping. But that was not the object of their true

147

devotion; no ... the golden calf, the graven image before which all must bow was the name of De-Thaine, that above all must remain untainted, everyone must sacrifice to that end–'

'As your father sacrificed!' Quiet as her son had been loud, Amelia's retort cut the tirade. 'As he sacrificed to save you ... committed murder to prevent you having to answer for the death of a young girl, thrown into an abandoned mine-shaft, of the woman and child you rode down until they fell into disused workings, the wife and son of Joseph Richardson. Oh yes ... I knew, but not until your father lay on his deathbed, lay where shame and self vilification brought him long before his due. You lied then, Marlow, and God knows you have lied since, but if I find you have once more committed that same terrible act–'

'I have not!' His expression revealing nothing of the leap his nerves had taken, Marlow shook his head. 'I confess to having been stupid but that was a lesson well learned.'

Well learned! Amelia watched the head turn to a slight angle, the eyes slide away from her own. Yes, he had learned well, learned to practise the art of lying even more expertly; and she had learned too over the years, learned it would be useless to continue to question him ... learned that truth and her son were total strangers.

'Very well,' she conceded. 'We will not speak of it again.'

A breath of relief eased slowly from Marlow's lungs.

The matter of rape truly had not been the subject of the meeting between his mother and

148

that girl or Amelia would not have let it slide so quickly ... and the bitch he had pleasured himself with? He would find her and when he did she would not speak again ... ever!

'I heard from Jamaica today, it appears the cane harvest will not be what I had hoped ... a tropical storm has devastated a great part of the acreage.'

He had swung the conversation ... now to swing the rest. Allowing what he hoped appeared as a frown of worry to crease his brow he shook his head yet again.

'That was bad enough but when I checked the price of sugar and found that fallen by almost twenty per cent on the ton...!'

He paused, drawing a breath deliberately harsh and ragged, a fist driving into an open palm.

'What exactly does this mean?'

A few seconds of silence, a gulp before answering, Marlow played the moment as he had planned.

'It means...' he swallowed again then met his mother's eyes, the son reluctant to bear bad news, '...it means the end ... unless...'

Real or false? Amelia's distrust of her son's word flicked her senses.

'Unless?'

'I hadn't wanted to tell you this...' he paced dramatically the length of the room before continuing, '...but without this harvest there will not be sufficient money to meet estate commitments, Bancroft...'

This would be the coup-de-grâce, the one stroke which would end any opposition. But it must be delivered carefully ... must seem to be

149

causing him a great deal of heartache ... which of course it would should it fail!

'Bancroft,' he gulped again, '...the estate will have to go!'

It had driven home as he guessed it would. The blow of execution! Seeing the distress cross his mother's face Marlow smiled inwardly. Lady Amelia Harford-De-Thaine-Bancroft! She could face up to anything except the loss of her precious prestige; lose Bancroft and she lost everything. His frown deepening, his eyes echoing pain he did not feel, he looked at the woman sitting so erect on her chair, the lies he had gone over again and again in his mind sliding glibly between stiff lips.

'Last year's poor crop hit us badly, it meant drawing heavily on capital. Now with virtually nothing to come this year then I see no other way than to sell the Hall and its land. Believe me, I have tried to find some other solution but the banks all refuse to grant a loan on the plantation. They view that as insecure collateral, and it was useless my taking a loan against this place for should the plantation fail again...' He shrugged, leaving silence to say the rest.

Foreclosure ... disgrace of being unable to pay one's debts. Amelia's hands tightened further on the delicate lace of her gown. This was what marriage to a man below her station had brought her to ... a life not only of social degradation but now one which threatened her name as well.

Across from her Marlow could almost read the thoughts flooding through the head held so firmly upright, the straight figure which had not so much as flinched an eyebrow. The genteel,

150

well-bred daughter of Whitchurch Abbey, the so bloody aristocratic Amelia... she would not fail to do as he asked.

Slumping to a chair he splayed both hands on his knees, giving a moment's grace before saying, 'There is a way ... I hesitate to put it but try as I will ... as I have ... I cannot perceive of any other, the jewellery–'

'No!'

Sharp and decisive it surprised Marlow. This he had not expected.

'No!' Amelia repeated. 'Those were gifts made to me, I will not part with them.'

Another scene! Marlow breathed hard to control the coil of anger beginning to loop along his veins. But this scene would be one he and not his mother would control.

'If I am not mistaken each piece is listed as being the property of the wife of the owner of Bancroft Hall. You, Mother, no longer come under that category, therefore you have no claim to them. They now belong to my wife and as her husband I have the legal right to do with them as I see fit.'

'And you see fit to sell them as you have sold everything of value this house held, sold only to throw the money away. Has the sugar crop really failed or is it yet more of your dissolute ways, more of your gambling debts my jewels are needed for? Is it for Bancroft you ask for them or to save your own skin? Well, this time, Marlow, the answer is no, I will not give you my jewellery.'

On his feet, eyes glinting grey ice, Marlow let the inner smile break across his mouth, a hard cynical depraved smirk.

'Not *your* jewellery, Mother, and not your decision.'

'I–'

'Enough!'

It was the crack of a whip, the snap of a pistol.

'*I* am the master of Bancroft Hall, I, Mother, it is my will that is obeyed here; if that is not suitable to you then you may return to your precious Abbey, see how your heritage serves you there when you return a pauper!'

'*I am master of Bancroft Hall...*'

Words to which she had no argument echoed in Amelia's mind as she watched her small private safe emptied of every last gift her husband had made to her.

'We deserve no more.' The whisper followed Marlow as he strode from the room. 'You, Saul, wanted the prestige of marrying into a titled family while they wanted only your money, and I...? I have loathed being brought to this house, this town ... hated you for marrying me... Is it any wonder life has taken its revenge, any wonder the son we created has become what he is, a liar, a gambler and a murderer? We deserve him, Saul. We both deserve him!'

Fingers closing on soaked skirts, Alyssa drew the soaked mass close against herself. How long could she hold on with fingers numbed by the icy water? As though hearing the thought, as if to mock her efforts, the breeze revived the stilled surface, building wave to follow wave, flinging them against her, each impetus having her feet slide a little further on the treacherous hidden shale. She should get out of the water, climb back to firmer ground. Somewhere in her brain common-sense murmured. A few minutes longer and it would be too late. Once again water slammed into her, tearing at the bundle held in her hands, almost wrenching it loose.

'I can't...'

Near-exhaustion made her sob the words helplessly.

'I can't ... I can't!'

She had tried but hadn't the strength to go on, she hadn't strength left to pull her mother from the water. She would have to let go...

'...*remember*...'

It came like a kiss in her mind, a whisper quiet and soft as breath, calming as a loving hand.

'...*remember, my little love, our minds don't always be a' tellin' of the truth.*'

Again those words! Alyssa felt them lift the heaviness of despair. 'Help me,' she called into the wind. 'Help me, Father.'

She had not felt the tug of it, the resistance of the water, the drag of heavy weight over rough ground, had not been conscious of her own laboured breathing or the pain screaming in every muscle, but only the warmth which had seemed to enfold her, lending her strength to pull her burden onto the bank, to sink beside it on the ground, to take it in her arms. But now the warmth was gone. She had come too late. Pond water which had splashed onto her hair trickled down her face mixing with tears. She had come too late. As though nursing a sleeping child Alyssa rocked back and forth, one hand freeing the wet grey hair of its

153

ribbons of weed.

'I'm sorry, Mother,' she whispered. 'I'm sorry I left you in that scullery, it's my fault … it's all my fault!'

Settling in the branches of the tree a small flock of starlings sang their evening hymn. Lifting her head Alyssa watched the last lingering rays of sunset lance across the flooded mineshaft.

Maybe a few moments … had she seen her mother floating in that water just a minute sooner, pulled her from that pool, might she have warmed life back into that thin body?

'I'm sorry.' She whispered her lips against the cold face. 'I tried, Mother, I tried so hard.'

It filtered into the gathering dusk, slipped among the sounds of wind-blown water, a cry which died into silence. But deep in Alyssa's heart another cry echoed a pain too deep to speak.

I tried, Mother … tried so hard to make you love me.

14

'It be right good of you and Laura to be taking the wench into your home and I thanks you for the doing of it, I knows Alyssa would have fretted over what would be said were her to be at Hall End along of nobody but meself there with her … folk have wicked tongues.'

Had it been someone's wicked tongue had sent that girl running from Bancroft Hall, had her look at him with terrified eyes before pushing away to race off as though the devil himself had reached for her?

Questions still hovering in his mind Paul Tarn answered, 'There is no need for thanks, Joseph, the young woman may stay...'

'Won't be no more'n a day.' Joseph interrupted then shook his head sheepishly. 'I don't be meaning that the way of its sounding; I meant only that Alyssa don't be a wench to take advantage of folk. It might be thought by some as that were what her were doing of me with being at Hall End but the wench paid for the lodging of 'erself and her mother.'

'That was her mother ... the woman whose body she was holding?'

'Ar, that were Hannah, God rest her. Poor soul were sick in the mind. Her would call to husband an' sons though they died in a pit accident these many years. I reckons that'll be behind her finishin' up in that flooded shaft, her'll probably have thought to be tendin' after them.'

'Would that be the Marshalls' place?'

'Ar,' Joseph nodded. 'The Spindrift mine, left Hannah with two young wenches to finish the rearin' of and her not the only widow. Took a few men did that explosion.'

'I remember, a sad business all round.'

'D'ain't do Laban Marshall no good neither, weren't the same man no more. Give him his due, he done what he could for the families left without a man as well as leaving them that were maimed to live the rest of their lives rent free; but that never lifted the weight from off his

155

shoulders. Pressed hard it did, pressed him into his grave. But the Spindrift won't go doing of the same for that nephew of his'n ... he be a no good if ever I knowed one!'

'Lindell isn't it?'

'That be the name his father give him!' Joseph sniffed with asperity. 'But it don't be what many men in Darlaston be callin' him, they be more like to use the devil's own name when speakin' of Cain Lindell. The man don't be satisfied with just the colliery, he wants the rent from the properties his uncle said should be free so he gets it by puttin' folk onto the streets or in the Poor House. I tell you he be a bad 'un ... him and the one he keeps company with, though I asks your pardon for speakin' as I does.'

'But Laban's wife, surely she is not in agreement with what Lindell is doing?'

Joseph gave a small negative shake of the head. 'From what be said, her be little better off than them folk already put out of their homes; the Spindrift Colliery and all that goes along with it belongs to Laban's nephew, that much has been made very clear to Emily Marshall. Her keeps a still tongue or her too will be out on her backside.'

Nice man! A grim smile edged the corners of Paul Tarn's mind, his next words left unsaid as a young woman entered the room.

'I left the doctor with her.' Laura Tarn smiled at her brother before turning to Joseph. 'Florence and I made her as comfortable as possible, I don't think there is any bodily injury.'

Bodily injury! Joseph felt his nerves jar. Did that mean there could be some hurt done to

156

Alyssa's mind? Had this last bout of worry been too much?

'Even so,' Laura Tarn went on, 'she needs rest after such a terrible experience. She must stay here at Lyndon, don't you agree, Paul?'

Impetuous as always ... but kind as always. He had known his sister would react just as she had. Paul Tarn's glance stayed on the face unhappiness had marked. 'Of course I agree.'

'Then you must agree also, Joseph.'

'Ain't for me to go saying what the wench be to do,' Joseph answered. 'Alyssa Maybury has a mind of her own and I reckon her'll do the deciding for herself, but that don't go to say you don't have the thanking of Joseph Richardson, I 'preciates all you be doing, you and your brother.'

'We are happy to help, Joseph, now if you will excuse me.'

Paul waited until the door closed behind his sister then turned again to the man sitting in his study. 'The cost of a funeral ... it would appear the girl has not the means, so I will take care of it.'

Rising from his chair Joseph stood with cap in hand but his eyes met those of the younger man with a steady determined look.

'That won't be necessary.' Tone as definite as his stare, Joseph gave a half-shake of the head. 'There be money enough for seeing Hannah Maybury to her rest though I be of a mind to say her daughter would thank you for the offering.'

'The same, Joseph.' Paul Tarn lifted easily to his feet, his smile evident now on his lips. 'Proud and independent as ever.'

'Then I be no different to the man standing

157

nobbut five feet from me. Them be your characteristics and they've med a good man of you!'

A good man!

Walking home through streets robed in the colours of night, Joseph let the words play in his mind.

Yes, Paul Tarn was all of that ... unlike the master of Bancroft Hall.

There was no child!

Eyes closed against the possibility she had heard wrongly, Alyssa held the words to her.

There had never been any child, she had not been pregnant!

The doctor had finished his examination of her. There was no physical injury but a few days of complete rest would help offset the drain of energy a heavy loss of blood resulted in.

Had he known her fear? Guessed the reason for the gasp which had slipped from her mouth?

There was no cause for concern.' He had told her quietly. *'It was a normal occurrence given account of the trauma you have suffered, perhaps a little heavier flow than a usual monthly cycle but no more than that.'*

He had closed his black Gladstone bag ready to leave then had returned to the bedside to press her hand reassuringly, his eyes filled with that same sympathy they had held when telling her David could not be saved.

'Consistent worry has many effects on the human body as well as the mind,' he had said. *'Losing a loved child combined with caring for a mentally ill mother could have one such effect, namely the*

158

withholding of the natural cycle for quite some time, while a sudden shock could prove the opposite, but it is all quite normal.'

Quite normal! Relief trembled fresh in Alyssa's every vein. She was carrying no bastard ... fate had spared her that. The sudden churning, the painful lurch which had rolled her stomach on seeing her mother...

Her mother! Eyes springing open she sat up sharply only then aware of her surroundings... This was not Hall End Cottage, not the room she shared with her mother; but Joseph ... she had heard Joseph's voice, he had called to her; or had that been hallucination? Joseph would not have left her in some strange place.

Perhaps it was not hallucination, perhaps the voice she had heard had not been Joseph but of the man she had seen in Amelia Bancroft's sitting room, the man who had raped her. He had followed across the heath, found her and now–!

Relief turning to panic she threw herself from the bed, tearing off the delicate lawn nightgown and flinging it away.

Where had he brought her? What did he intend to do with her?

Each thought a brand scorching her mind; she reached for the clothes draped on a stand beside a large dresser.

Her clothes ... her own clothes ... but these were not caked with mud, not wet from the waters of that pool, they were perfectly clean and dry! How? How could that be? They had been soaked through, they would need hours to dry.

Hours! Fingers struggling with the tiny buttons

of her blouse suddenly stilled. Her clothes, they did not smell of brackish water but of lavender; they were not only dry but had been laundered. How many hours had she been here? What had happened to her mother?

She had run from Bancroft Hall, run from the man who had grabbed her as she passed a gate in the wall...

Slowly, as though turning the pages of a picture book, memory returned showing one after the other the events which had followed.

She had held her mother, held her close in her arms, smoothed the wet strands of hair from her pale face, begged her to wake, to live ... cried out a daughter's love; but there had been no sound, no movement of that cold wet body, no smile of recognition in the wide open eyes, only silence ... silence broken by—

'You shouldn't be up...'

A cry of fright bursting from her, Alyssa swung to face a door she had not heard open.

'...doctor said for you to rest some more.'

Fear receding into weakness, Alyssa swayed, her head swimming.

'There now, didn't I just be tellin' ... you shouldn't be up from your bed.'

With legs as wobbly as an infant taking its first steps, Alyssa caught at the bedpost, holding fast while her brain swirled.

'There now, sit yourself down, you can't expect to go rushin' about after near enough a week in bed.'

Who was this woman pressing her to a chair?

'I expects you be wonderin' where it is you be

at.' As though reading Alyssa's thought the woman answered. 'This be Lyndon, the home of Mister Paul Tarn and his sister Miss Laura, Oh, and I be Florence Adie, I keeps house for them; but there I go runnin' off at the mouth and you not havin' had your breakfast, you sit there while I brings–'

'Wait, please!' The reeling slowing in her head, Alyssa called to the woman set on leaving the room. 'Lyndon ... I don't understand, who brought me here...? Where is my mother?'

'No more would I reckon you to understand...' Florence Adie's pleasant face wreathed in sympathy, '...the state you was in when the master fetched you to this house.'

The master! Alyssa's senses jolted again. He had caught up to her, had brought her into his house...!

'...handed you over to meself and Miss Laura then sent Mister Adie to bring the doctor ... but the rest can wait 'til you be fed.'

Strength seeping back into her limbs Alyssa rose from the chair. 'Missis Adie ... how long have I been here?'

Deterred from fetching a breakfast tray, Florence Adie's plump figure moved surprisingly quickly throwing back covers of the bed, shaking pillows then smoothing them neatly into place, her answer keeping pace with the deft movements of her hands. 'Like I says, the master brought you here near enough a week since.'

A week! It rang like a bell in Alyssa's mind. She had been in this house a week ... and her mother? Alarm painting dark shadows in her eyes she

161

looked at the woman busily settling bed covers into place.

'Missis Adie.' She paused, dreading the answer to the question she knew had to be put. 'Missis Adie,' she swallowed against the sudden dryness attacking her throat, 'what has happened to my mother?'

She was to come face to face with the man to whose house she had been brought, face to face with the man who had raped her! Following the housekeeper down a well-polished staircase Alyssa felt her nerves tremble. She wanted only to run, to get away from the man who waited for her.

'Thank you, Florence.' Laura Tarn smiled up from her place at the dining table. 'Please sit down, Miss Maybury.'

It wasn't him! Alyssa stared at the man sitting opposite a younger woman, her dark hair caught beneath a white lace cap, hazel eyes warm with welcome. It wasn't him ... it was not the man who had raped her... Then who was he, why bring her to his house?

'Will you not sit down, Miss Maybury, I assure you neither my sister nor myself will eat you.'

It was meant to bring a smile but trapped in confusion Alyssa could only stare.

'There you go, now you put that inside of you and it'll have you feelin' a lot brighter.'

The arrival of the housekeeper with a fresh serving of breakfast broke through the turmoil raging in Alyssa's brain and she asked, 'Why was I brought to this house ... where is my mother?'

'So you see, Miss Maybury, Mister Richardson

162

and I thought it more suitable you be taken some place where a woman could take care of you ... it seemed Lyndon House could serve that purpose.'

'Joseph...?' Having listened in silence to Paul Tarn's explanation of her being found on the heath, Alyssa put her question, 'You know Joseph?'

For the first time since the pale, slender young woman had joined them in the breakfast room, Paul Tarn smiled. 'Joseph Richardson and I have long been friends, I could say almost like brothers. He took me under his wing after my father died, kept me on the straight and narrow though my scamp of a sister tried his patience.'

'Oh ... and how much of my misbehaving was in reality a cover for a brother's mischief?' Laura Tarn's laugh sprinkled into the room.

'We will discuss that later.' Pretended severity was lost in the touch of his hand on that of his sister, his smile resting a moment on her own then he looked again at Alyssa.

'Joseph was aware that to return you to Hall End Cottage, to have you there with no other person but himself, would give rise to fresh gossip. Wednesbury is a small town...' he had seen the swift rise of colour to her cheeks, '...gossip is its one source of amusement for many I am afraid; Joseph would not have you exposed to that.'

Fresh gossip ... he had said fresh gossip, so he knew there had already been talk. Colour deepened, the heat of it warming through Alyssa's veins.

'For that reason Joseph agreed to your coming here.' Laura Tarn took up her brother's explanation. 'He had wanted for you to be taken to Hall

End, said he would stay in his gardener's hut at Bancroft Hall, but as my brother pointed out, who would be at Hall End to care for you, but Joseph has not abandoned you, he has called here each evening asking after your welfare.'

Joseph had wanted to give up his home for her. Alyssa's throat tightened. Fingers clenched into her palms she fought back the tide of emotion threatening to overwhelm her.

'Mister Tarn.' She looked straight into a pair of deeply brown eyes. 'I thank you and your sister for your kindness, you must allow me to repay you.'

Brown eyes lost their warmth. 'Miss Maybury, neither Laura nor I require reimbursement, we were taught help genuinely given is its own reward.'

She had made him angry. Embarrassment at her own thoughtlessness increased the colour staining Alyssa's cheeks. He had the same fierce pride as Joseph, but then she had pride also. Rising from her chair, the meal she had been served still untouched, she faced the man watching her intently.

'Mister Tarn,' she answered as calmly as her feelings would allow, 'I also was taught never to take unless payment was given in return; I have lived by that teaching, I do not intend to forsake it now.'

Joseph Richardson had not exaggerated this girl's spirit. She had self-respect, a quiet dignity which at the same time expressed no humility. Paul Tarn faced a replica of himself, of his own approach to life, and respected it. Laying aside his linen napkin, hiding the regard threatening to result in a smile, he rose from the table. 'Then I will leave you to determine any such payment with my sister.'

'Thank you.' Alyssa nodded briefly. 'But there is one thing I would prefer you to do yourself... Tell me what has happened to my mother?'

15

'You should not be out of doors ... if you must go out then take a walk in the garden.' Amelia Bancroft watched her daughter-in-law adjust the skirts of a dark green velvet costume.

'There is no cause to fret, I have some months to go before the child is born. Besides you know Marlow, he dislikes my staying indoors.'

He also disliked having his word questioned. Amelia caught the quick turn of the head, the extra unnecessary twitch of the velvet skirt that said her son had insisted his wife take a morning walk. She had hoped marriage would bring about a change of behaviour in him, that the pretty Felicia would have him realise his responsibilities and settle to them, but that hope had gone the way of all the rest.

It had been a little over three years. A brief return from the plantation had seen Marlow introduced to Felicia Talbot, the twenty-year-old daughter of an iron and steel manufacturer. Continuing to watch her daughter-in-law tie on a green-feathered bonnet Amelia remembered her own aversion to the resulting courtship. She had wanted more for her son, a marriage if not within the aristocracy then at least to a daughter of landed gentry; but Marlow had seen the money behind the girl, the wealth bequeathed to her by parents dead of some illness while travelling the Continent, money he had made play for.

Small framed, delicate in her movements, pale gold hair falling in soft ringlets, almond-shaped eyes the same blue as hyacinths, Felicia Talbot had been lively as she had been pretty; but where was that prettiness now ... and what had caused liveliness to become reticence, almost a with-drawal from life? It was expected when carrying a child that a woman would not indulge too much in social gatherings but since their return from the Sugar Islands any sort of social life had been shunned by her daughter-in-law.

Shunned or denied? Returned to her private sitting room Amelia stood at the high window looking out over what had once been sculptured flower gardens but now showed unmistakable signs of neglect.

Marlow had married his money, squandering it as he had that left by his father ... and Felicia! Despite the warmth of the sun-filled room Amelia felt her blood chill. With her wealth gone had Marlow's wife become an encumbrance, one more mistake to be rectified?

She should not think such a thing, Marlow was simply being protective of his wife, of the child which would be born to him.

Turning from the window she stared at the

small safe he had rifled of every piece of jewellery.

She should not think! Amelia's hand tightened. She should not think ... but then she could not hide the whispers in her heart.

'You was soaked through and the lanterns showed you blue with cold. I had no way of knowing how long you had been sitting there and I was feared of you getting pneumonia. Maybe I should have waited 'til you could speak for yourself, but at the time ... could be my thoughts d'ain't come straight.'

That was about as near truth as he would be to getting angel's wings! Joseph Richardson looked at the young woman he had found sitting beside a flooded pit shaft nursing a corpse, crying into its wet hair, kissing its cold face. That had been enough to twist any heart but it had been the words coming with every sob had wrenched his ... the soft heartbroken phrase cried over and over through the darkness. *'Why couldn't you love me, mother? Why couldn't you love me?'*

In the short time of his acquaintance with them he had seen nothing on this girl's part but love, the real love of a daughter for her mother, word, action, even every thought had been for the comfort and welfare of her mother. Hannah Maybury had suffered from pain of the mind which undoubtedly accounted for her behaviour, her seeming to have no knowledge of the girl who rarely left her side; but Alyssa, the daughter who had clung so desperately to that cold dead body, she suffered pain in the heart... pain every sense told him had ached there many years.

167

'I be sorry if I done the wrong thing but there were no telling how long it could be afore you could take matters into your own hands.'

'Why was it so long? I mean...'

'I knows what you mean.' Joseph answered the half-spoken question. 'Why near enough a week afore you come full to your senses? That were the doctor's advising. You were near total exhaustion of the body and he feared that to have you faced with more emotional upheaval ... well there was a chance you might break under it so he prescribed a few drops of poppy juice each night and morning so you would sleep deep...'

'*...a chance you might break under it.*'

A chance she might suffer the same illness which had eaten away at her mother's brain, which slowly day by day had stolen her further from reality until she had not known present from the past.

'...that were the only reason of my agreeing to you being given that medicine, and as for having you stay at Lyndon...'

'Mister Tarn has already explained the reason.' Alyssa spoke quickly seeing a shadow of regret settle in clear blue eyes. 'It was very kind on the part of himself and his sister taking a complete stranger into their home.'

'Laura Tarn would have acted no other way; her be the gentlest of folk...'

Had the shadow in his eyes deepened? Had he been about to say more then caught back his words? Alyssa recognised the swift recovery, glimpsed the distress pull slightly at a mouth suddenly taut... Joseph Richardson walked a path

168

much as she walked!

'She is very understanding.' Alyssa filled the gap of silence. 'But like her brother she does not easily give way to argument.'

'Headstrong...' Joseph smiled but the shadows remained. 'Ar, that be Laura Tarn, time was her would go her own way though a snorting bull blocked her path, and Paul ... he still be resolute as when he were a lad, but there be commonsense to go along of a strong will; he be a fine man does Paul Tarn and his sister ... her be from the same mould.'

The hesitation had been seconds long, as if Joseph had wanted to say other than he had, as though he would have given a different explanation of Laura Tarn but again withdrew.

'Laura could be said to be much like yourself.' Hesitation gone Joseph smiled. 'You both have a mind of your own and that be my worry.'

'Worry?'

'Over what were done with your mother, if the decision I come to were the right one.'

Given the doctor's prognosis, his uncertainty as to the length of time it would take for her to recover physically, maybe even more should he think it necessary to shield her mind from yet another paralysing blow, Joseph had agreed to her mother's burial being conducted without her being there.

'Mister Tarn explained your reason of having my mother buried in my absence, you could have made no other decision... You have my thanks, Joseph.'

'That be all well and good,' Joseph shook his

169

head, 'but you haven't been given the all of it.'

The account related to her by Paul Tarn as he had driven her to Hall End Cottage, it had been incomplete? But why ... what was there he could not bring himself to tell? It would have been obvious she had little money, too little for a proper funeral. Alyssa's heart tripped in its beat. That was what Paul Tarn had kept from her; without money with which to pay for church and priest her mother had received a pauper's burial, she had been laid in an unmarked grave without benefit of any word, with no commendation to the Grace of God. Hannah Maybury had gone from the earth having no one to stand beside her grave, no one to mourn her ... no daughter to whisper a last goodbye.

'There is no need to say any more.' She forced the words, anxious not to hurt the feelings of a man who had been so kind, who had acted in the only way he could.

'There be every need if I be to know a minute's peace with meself.' Joseph glanced to where the window of his house showed a carriage, a tall dark-haired man gentling a horse that struck the ground with an impatient hoof. 'Paul Tarn told only a part,' he went on bringing his glance back to Alyssa. 'That were not from any wish to keep you from the truth but from the fact he himself d'ain't know all of that truth and that be due to my not speaking of it. For that I will be called to stand before my maker, to give Him my reason as I give it now to you. I told Paul there were none to lay Hannah beside in that churchyard on the hill, that no one of her family were buried there.

170

That were the lie I spoke, yet I thought it worse to speak of that little lad you buried there, a child Hannah's mind never let her have the knowing of; to have her laid to rest there seemed to me to be a denial, a breaking of trust. Hannah's mind let her know only the past, only the husband and children she had lost; had the Lord given her the time, the means to ask, then I believe her would have asked to lie with them; that and no other were the reason of my taking her home to Darlaston, to have her service of burial in the church of Saint Lawrence and her body set to lie alongside them of her family.'

It had not been a pauper's burial! Alyssa stared unable for the moment to take in what she had heard. Her mother had not been taken on the pauper's cart and buried without a coffin in the furthest corner of some cemetery. A cry of gratitude caught in her throat, a cry which became a sob of the realisation her mother would not lie in a lonely grave dawned in her brain.

Joseph ... Joseph had taken her mother home.

Tears spilling uncontrollably she flung herself into his arms, her muffled thanks lost against his shoulder.

Standing in the doorway, his tall figure blocking the sunlight, Paul Tarn stared at the couple, the man's arms holding the woman tight against him, then, lips set in a tight line, he turned away.

'There be pride and there be foolishness, you be certain you don't go mixin' one with another.'

Joseph's quiet words while standing beside her in St Lawrence churchyard echoed again in

171

Alyssa's mind.

She had broached the subject of the cost of her mother's burying and her speaking of repaying every penny made Joseph answer more sharply than he had spoken before. His brow had creased as it had the evening he had confronted those women outside the church in Wednesbury, his mouth set in that same determined line. He would take no money for what had been a parting gift to Hannah and he would take none of that which had been left in a pot above his fireplace.

'I don't go a' selling of good deeds.'

He had seemed near anger when she tried, refusing the money.

'...a kindness don't be a kindness if it be done only for what it brings to them as does it.'

It had sounded so much like the words her father had often used that her eyes had filled with tears. He had followed that same creed all of his life, had taught it to each of his children; but he had also taught they accept no charity.

Standing beside the grave, its headstone now bearing her mother's name along with that of her father and brothers, Alyssa had spoken quietly of her father, of what he had tried to instil in his children. Joseph had listened in silence then when she finished had taken her hand between both of his own. Would her father deny another man an act of kindness, he had asked, would he refuse to give charity of the soul?

Charity of the soul!

Alyssa rested the cloth she was mending in her lap.

It was a strange saying but somehow, standing in

172

that churchyard, the gentleness of afternoon spread like a soft veil around them, it seemed she had understood. To accept what Joseph had given, what he had done for her mother and herself from their first meeting, would be her kindness to him.

'You really don't have to do that.'

Startled by the voice Alyssa's hand jerked, pushing the point of the needle into her thumb.

'You made me jump!'

'So I see, I'm sorry.' Paul Tarn apologised.

Forgetting the thumb she had thrust instinctively into her mouth Alyssa freed the needle then gathered the cloth and thrust it into the scullery sink.

'What do you think you are doing?'

Hard and demanding the question flew at her back.

'Blood,' she answered pumping cold water over the fabric. 'The stain is more easily removed if soaked immediately in cold water.'

'Damn the cloth!'

The coldness of it had Alyssa turn from the sink. Eyes normally the colour of ripe damsons were now almost black, the mouth she knew could smile was hard, the strong jaw set. Paul Tarn stared at her.

His annoyance was obvious and it appeared she was the cause of it. She swallowed to control the flicker of apprehension along her nerves. But what could she have done to cause him vexation? She had not seen him since that drive to Joseph's cottage, had not exchanged a word.

'I asked what do you think you are doing ... and I am not referring to any damned sewing!'

173

A slightly deeper breath adding its measure of control, Alyssa held the glacial stare.

'I might ask the same of you, Mister Tarn, what do you think *you* are doing speaking to me in that way?'

She had taken the game right out of his hands. This slip of a girl had faced up to him ... she had thrown his own question in his face delivering it with an extra verbal slap. Beneath his irritation, Paul Tarn felt a smile. Like his sister this girl would not be put back by a sharp tongue.

'I apologise.' He inclined his head slightly. 'Rudeness is unforgivable whatever the cause.'

She had not said his apology was accepted. His glance took in the frost sparkling in violet eyes, the challenging lift of the head, a touch of daylight from a window sending darts of crimson from its wealth of red-gold hair. Standing facing him now, dignity in every line of her, he felt a tug at his insides; admiration, approval, respect...? It was all of those feelings yet none of them. Yet if it were none of those emotions then just what was the reason for the uncertainty, the perplexity posing riddles in his mind?

'I hear you spoke to my sister regarding the renting of the old keeper's cottage.' He pulled his mind back.

'Yes.' Alyssa nodded.

'It is not within my sister's jurisdiction to rent or allow sub-tenancy of Lyndon property.'

So that was what was annoying him. His sister had trodden on his manly toes. Had that kind woman been subjected to this same displeasure? Had her own insensibility brought disharmony

174

between brother and sister? Grieved by the probability Alyssa replied quietly. 'I should have realised that as the owner of Lyndon it was you I ought to have enquired of. Please do not allow my thoughtlessness to give distress to your sister, she acted only from kindness.'

'I place no blame upon Laura.' It was said sharply, the underlying implication being he placed all blame on her.

'Then I thank you for that,' Alyssa replied softly.

There she went again, taking the wind from his sails! Aggravation drained but the determination which had brought him to speak with Alyssa remained hard and stubborn. His tone still cold despite the change of feeling he asked, 'Why do you wish to rent Keeper's Cottage?'

Why not say what he had come to say, that he had changed his mind, she was no longer welcome to say at Lyndon! Well, she could spare them both the embarrassment of that. Her head lifting a mite higher, her look still holding his dark gaze, distinct coolness replacing the softness of her previous answer, Alyssa replied.

'I do not. I would have spoken with your sister telling her I no longer wished to rent the cottage but my conversation with you renders that unnecessary. It remains only for me to express again my gratitude for the hospitality I have been given.'

'Hospitality you now reject,' he countered harshly. 'You have been offered a place here in this house yet you refuse ... is it Joseph Richardson has made a better offer!'

Eyes which had been frosty became violet ice. Though blood pounded rapidly along her veins,

Alyssa's limbs were suddenly tense with anger.

'Mister Tarn,' she forced the words from stiff lips, 'my association with Joseph Richardson is in no way any business of yours, as anything I do or any place I go is nothing to do with you. I am no servant here, no employee accountable to you for my actions nor do I have any obligation as to explain the reason for my decisions. You have already received my thanks for the assistance you have given.'

'Assistance you have insisted upon paying for ... yes, Laura advised me of that also; a swift change of fortune, Miss Maybury.' He smiled a look of pure contempt. 'Allow me to congratulate you.'

16

Why had she let him affect her that way? The cloth wrung out and set to dry, Alyssa wiped her hands then removed the apron Florence Adie had given her to wear. Worse than that why had she said she no longer wished to rent the cottage? It had seemed the perfect solution. The shillings Joseph had returned to her would have paid for its rent until she found permanent employment.

She paused in her folding of the mending she had completed earlier, the accusation behind the words thrown at her bringing a touch of colour to her face.

'...is it Joseph Richardson has made a better offer.' He thought she and Joseph...! He thought the

176

same as those women at the church had thought, that she was Joseph's mistress! Shame deepened the tinge in her cheeks. Then of a sudden it seemed her whole being stiffened. What did it matter what Paul Tarn thought of her! What did it matter what the whole town thought! Joseph Richardson knew her character and that was enough. The mending she had agreed upon to pay for her stay at this house was done. Now she was free to go her way.

But to go where? The same problem had dogged her since the house in Booth Street had been taken from them.

'That be the last of it, I've gone through the linen twice and can't find another piece that be in need of bein' mended.'

Caught in her own thoughts Alyssa started at the sound of the voice.

'Eh, wench!' Florence's quick frown was one of concern. 'Y' be jumpy as a cat wi' its tail in the fire ... do there be summat worryin' you?'

'No.' Alyssa shook her head quickly. 'No, I...'

'I knows, wench ... I knows.' The frown gave way to a smile of sympathy. 'You still don't be over the losin' of your mother an' your 'eart will ache for many a month. I ain't one to tell you to forget what 'appened for the eye 'as seen and the brain knows; but this much I does counsel, remember the Lord sent His holy angels to tek your mother from this world and set His blessed saints to welcome her into the next and that be where one day her'll tek you once more into her arms and whisper that mother's love we all longs to hear again.'

Mother's love! Alyssa's look dropped to the

177

folded linen held in her hands. That had not been her mother's murmured goodnight, not her morning welcome when waking two little girls from their sleep ... Thea ... Alyssa swallowed the pain that was a lump in her throat ... only Thea!

'Eh, but you 'ave a fine hand wi' a needle.' Florence patted the linen she had taken from Alyssa. 'I must say I've seen no better, no not nowheres; you could mek y'self a living with it, there be one or two dressmakers along of the town would be pleased to tek you on should you be of a mind.'

Half lost in an unhappiness she had known so long, Alyssa struggled to bring her mind to what the woman had said. 'What ... oh no, you see I am not staying here in Wednesbury.'

'Ain't a' stayin'!' Missis Adie's brow registered her confusion. 'But Miss Laura, her told me only this mornin' you was after rentin' that old cottage along of Hobnail Brook.'

'Yes ... yes that had been my intention but since speaking with Miss Tarn I have had a change of plan.'

'Oh well, don't do for me to go tellin' you what to do, you young folk be much of a muchness when it comes to advice, you mostly leaves it where you found it, but though I says it as shouldn't you'd do well to think afore you goes leaving. The Tarns be good friends to 'ave, you'll find no better wherever you lands.'

'They have both been very kind.'

'Then why go wrostlin' off lookin' for some-wheres else to settle? Seein' you couldn't tek the offer to bide 'ere at Lyndon – though for the life o' me I can't see why – then that old place you was thinkin' of don't be much but it would provide a roof over your 'ead an' a fire to warm you nights. You mark what I says an' think 'ard afore you decides anythin'.'

It was already decided. Alyssa watched the plump figure leave the scullery. She had told Paul Tarn she no longer wished to rent Keeper's Cottage but perhaps she could speak with him again, say she had spoken in haste, ask could she rent the house after all.

For a moment only the idea played in her mind then the tightness which had gripped her every muscle minutes before returned to hold her tense, to lift her head defiantly. She could ask but she would not! She would go cap in hand to no one ... especially not to a man who had already made up his mind she was no more than a whore!

It was she, the height, the slenderness of form, but most of all the hair, that lovely red-gold hair marking her unmistakably. He had seen it glint in the afternoon sunlight, a glorious Titian hallmark.

Nearing the colliery he had inherited Cain Lindell reined in his horse and held it on a short bridle. He had observed the women and young girls of Darlaston but none he had witnessed boasted that deep flame-coloured hair, except one: the girl Marlow Bancroft had raped, and since that day had become one girl Cain Lindell wished to take for himself.

In the near-distance the great wheel of the winding shaft rotated slowly, its shape slightly distorted by the haze of dust and smoke which

179

draped a perpetual fog over the colliery and the houses surrounding it.

Yes, he wanted the girl with auburn hair; but not for the reason Bancroft had. Cain Lindell had different plans. True, he might take a tasting but only a tasting; to gorge on the goods would be to spoil them and selling spoiled wares was difficult, especially to the market he catered for.

He could have taken her then, had begun to move towards the house he had seen her emerge from but had checked himself when a tall figure had stepped forward. He had not noticed the carriage half hidden by heavily leafed trees or the man who had seemingly waited beside it. It had not been Bancroft, the dark hair and lithe easy movement of the body had dismissed him as the man waiting for the girl ... yet it was someone if not of quality then of wealth ... so who was the man had handed her into that carriage? What did it matter who he was! His mouth set in a hard smile, he jabbed a sharp heel into the animal's side while snatching on the rein. The dark-haired man would soon be losing his flame-haired beauty!

'There be a visitor a' waiting of you, Mister Lindell, sir.'

Cain Lindell had ignored the man coming to take the horse as he dismounted, but now glanced at the coal-blackened face.

'I said as you wasn't 'ere but the fella ... well he shoved past...'

'Pushed past?'

Sharp and condemning the query had the workman touch his cap in nervous salute, a mark of trepidation often seen since the new owner of

180

the Spindrift mine had taken over. Anxiety of dismissal adding a tremulous quiver to his voice he answered, 'Wouldn't tek no sayin', just barged straight past 'e did, walked into the office like the Spindrift were his'n, be in there now 'e does.'

Like the Spindrift belonged to him!

Cain Lindell's glance followed the direction the quick nod of the dust-caked head indicated.

Like the Spindrift belonged to him!

Was the visitor waiting in that office some other of Laban Marshall's relatives, some forgotten nephew come to lay claim to the mine ... a child of some illicit love affair wanting a share of the spoils? Improbable ... maybe ... but not beyond the bounds of possibility.

The grip of his mouth the only witness to a swift surge along his nerves, he walked across the hard-packed earth that was the colliery yard and into the small brick building comprising its office.

'So you came here.' The nervous flush which had tripped his nerves now calmed, Cain Lindell looked at the figure sprawled in the one comfortable leather armchair the small office held.

'I thought it wiser.' Marlow Bancroft tapped a riding crop against an expensive hand-made boot.

Wisdom! That was an asset entirely lacking in Marlow Bancroft! Lindell almost spat the thought, glancing instead towards the one glass window set in the room's partitioning wall beyond which a clerk was bent over the accounts he would be called upon to submit once the master's visitor had departed.

He returned his glance to the figure flicking the crop casually against a boot. Bancroft needed an

181

alibi and was here to obtain it. Like his other gambles this latest venture needed the support of Cain Lindell and support would be given ... at a price. Settling into the chair behind a heavy oak desk he asked, 'Why choose that way, and why now?'

'Why?' Marlow snapped upright, the plaited leather of the short-handled whip smacking against the side of his chair. 'You know damn well why! She knew what was going on, the least accusation on her part, the slightest imputation and the whole thing would be over; that was the why of now, and as for method, how else would you have had me do it? Tell me, Lindell ... how should I have done it ... poison ... a knife in the heart and an open bedroom window to suggest a thief seen in the act? I don't think so! No, I killed her in the only believable way, an accident made the more acceptable by your having been present when it occurred.'

She missed the company of Laura Tarn, the easy companionable talk when together they had visited Joseph, the smile which might once have been an infectious giggle yet now reflected no girlish joy, no delight in dreams waiting to be realised but rather a smile long used to cover the wound of something lost before it could be lived.

Shawl hanging loose about her shoulders, Alyssa walked briskly along Jowett's Lane glad to be free of open heath, to be free of Lyndon. But how free was she when every thought since leaving had been of the people who lived there, of the kind sensitive woman and more of the dominating brother who thought Alyssa Maybury to be the mistress of Joseph Richardson.

Laura! Determinedly she pushed aside thoughts of the man who had glared so disapprovingly in that scullery. Laura Tarn had a good home, a brother who obviously held a deep affection for her, in fact everything a woman could want ... except for a husband. Was that the reason behind the sadness which shadowed that smile, which sometimes showed in those hazel eyes? Her name said she had not married but surely—

'Excuse me.'

The words quiet yet urgent came from a young woman stood beside the Gough's Arms, a hostelry set at the junction which merged Jowett's Lane with Witton Lane, the route Alyssa had chosen to bring her to the tramway which would take her to Birmingham, a town Laura had told her was frighteningly large, so large a body could lose itself there.

'Excuse me.' Dressed in a coat of midnight blue, a straw bonnet covering almost all of her black hair, a large cloth bag clutched in a gloved hand the two words were repeated, the free hand extending to halt Alyssa. 'It is you, isn't it ... you are the girl sent for by the mistress of Bancroft Hall?'

Taken aback Alyssa made no reply.

'I don't be mistaken do I?' Indecision showed in the blue eyes and the hand reached to Alyssa's sleeve dropped quickly away. 'I ... I saw the hair, it be so unusual in its colour ... it had me think you were the girl I showed into the mistress's private sitting room; I thought you were Miss Maybury.'

Memory clicking open its doors Alyssa nodded.

183

'You are the maid—'

'Then you do be who I thought,' the woman interrupted. 'I told the mistress there couldn't be no mistakin', then when you come to the Hall and she saw for herself ... well that were that.'

'That was what? I'm sorry but I really don't understand. Is there something your mistress had wanted to ask but didn't? Does she wish me to revisit?'

'No!' So sharp it cracked like a pistol bringing glances from people passing the busy crossing, the woman's answer cut Alyssa's question. Then more quietly as if speaking to herself murmured, 'Be best never to go to that place again.'

There was nothing more to be asked, but the rest ... that sounded more like a warning. Was this something to do with the man who had come into that room, the man who had called the woman 'mother'? The acid taste of fear was suddenly in Alyssa's throat. He must have discovered where she had been living, but he would not send a maid to make sure, and surely not to waylay her in a busy street. Confusion and fear made Alyssa begin to turn away.

'Wait!'

Turning towards a call little more than a whisper, Alyssa caught the swift glance the other woman cast back along Witton Lane then another, more searching, over the expanse of heath stretching away on three sides of it.

'Wait!' Clearly disturbed, the woman sent another glance after the first. 'There is something, something I needs to ask.' She paused again as though unwilling to put voice to the rest then with

184

Alyssa's shuffle of impatience went on. 'Afore I do what I've come to do I asks your promise, your solemn oath, you will never tell a living soul what passes here between us, you will never say who come to you or why; do I have that promise?'

No one must know! No one was to be told! Alyssa's nerves jangled. Why such secrecy? Unless ... it had to be him, the man who had raped her. He wanted to be certain of her whereabouts and then...

Blood pounding, eyes sparkling her intensity of feeling and her tone a razor's edge, Alyssa shook her head. 'You may tell your mistress's son he will get no pledge from me.'

Had that been a flicker of understanding? Alyssa saw the nuance flash across the woman's eyes.

'Don't be that one be asking.' The return was made quickly, the moment of inner perception dismissed. 'That be my word, now I asks yours ... do you give it or do I be on my way?'

Did she trust this woman? Was this some sort of trap? Caught in a tangle of emotions Alyssa hesitated.

'I see you have doubt, you thinks I might be lying ... and if I read your face right then I understands your reason. Him up at the Hall be a no good ... I would as soon chuck meself in the canal as do anything for him. No, I be acting on no instruction from Marlow Bancroft.'

Not the mistress and not the son, then who? Who other than those two could possibly have any interest in her?

Across from them the whinnying of a horse rang from the heath, visibly startling the woman whose face paled as she lifted her glance to follow the source of the sound. She was obviously afraid of something or someone. Alyssa watched the colour fade from her cheeks. Could she also be in fear of the man she had named as Marlow Bancroft? Wanting to end this for both of them Alyssa began to speak but a gloved hand halted her.

'I asked your promise, without it I says only this. I trusts Marlow Bancroft no more than instinct says you trusts him; you can tell that to whoever you will and I will deny it.'

The look of hatred flashing in the eyes watching her, the ring of contempt with which the words were spoken, that surely was not contrived. Trusting to her own conclusion, Alyssa apologised. 'I'm sorry to have given the impression I doubted you ... of course you have my promise to say nothing of this meeting.'

Gloved fingers closing again over Alyssa's arm drew her to a side of the building out of sight of the street. 'Tell me,' the question was low, 'do you have a sister?'

Thea! Alyssa's veins throbbed. This was somehow to do with Thea!

'I sees you have.' The woman went on, her words stumbling over each other in their bid to be said. 'That sister, would her be a few years younger than yourself with eyes blue like hyacinths and hair of a colour such as your own?' Low and with an urgency the words ran on, flowing over Alyssa like a warm tide, a breathlessness leaving her without answer.

'...would that sister be a laughing carefree girl ... one by the name of Thea?'

'Thea,' Alyssa almost cried the name, 'Thea is my sister, is it she sent you to find me?'

'No.' The straw hat bobbed the denial.

'Then who!'

'Shh!' The shrill demand brought a swift return, the woman again glancing nervously past Alyssa's shoulder. 'The Gough's Arms sees a lot of trade passing from one town to another and not all ears be closed to the conversation of other folk, there be some would pass what they heard to the devil should he pay them a shilling.'

This woman knew Thea! Alyssa's brain whirled. She must have met with her to know her name, to describe her in such detail; Thea must be here ... at Bancroft Hall!

The awfulness of it, of what it might mean halted the rush of thought with the impact of a blow sending a shudder rippling along every nerve. 'Where?' she asked, a half-sob choking her throat. 'Where is my sister?'

The sounds of men talking from the doorway of the public house had the other woman shake her head, a finger already to her mouth in a gesture for silence.

Strung tight as a wire, every fibre screaming under the stress of having the woman say no more, to have her possibly turn and walk away, it seemed to Alyssa the men she could hear laughing would never leave! Please, she begged silently, please let them move on! The scrape of a match against stone grated like thunder, the curl of tobacco smoke drifting on the air seemed only to mock the silent plea. Then another burst of laughter and calls of goodbye allowed the breath

187

to surge back into Alyssa's lungs.

'Listen!' The prudent finger had lowered with the cessation of men's voices but caution remained in the woman's tone. 'The mistress give me a note...'

'But you said...'

'I knows what I said.' The retort was curt, admissive of no interruption. 'But that be water under the bridge. The mistress, she give me a note to pass to you; it don't have no address nor no signature neither but you have my God's honest word it were meant for you.'

'A note.' Alyssa frowned. 'Why would Lady Bancroft write to me?'

'That be for you to find out when you reads it.' Another glance about them preceding the dipping of a hand into the pocket of her coat, the woman thrust an envelope at Alyssa.

'Wait!' It was Alyssa who now stretched a hand, catching at a brown sleeve. 'Are you not to take back an answer?'

'Not me.' The woman freed her arm. 'I don't be going back to that place not never.'

'But your mistress...'

Her back already turned on the protest the woman looked briefly over her shoulder. 'I don't have none ... the mistress of Bancroft Hall be dead!'

17

'I feel responsible, Paul. I feel it must be something I said that made her leave so abruptly.'

She had said goodbye to his sister but had made no mention of speaking with him. Paul Tarn listened to his sister come into his study, his resentment of earlier that day still smouldering. Alyssa Maybury had refused a place in his house, refused his hospitality but not that of Joseph Richardson. She must have gone to him, to the man whose arms had held her.

'We brought her here, Paul, she did not ask to come,' Laura went on. 'I can't begin to imagine how frightening it must have been for her waking to find herself in a strange house with no one she was familiar with to comfort her.'

As she was obviously familiar with Joseph Richardson, as she was with the comfort of that man's arms! Paul fiddled with the pen he was holding, twisting it around in his fingers.

'...and then the added horror of remembering what had happened to her mother, of finding her drowned in that flooded pit; I shudder when I think of the girl all alone on the heath, of pulling her own mother from the water. I could never get over an experience such as that and now Alyssa is alone again and it is my fault. I must have hurt her...'

'You did not hurt her.' He threw the pen on to

the desk, the sharp nib scratching a line on the polished surface. 'You are not the cause of Miss Maybury no longer wishing to rent Keeper's Cottage, I am–'

'You?' Hazel eyes darkening with sudden concern Laura Tarn's brow creased. 'But how?'

Not how but why? Paul Tarn heard the question loud in his mind. Why had he felt so angry ... why had he made an issue of Alyssa Maybury consulting his sister and not himself?

'I...' This was going to sound so foolish. He picked up the pen needing something to focus on, to avoid having to meet the look which would tell him his sister was a little ashamed of such behaviour. '...I was short with her when we spoke this morning; I told her it was not for you to grant lease of Keeper's Cottage, that it would have been more prudent to have spoken with myself.'

'Then it *is* my fault, I should have known to have sent her to speak with you.'

'No, Laura, you did nothing to blame yourself for. I acted boorishly with Miss Maybury; I shall of course apologise.'

He had seen that expression on his sister's face many times. Paul met it again now. A look which said that although he were the older by five years he was very much her junior in commonsense.

'I am glad to hear that.' Her frown disappearing, Laura raised a quizzical eyebrow. 'But tell me, how do you plan to apologise when neither of us has any idea of where it might be Alyssa has gone?'

There would be only one place the girl would go to! Concentrating his gaze once more on the pen,

190

Paul Tarn tasted the acid of the thought. She had demonstrated the feelings she had for Joseph Richardson; it was to him she would go. But why had not Laura supposed as much? She had accompanied Alyssa Maybury, going with her to visit Hall End on several occasions during the girl's stay at Lyndon ... a stay only long enough to repay an imagined debt! A flicker of anger he had been unable to dismiss entirely since that encounter in the scullery rose again in his chest; she had repaid what she felt she owed to Paul Tarn by repairing household linen ... but just how had she repaid her debt to Joseph Richardson?

'I can only hope she may have decided to speak with Joseph, that he may have knowledge of Alyssa's intentions. In any case I shall go see him.' Laura rose to her feet.

Relieved he had not had to put his own supposition into words, Paul returned the pen placing it in a crystal pot encased in a brass inkstand. Laura had been friends with Joseph as long as he had and would be the first to defend his or Alyssa Maybury's association as being their business and that of no one else. Nor would his sister be wrong. Joseph was his own man, what he chose to do was solely his concern, but the girl ... why did what she might choose to do be of so much concern to Paul Tarn?

The question came so readily, a question it seemed had no answer. Impatient with himself Paul also rose. 'I will drive you.'

Laura shook her head, her smile saying she had already forgiven her brother's abrupt attitude of that morning. 'There is a bonnet I wish to try on and I have gloves to collect from the glovemaker in Wednesbury town ... but if you wish to come shopping...'

'No ... spare me that.' Paul lifted both hands in mock horror then caught his sister in a hug. 'Give my regards to Joseph, remind him we do not see him often enough here at Lyndon.'

True they did not enjoy the company of Joseph Richardson as often as would be liked. Paul watched his sister leave the study. But was it him he hoped would visit this house, the man whose company he wished for, or that of Alyssa Maybury?

It had all gone remarkably well. Marlow Bancroft slid into a charcoal-grey morning coat, easing it across his shoulders and smoothing its line over matching trousers before fastening its single line of buttons. He liked these new fashions of 1895, the cut-away line of the coat complemented his thighs. It was unfortunate he must wear a black necktie and armband but to be seen without that touch of mourning would give rise to speculation. Not that there could be any with regard to the sudden loss of the mistress of Bancroft Hall ... a loss the son and owner of that residence did not have the slightest regret for. Tucking a perfectly folded handkerchief into the breast pocket of the coat, he smiled at the reflection looking back at him from the long Cheval mirror of his dressing room. It *had* all gone very well.

'You have a visitor, sir, will I say it is too soon yet for you to receive callers?'

A visitor! Despite his convictions of moments

ago Marlow felt a tremor of apprehension ripple the length of his spine. Had it all gone so well after all...! Was there something he had overlooked, something which could give rise to speculation? But there was nothing ... he had been too careful! Unconsciously he reset the mauve handkerchief in his pocket. It was perfectly natural for people to call, to offer the condolence on his loss ... but so soon? He would not have expected news of it to have spread quite so quickly ... but why else a visitor? Sending people away unreceived would not answer the question in his mind but might serve to raise some in the minds of others. Forcing his brain to clear he dismissed the manservant telling him to show the caller to the morning room.

Why the hell hadn't Lindell shown? Alone once more Marlow juggled with a fresh torrent of thought. He had said he would return so why hadn't he? Was he regretting having given his word ... was he going back on it? Christ, that could make things sticky! With Lindell claiming they had been together the whole time no one could say other than that death had been an unhappy occurrence, an occurrence neither of them could have foreseen or forestalled. Damn Lindell! Marlow kicked savagely at the foot of the bed. If he reneged now ... but he would not! The last brought a smile to Marlow's mouth. Lindell would realise that only by playing the game Marlow Bancroft's way was he ever likely to be paid the money he had loaned.

Something was not well with his sister. Paul Tarn watched the agitated twist of fingers. She had been

193

distracted throughout the meal, her thoughts anywhere but on the conversation. It was not the fact she answered in monosyllables, half of them an incorrect return, not a worry she did not seem to hear much of what he said to her, but of what she was hearing or perhaps seeing in her mind. Something had affected her, there was little doubt of that, something which had left a profound expression ... Joseph and Alyssa Maybury? Feeling contempt at his own thought he pushed it away yet he knew he had not driven it so deep it would not return.

'How is the new bonnet?' Driven to break yet one more silence Paul tried the trivial. Maybe it would lead to what was disturbing his sister.

'Yes.'

The answer again given with no recognition of what had been asked, Paul set aside knife and fork. 'Laura!' He spoke sharply hearing the sound of it ring against delicate glassware placed alongside each plate. 'Laura, what happened today? And please do not tell me there is nothing, we both know each other too well for that.'

'I...' She looked at him then quickly away, her glance resting on fingers she clearly was not seeing.

God Almighty! Paul felt the tingle of fire in his throat. If any man had spoken meanly to his sister, if any man had offended her then by God he would pay for the doing!

Leaving his chair he took her hand leading her gently to the sitting room. With her sitting beside the fire, the play of gaslight glinting tiny brown darts through her hair, Paul felt the deep

194

protection he had felt since their parents' death had left him the responsibility of a younger sister. Laura had not always behaved as he would have her behave, she had been headstrong and obdurate with a tenacity of will not even Joseph Richardson with his commonsense advice could overcome, but all of that was in the past. Laura left those ways behind after... But that also was in the past, he would not think of that again.

Nodding thanks to Mrs Adie who had thoughtfully brought a tray of tea, he waited while a cup was poured and given to his sister, then as the door closed behind the woman who had been part of the household from his childhood, Paul spoke quietly.

'Laura, what happened today?'

She could have been carved from marble. A touch of real fear pressed cold in Paul's stomach. The fingers which had twisted and worried all during dinner were now unmoving, the face still as a painting, but the eyes ... the eyes flitted like dark moths, eyes filled with pain. Pain from what? Paul took the cup from nerveless hands and replaced it on the tray. What had his sister looking as if she had seen beyond the grave?

'Laura,' he held both of her hands in his own, 'Laura, I know something has happened, please won't you tell me.'

A half-burned coal tumbling deep into the fire his only answer, he tried again.

'Is it something someone said to you?'

What on earth could he do? If she would not speak, would not say what it was had upset her to such a degree? Had she spoken to Mrs Adie, perhaps confided what was wrong to her? Almost as it came Paul rejected the thought. Florence Adie had been like a mother to them both since they were orphaned, she would prevent the wind from blowing on either if she could; had Laura spoken to her of receiving any slight then Florence Adie would have gone after the culprit's hide be it man or woman.

Sitting in the quiet room, his sister's hands in his, he could not fend off the thoughts manoeuvring their way cunningly up from the depths of memory, thoughts contriving to force their way into his conscious mind, bringing with them the quiet heartbreak of the sister he loved. He had vowed when watching her suffer the trauma of unhappiness six years ago, had made a solemn promise to himself that never while he lived would Laura be hurt again. She had hidden herself behind a barrier, a wall of pain it had seemed impossible to penetrate, a world he dreaded she might slide back into when that old sorrow showed in those soft eyes or trembled behind a smile. Watching her now he felt that dread pull at his heart.

He had been much to blame. His glance shifting to the fire he stared into yesterday. Laura had been visiting a former school friend at her home in Buckinghamshire and while there had been introduced to a young man and had, she professed, fallen in love with him. Returned home to Lyndon she had expressed the desire to become engaged to marry. In the heart of the fire Paul watched the glitter of flame. Laura's eyes had flashed as vividly. At twenty years of age she had all the spirit of youth, the confidence that what she wanted was right for her, that she should be granted what she asked. But he had not granted what she asked. Her brother and guardian, he had refused permission for her to marry. There had been tears and tantrums, her eyes flashing anger, but he had refused to be moved. She had confided in Joseph Richardson then perversely dismissed his advice she be guided by her brother as 'old fashioned'.

'*Why should we wait?*' It seemed the words she had flung later that evening, when he himself had supported Joseph's reasoning, resounded on the silence and winged about the room as they had all those years ago. But their only sound was in his head. '*I will feel the same in a year's time!*' Laura's tempestuous cry swam back from the past. '*I will feel the same for the rest of my life. I love him and nothing you say will change that nor will you prevent our marrying!*'

The next day she had run away.

It had been Joseph again, quiet sensible advice stilling the swell of anxiety ... and of anger. Yes, there had been anger. Paul admitted what had been so hard to admit then. The man was a fortune hunter and Laura ... Laura was an impetuous little fool who needed to be taught a lesson!

But he should not go after her like a bull in a field. Joseph's words were as clear now as they had been the moment he had spoken them. Anger will only bring anger, Laura would retaliate in kind maybe causing a rift which might never heal. Instead he, Paul, should go to Buckinghamshire, meet with the man, tell him of Laura's financial circumstance, of the Will which had left Lyndon House and precious little else; advise him the young woman he had known for such a short time was totally dependent upon her brother, then listen in turn to what was said in reply. Give the fellow a chance, had been Joseph's advice.

And he had followed it. His glance still deep in the scarlet bed of the fire he allowed memory its moment. He would meet with the man his sister claimed loved her, give him the opportunity to speak for himself.

But they had not met. The man had been advised property abroad needed his immediate attention. He had left that week leaving behind a letter for Laura.

'...*nor will you prevent our marrying.*'

Shifting his glance back to the face devoid of colour despite the warmth of the room, sympathy for his sister welled inside him.

He had not prevented their marrying. Power and intent had in the event been taken from him. The man his sister had run away to join had sailed from England and Laura had seen nothing of him, received no further word from that day to this ... like the stuff of dreams he had faded from her life.

'I did not find Alyssa...'

So quiet it might have been just another whisper in his head Laura's words fell into the void of silence.

'...I looked but I could not find her.'

She had not seen the girl! The seconds of ease it afforded were instantly swept away. Not seeing Alyssa Maybury did not necessarily mean she was not with Joseph Richardson!

'She is a sensible young woman, she will take care for her safety.' Had she already done that? Was she even now settled in Hall End Cottage? Like shadows thoughts flicked in and out of Paul's mind.

'I met with Joseph.'

Doubts reared again sharp and forceful, refusing Paul's attempt to clear them. Laura had met with Joseph. Had he seen the pony cart driving towards his home? Gone to meet it before Laura reached the house and so prevented her from seeing the girl inside it?

'He had not seen Alyssa.'

Disgust at himself, at the thoughts he had harboured, mixed with an emotion he could not name, swept hotly through Paul Tarn. There was no question of truth, Joseph Richardson was not a man to lie; so if the girl had not been at Hall End then where was she gone?

'Did you spend some time at Joseph's place?'

Was he deliberately trying to punish himself? Was the question a lash used to whip himself ... retribution for his mental accusations?

'I did not visit Joseph's home.'

His sister's answer a fresh barb in his flesh Paul drew a hard breath. Using it to barricade his mind against a further invasion of doubt he remained silent.

'It was not there I spoke with Joseph...'

Held between Paul's hands her own fluttered.

'...I knew he would not be home at that time of day, that he would be at his work...'

Had Alyssa Maybury made her way to his house? Had she been waiting there against

199

Joseph's return? Determined to keep his mind clear of further accusations Paul repelled the mental onslaught, only the slight pressure of his hands relating to its presence.

'...so I drove to Bancroft Hall...'

Laura continued to speak, her voice quiet as though it came from some place far away.

'...I did not present a card having no wish to impinge upon Lady Bancroft's time. I went instead to the kitchen garden and there spoke with Joseph. He promised he would bring word of Alyssa should he see or hear from her.'

Joseph would not have spoken sharply, given no reprimand for her entering the grounds of Bancroft Hall and seeking him out before first obtaining permission, and certainly no other employee would risk his wrath by daring to do so. Yet something had caused Laura to be distressed, the marks of that showed only too well.

'Did you go anywhere after leaving Bancroft Hall?' Paul posed the question, then when it seemed she would not answer asked again, 'Did you call anywhere ... speak to anyone?'

She lifted her head, the light from the gasolier showing the pain in her eyes. 'No,' she answered softly, 'I did not speak to him...'

Him! Paul's whole body tightened. So whoever had caused his sister's present state of mind was a man ... but who? And what was it he had done?

'...I saw him...' Laura's voice trembled, '...I saw him ride towards the house.'

'Did he stop ... ride across to you?' Paul felt anger begin to churn along his veins. 'Laura, did this man follow you from Bancroft Hall, did he ...

did he force his attentions upon you ... is that it, is that what has you so upset? If so then by God I'll beat the life out of him!'

'He did not follow, he did not approach me.'

Confused, Paul stared. The man had not attempted to speak, he had not imposed his presence in any way so why was Laura so agitated?

'This man,' he asked again, 'the one you saw riding up to Bancroft Hall, can you tell me who he is?'

For a long moment only the gentle hiss of the gasolier penetrated the silence then a breath helping the words from her mouth Laura answered, 'Joseph told me his name. It was Cain Lindell, the man I had wished to marry.'

18

She had not expected it to be like this; the sights the sounds, it was all so foreign. Taking that letter she had not stopped to think, to plan ... but how did she plan for something she did not know? Asking directions while in Wednesbury had not come easily, here it felt virtually impossible. Nerves threatening to get the better of her, Alyssa glanced to where a narrowboat was moored at a jetty where the river fed into a wide channel.

She could ask those boat people to take her with them, to take her back to Tipton. They had been so kind giving her a place on the boat asking no question why she would be travelling so far.

A breeze catching at her skirts, she touched a hand to hold them, feeling the pocket containing the letter ... the letter she had read while standing in the Street and on finishing it had immediately enquired where it was she could get the tram to Birmingham. The woman she had asked glanced to the doorway of the Gough's Arms Inn then back to her, seeming for a moment unwilling to reply. Alyssa remembered the flush rising to her face when she had realised she might be thought a woman of the streets.

Perhaps it had been the bundle of clothing for the woman had looked at it with a flash of pity in her eyes. Times were hard for folk, forcing them to leave their homes to look for work in other towns, she had said, then agreed to show her the place where the tram could be got.

Her moment of suspicion passed the woman had chatted the whole time it had taken to walk the length of Witton Lane, the steep rise of ground causing her to breathe heavily though not proving sufficiently difficult as to halt her flow of words.

Reaching the point where the Lane joined the wider Holyhead Road the woman had halted. Placing her basket on the ground she wiped her forehead with a large handkerchief as red as her cheeks.

'*You ain't said much wench...*' She had paused in the mopping of moisture glistening on her face, the glance she directed one of understanding.

'*...and I ain't goin' to ask of no question, but I don't think to be far wrong in sayin' you don't go 'aving a deal of money to your name.*'

Her worn boots and skirts had been answer in

themselves and the woman had gone on.

'*There be another way of getting to Brummajum and further than that should you be wanting; a way that'll take naught from your pocket should you be willing to work.*'

A way of saving her precious few shillings ... of course she would work.

'*The Tame Valley canal be not far and most any boat'll pass through Brummajum.*'

The woman had pointed to where open heath backed a line of straggly houses, her handkerchief fluttering like a flag.

'*...a polite askin' will get you a lift for free, though if you should be of a mind to go somewhere's further then you looks to find y'self a monkey boat. Don't be no chimpanzee operates it!*'

The woman had laughed at Alyssa's startled glance.

'*They be called monkey boats cos they be owned by a carrier the name of Thomas Monk. These be used for journeys to London and the like so they 'ave a cabin for to live in. You look for one wi' a family, they be grateful for the extra help.*'

They had been grateful and she had shown her own gratitude by working alongside them dawn to dusk, the younger children accepting her almost immediately as family, the twelve-year-old son gravely instructing how to steer or operate a lock.

The cloth-wrapped bundle she had brought with her from Lyndon House held in one hand, Alyssa waved goodbye to the family who had made space for her in their cramped home, who had brought her here to Bristol, the port they said saw boats come from and sail to all parts of the

203

world, but they were each of them already busy loading cargo to be carried back to the Midlands.

Standing, uncertain of what her next step should be or even how to take it, she pulled her shawl close across her chest.

'Outta t'way!' The shout accompanied the shove of a body hurriedly pushing past her, the head of the man hidden by the huge sack balanced on his shoulder. Stumbling awkwardly from the collision she was instantly caught in a second one, this from a woman whose black skirts were covered with an apron of coarse sacking and wearing what once might have been a prettily red and blue chequered shawl but now was tattered almost beyond recognition.

'Y'go standin' about gawkin' and you'll find y'self in t'warter!'

Shouted irritably the words drifted after the woman now hitching a large wicker basket higher on her hip.

She was standing and staring. Alyssa's gaze followed figures scurrying like so many ants fetching and carrying, constantly unloading crates and containers only to have them whisked across to high-built warehouses or to canal boats waiting to transport them to towns across the country. How could she not stare! Never in her life had she dreamed ... never known boats as large as this! Fascinated, she let her gaze wander over the vessels moored at what the boating family she had travelled with had called the docks, her head tipping back on her neck as she scanned huge masts, their sails furled, then at others, their huge canvas sheets spread to the wind, moving as gracefully as great winged butterflies down the channel giving onto the sea. They looked so beautiful, more beautiful than anything she had ever seen. Forgetful of the bustle all around her, as if responding to some soundless call, wanting only to be part of the beauty her mind cried to, she had reached the edge of the stone-built quay and would have stepped off had not a hand caught her arm.

'You really ought not to venture so close, accidents happen very easily at the dockside – and once in there...'

Brought sharply from her reverie Alyssa glanced at the water. Crusted with oil and tar its surface undulated slowly like the breathing of some great slime-covered sea serpent.

'Not so pretty when you get a closer view, eh?'

Alyssa looked again at the dark water lapping the side of a tall ship, each swell washing floating debris against its timbers in some macabre offering ... an exchange for life! The thought bringing a shiver she stepped quickly away, turning her back to the slimy mass.

'I ... I wasn't thinking.'

'It happens to most people seeing sea-going ships for the first time ... this is your first time if I am not mistaken.'

'No, you are not mistaken.' Alyssa freed her arm. It was all so strange, so different from Darlaston. The way people spoke, so difficult to understand ... the tang of sea air added to by the scents of tea and fruits, raw cotton and spices, exotic yet at the same time frightening. And rising above it all those huge ships, any one of them would hold a dozen of the narrowboats she had so often seen drawn by horses along the canal where her father and brothers had fished. Her mother would have called upon heaven to protect them while Thea would have squealed delight... Thea! Instantly all else was gone from Alyssa's mind. Thea was the reason of coming here, Thea who had run away ... Thea who had not once written to say where she was or to ask of her family.

'You are travelling on?'

Quietly asked, the question seemed somehow to have no competition with the hurly-burly noise all around and for the first time Alyssa looked at the man who had prevented her stepping from the quay. Mouse-coloured hair receding from a high forehead lent a prematurely balding look while eyebrows bushy and of a much darker brown seemed incongruous above eyes so pale they might have been without colour.

Suddenly aware of her scrutiny Alyssa turned an embarrassed gaze in the direction of narrow streets leading warren-like from every angle of the busy dockyard. 'Yes,' she nodded briefly, 'that is my intention.'

'Then allow me to assist you, or has your baggage already been taken on board the *Dolphin?*'

'*Dolphin?*' Concentration drawn to the streets, her mind juggling with the problem of which might lead to a lodging where she could spend the night, Alyssa answered vacantly.

'The schooner.' The man smiled, pointing to the ship in whose long shadow they both stood. 'With you coming to stand here I naturally thought you to have passage on her.'

'No...' Alyssa's reply trailed as she was

206

brusquely pushed aside yet again.

'Y' gets y'self a step nearer the edge an' it'll be a cold bath y'll be tekin' ... owt getting' in t'way o' folk workin' finds itsel' chucked over t'side.'

Already several yards away the man who had shoved roughly between them muttered, striding on towards a line of warehouses, their arched entrances sealed by heavy wooden doors, windows set only in upper storeys crossed by metal bars. But it was none of this that held Alyssa's wide-eyed stare, not the man's rudeness, not his continued threats but the line of men following behind, their backs bent beneath large and seemingly weighty sacks. Their skin...! She stared at the figures moving in silence behind the man tapping a cane against a leather boot as he marched dominatingly on ... the men carrying the sacks ... their skin was black! It was not the thick layer of coal dust which had plastered the hands and face of her father and brothers, not the powdery legacy earned from working in the bowels of the earth, this was unstreaked by sweat, unmarked by rivulets of perspiration coursing down their faces... this skin gleamed as rich and dark as newly turned earth.

'I see ships are not all that is new to you.' Standing beside Alyssa the man who had kept her from the water now drew her out of the path of a second convoy of goods. 'The men you saw just now, they came originally as slaves...'

'But slave trading was abolished many years ago my father told me!'

The man looked in the direction the line had taken. 'Perhaps I should explain. Those men are the children of slaves imported into this country but thanks to William Wilberforce and his untiring campaign slavery is no longer legal anywhere in the British Empire.'

'Then why–?'

'Do they not return to their native Africa?' Having reached the fringe of streets he halted. 'Some of the men you saw carrying cargo to the warehouse were small children when brought to England, some of them were not even born; consider then their position supposing they could afford passage. Africa is a vast continent. With no knowledge of their ancestral villages, of where parents or grandparents were taken from, how do they find their roots, their own people? And then how do they make their living? At least here they have employment, a roof and a meal ... here in England they are free.'

Free as her father had been, free as most others in Darlaston and in Wednesbury, men who worked their hearts and souls out in order to keep their families! Alyssa's mind answered acerbically; there was little freedom for them, as those men labouring here at the docks they wore the invisible chains of poverty.

'Man's cruelty to man has been legendary through the ages, but the taking and selling of others was, I fear, the worst of his sins ... but I must not keep you, night comes quickly to the docks and sadly it is not safe for a young woman alone; if you say which vessel you are to take I will accompany you to its berth.'

Wanting to tell him, yet not wanting to tell him she had no passage booked on any ship, Alyssa hesitated. He was a stranger but then wasn't everyone in this town a stranger to her? But what was to be gained by lying, by saying what was not true? Trust had to begin somewhere and if not here with him, then where?

'I ... I arrived only a few minutes ago...' She had begun truthfully enough yet the feeling she should not confide her situation still hankered in her mind. It must be obvious she had no previous arrangements; if she had she would have taken advantage of it not stood around with her small bundle of clothing tucked beneath her shawl.

Caught by a breeze whipping in from the broad channel of water, a torch set in an iron sconce fixed to the wall of a warehouse flared sending the acrid smell of pitch wafting across the quay, the brilliance of flame lighting the pale eyes watching Alyssa's face.

'I should have realised.' The eyes narrowed slightly, a smile touching a face becoming rapidly lost beneath the gathering night. 'You have yet to make your arrangements. In the meantime perhaps I might suggest the Mission Hall, it offers tea and a slice of bread with a bowl of soup. Betsy and Tom Fletcher run the place and, though not perhaps with an iron hand, Betsy wields a pretty formidable metal ladle as many a seaman using the port of Bristol has found to his cost, should his language not meet with Betsy's approval.'

A cup of tea! Alyssa mentally counted the money still in her pocket. She would need every penny ... but a cup of hot tea ... it would surely not cost more than that.

'The Mission Hall is this way.'

He had turned about on saying it. She either had to follow or find her own way. Alyssa glanced again at streets which in the few minutes of her conversation with the man now beginning to walk away from her, had already become tunnels of darkness, the buildings on either side seeming to close over them and shrouding away what little was left of light.

'...*it is not safe for a young woman alone*...'

So clear they might have been spoken aloud the words echoed in her brain. Waiting for no more she followed.

Sitting on a tiny iron-framed bed, in a pocket-sized room lit only by a candle and the greyness of a moonless sky, Alyssa hugged her shawl close about her shoulders.

'It don't 'ave the mekin's of a decent cupboard,' Betsy Fletcher had said on offering the room for the night, 'but y'll 'ave a safer night than you'd 'ave out on the streets.'

The Mission Hall had been full of men sitting at trestle tables drinking steaming hot tea from tin mugs held between their hands or eating thick meat stew from tin bowls. Betsy had directed her to a smaller table wedged into a corner then had gone into the kitchen to fetch food.

Beyond the window the raucous shout of a man and the high-pitched laughter of a woman had Alyssa shudder. That man's voice had been hard, his hand on her wrist like the talons of a vulture.

'...*ya don't want to go sittin' all by y'self*...'

Like boots crunching over stones the words repeated now in her brain.

A woollen hat pulled low over a heavy brow, particles of stew dripped onto an unkempt beard, one of the men had caught her as she made towards the smaller more isolated table, snatching her down so hard she had fallen backwards across his lap.

'*...now that be more friendly...*'

He had laughed down at her, his hand clamping to her breast.

'*...I likes a woman to be friendly, 'specially one pretty as you.*'

She had tried to struggle free but the brute strength of those arms had held her, his laugh drowning her cries, his face with its grease-soaked beard lower over her own, mouth smeared with the remnants of a meal, rank breath sickening in her nostrils. But horrifying as that had been, the eyes were more horrifying still. Dark and menacing as the water which had lapped the stonework of the quay, they had bored into her, the message contained in their depths assaulting her senses – that same message she had seen in the eyes of Marlow Bancroft moments before he had raped her.

The intention had been there, it had been clear in the way that man had held her! Alyssa shrank into the shawl as though using its protection against the thoughts her will could not drive away.

The hand had cupped her breast squeezing painfully, words slurred by lust drooling between yellowed teeth his lips had all but touched her own when he had gasped, his grip releasing her as Betsy's ladle had smacked against the side of his head.

'Y'll be bringin' none of your filthy ways to this place...'

She had bellowed at the man, the ladle swinging threateningly close to the woollen cap while her other hand swung a meat cleaver.

'...nor will y'be tekin' no more meals at this Mission; now get yer stinkin' hide away afore y'finds yerself goin' back to sea with a hook fastened to the stump of an arm!'

The appearance of Betsy's husband, an iron bar beating a steady rhythm on an open palm, had prevented any reaction from the seaman. He had hastily left the hall and Betsy had taken her into the kitchen, her apology at having left her with those men profuse and genuine.

The meal which minutes before she had longed to eat had no longer appealed. Shivering despite the heat of a large cooking range she had fought tears she had not wanted the other woman to see.

That had been when Betsy had offered lodging for the night.

'I ain't a goin' to pry, I be one who believes a body's business be her own...'

She had brought two large mugs of tea and set herself at the table, pushing one mug across to where Alyssa sat.

'...but anybody wi' one eye missin' and blind in t'other can see y' don't 'ave no wherewithal for a lodgin' nor no passage on no boat neither an' while it don't be my place to go givin' advice I be goin' to anyways an' that advice be this, tomorrer get y'self back to where y' come from afore you 'ave cause to regret ever seein' Bristol town.'

212

Grief and sorrow of weeks, weariness of her body or just the dejection so heavy in her heart? She had not known which was the key that had opened the floodgates but sitting at that table with Betsy's comforting hand covering her own the misery of the weeks lived since being ejected from the house in Booth Street had poured from her.

Betsy had crossed to the fire and taken the large enamelled teapot from a trivet drawn beside it, refilling both cups before returning the pot to its place and setting herself back on her chair before answering.

'...*There be many a wench passes through...*'

She had stirred her tea the clank of a metal spoon against her cup sounding over the low hum of conversation seeping through the closed door of the kitchen.

'...*an' I gets to see a fair few as I comes an' goes about the port but I can't say as I've seen a wench the likes of you be describin', an' I don't be likely to forget one with hair the colour of yer own; y' be certain that sister come this way?*'

She could not be certain. Alyssa's hand closed over the envelope thrust deep in the pocket of her skirt, over the letter passed to her by the maid from Bancroft Hall, a letter she had shown no one.

Taking it from her pocket, she unfolded the single sheet of cream-coloured notepaper, a distinctive crest denoting its house of origin showing imperiously as she held the paper closer to the light of the candle.

The writing had the appearance of having been hurried, the characters sometimes scrawled as if the pen had rushed eagerly on to the next before

213

completing the shape of the one before. Had the author been afraid of being discovered in the task? The thought which had played ever since her first reading came now as she read again.

'Thea Maybury...'

Her pulse had throbbed on seeing the name and she had almost cried out for the woman who had brought the letter to come back, to tell her more of her sister. But the woman had gone, disappearing so quickly she might never have been there outside of the Gough's Arms Inn, but the thump of pulse told its story then as it told it now.

Candle flame caught by the swift exhalation of breath flickered, seeming to catch the words cavorting across the page in a wild dance, but imprinted on her brain they needed no steadying.

'I believe you to be the sister of Thea Maybury...'

Words motionless now on the page stared up at her.

'...If you have love for her then take her away from Jamaica before it is too late.'

There was no salutation marking its beginning, no signature at its end, just that plain warning – *before it is too late.*

What did it mean by too late? Was Thea ill ... perhaps terminally? Was this letter a means of saying that, of giving one last chance of sisters meeting before that death occurred? But if so, if this letter were sent purely from sympathy, why did it bear no name ... and why had it identified a country yet not said where in that country Thea was to be found?

As great a question rose as Alyssa returned the letter to her pocket. How was she to get to Jamaica?

19

As he sat at the desk in his study, Paul Tarn's hand rested on the letter he had received in the morning post. He had not doubted his sister's word yet given the unhappiness of being jilted by a man she believed had loved her, unhappiness he knew still clouded her days, she could easily have misheard, only imagined Joseph Richardson to have said the name Cain Lindell.

She had seen the face of the man briefly as he passed by; *briefly*... Paul caught at the word his mind offered, the word he had held to since the evening Laura had spoken of seeing a man ride by on his way up to Bancroft Hall. But many men travelled on horseback finding it more convenient than a carriage. Laura was as well acquainted with that as himself and until that day had paid little attention to a rider. So what was it had drawn her that day? Laura had been unable to explain, she had not known herself; she could only say something deep in her stomach reacted sharply to sight of the man sitting tall and confident in the saddle. The hopes of a woman loath to believe her fiancé would not return? Of course such hopes could give rise to misconception, an error of judgement which given the light of day would have been recognised and withdrawn. But Laura had withdrawn nothing.

Resting his head against the padded leather of the chair his eyes closed as he let the memory of speaking with his sister return.

They had talked again the day following her going to Bancroft Hall. He reckoned a night's sleep would have cleared Laura's brain of the image it had conjured, had her recognise she had been mistaken in her thinking.

'*I am not mistaken, Paul.*'

The denial had been given with quiet assurance, an assurance he also was beginning to feel.

She had watched the man ride on, stared after him until Joseph had drawn her back behind the high wall of the kitchen garden. The man she watched was best left to pass by, Joseph had said without adding reason to the words. She should wait for him to go inside the house before she drove away; only then had he said the man's name ... the name she had repeated in the sitting room.

'*I am not mistaken, Paul.*'

Behind, closed eyes Paul saw the figure of his sister, her hands folded and unmoving in her lap, her face composed and her glance steady. The sister he knew related only the truth of her convictions.

'*...the name Joseph Richardson spoke was Cain Lindell.*'

Why then? He had asked her, why if it was the man she had once vowed to marry, one who had promised to make her his wife on his return to England, why had she taken Joseph's advice, and left Bancroft Hall without making herself known to Lindell?

She had sat for a moment, lips closed on the long breath she had drawn. He had watched the nuances of emotion coming so swiftly to play over that face, the shadows of a heart still torn with longing. His own heart had swelled as it always did on seeing that sadness and he would have taken her in his arms except at that moment she stood up and moved to stand at the window.

The sun of morning had played on her hair sprinkling diamonds among the rich dark depths, her small figure held straight had shown no sign of the feelings he had known ran deep inside. Then when he would have gone to her she had turned about, one hand reaching into a pocket of her gown.

'*I did not make myself known,*' she had taken a small rectangular card from her pocket holding it out for him to take, '*...I did not make myself known because the face of the man I saw riding up to Bancroft Hall was not the face of the man you see there.*'

Not the face of Cain Lindell!

Paul opened his eyes. Laura had been so positive, so definite in what she had said, that he had talked himself with Joseph Richardson.

'*Ar, that be the name.*' Joseph had answered, a slight frown drawing his brows. '*Cain Lindell were the name my brother Elijah says and Elijah isn't like to make any mistake regardin' that man.*'

He had gone on to tell of the reason for Elijah Richardson's dislike of the man and Paul's own had not been unmistakable in his throat when hearing of Alyssa Maybury, her mother and a blind child being turned onto the streets.

217

A child! It had stunned him. Joseph must have noticed his reaction, must have seen the look flash across his face, but had made no comment, going on only to say his brother had written what Alyssa had said later, that the child was the son of her sister. Relief had brought a warmth which, though he had tried to repel it, had tinged his face, relief to hear Alyssa Maybury had borne no child ... or that she was not wife to a man? He had wrestled with that over and again. Why should it bother him? Why should he care? Only in the deepest reaches of him did he admit he did.

But the woman was gone from his home and his life and from this day must be gone from his mind! Annoyed with himself for allowing thoughts of Alyssa Maybury to encroach yet again, he took up the letter lying beneath his hand, re-reading it before placing it in an inner pocket of his coat.

Lindell had given the support he had promised. He had kept his word, telling any who spoke of it that it had been an accident; but then Lindell had realised which side of his bread was buttered, he wanted the return of money loaned; but that was not Lindell's only requirement, astute as the man was there was one thing he had not allowed for!

Marlow Bancroft turned away from the grave banked around with wreaths and sheaves of flowers laid by mourners, murmuring his thanks as they too turned to leave the cemetery.

It had been a difficult week. Setting his black silk top hat back on his head he turned to play a lingering look at the flower-strewn ground, at the same time releasing a long shuddering breath

218

while a black-gloved hand touched beneath his eyes and the softest of sobs trembled from his mouth. He sniffed then stumbled slightly as he turned finally away, congratulating himself inwardly on the display of grief ... grief he did not feel.

Events had gone as he had intended. There had been no suspicion that death had occurred in any other than unforeseen circumstances. The mistress of Bancroft Hall had suffered an accident. He and Cain Lindell had been present at the time. It had warranted no more than a brief enquiry by the local constabulary, an enquiry liberally laced with apology, the inspector repeating it was merely formality. Why would it be any but a brief formality? Marlow almost smiled openly. No one could ever suspect the Master of Bancroft of committing any crime, and certainly not that of murder.

At the lych gate, saying goodbye to the priest who had accompanied him, Marlow entered the waiting carriage.

There had been no suspicion and there would be no more mourning. A week of being shut in the house, of having people commiserate had been a week too long; now it was over and Marlow Bancroft could live again.

'Do you think it wise to be visiting the George on the same day as a family funeral?' Cain Lindell glanced at the figure leaning against the padded interior of the carriage after giving terse instruction to the coachman, a smile resting about his mouth.

'Wise?' Marlow's expansive smile remained. 'Why should it not be?'

'People are bound to view it as heartless.'

'People can bloody well think what they wish!' The smile vanished. 'Marlow Bancroft will do what pleases him and right now it pleases him to spend a few hours in convivial company.'

Convivial meaning the card table. Cain Lindell's glance stayed on the window, watching the medley of small shops lining Upper High Street, each of them suffocating beneath their coating of coal dust and smoke, yet despite the drab-ness of the landscape and the depressing business of a funeral a warm surge of satisfaction welled in him. Bancroft's convivial pastimes were as much a pleasure to Cain Lindell as to Bancroft himself ... after all they brought ownership of the Hall ever nearer.

'I'm in need of funds, just enough for a hand or two of cards, this week's bloody highlights have emptied the pocket...'

As he had guessed. Lindell smiled to himself. Yet one more loan, the man never seemed to learn! But then Cain Lindell would not offer to teach ... not while he was the one who stood to gain from another's stupidity.

'...Twenty pounds should be sufficient, will you do the honours, Lindell?'

Oh, he would do the honours. Lindell's inner smile deepened as he extracted four five-pound notes from a Moroccan leather wallet handing them to his companion. In a few more weeks he would have the honour of booting Bancroft out! Of taking ownership of Bancroft Hall.

'I shall be leaving next month. Business commitments abroad.' He returned the wallet to his pocket. 'I shall be away several weeks; perhaps by that time you will have your affairs settled and can recover your notes.'

Recover his notes! Lindell was asking for settlement of his IOUs. Settlement! Christ, that was a laugh. Marlow's teeth clamped hard holding the exclamation on his tongue. There wasn't enough of value left in the Hall even to begin to cover those debts and as for the jewellery he had taken from that safe, most of it had proved to be paste ... bloody fake! It had realised less than a couple of hundred and that had gone in a night; the land and buildings then? But he would not go over that, not even mentally. The carriage drew to a halt outside the impressive George Hotel and Marlow alighted, ignoring the uniformed doorman stepping forward to hold the door open. Lindell was in for an unsavoury surprise if he hoped to recoup anything from that direction.

'I 'opes as what I done don't be wrong, but it seemed to me you needed summat of an 'elping 'and if you was to get to that there Jamaica, so I went along and 'ad me a word wi' the reverend along of the church. He told me a party be leavin' today aboard the *Dolphin*, a man and his wife goin' to start a school for the edyookatin' o' the children of plantayshun workers an' should you be of a mind to 'elp get things started then you could travel along for free.'

It was beyond believing! Alyssa stared at the flushed face of Betsy Fletcher. It was too much to hope yet those kind eyes and smiling mouth said it was true, she had been given the means of

221

reaching Thea.

But how long would she be expected to remain at the school?

'...*if you have love for her then take her away from Jamaica before it is too late.*'

Rising swiftly to mind, the words written in that letter given by the young maid in Wednesbury snatched away her elation.

'...*before it is too late.*'

There was an urgency in that, one that said she could not agree to anything which would delay Thea's removal from that place. Spirits drooping, Alyssa shook her head.

'I can't,' she said, her glance falling away from the beaming face. 'I can't agree to staying while a school is established. I have to bring my sister home as soon as possible.'

'Which don't be goin' to be possible at all be Betsy Fletcher any judge o' things.' The reply was sharp. 'Do you know how much it costs to go a' crossin' of the sea? Well, I'll tell yer, it be a sight more'n you've got in yer pocket; so tell me, 'ow if'n yer don't go along of that couple, 'ow be you goin' to get to fetch your sister at all?'

How? Alyssa stared at her hands. Familiar as Betsy must be with coming and going, the daily business of the port, she would doubtless have a very good idea of the cost involved in taking a sea voyage, just as she had formed an accurate idea of the amount Alyssa, had to spend.

'I don't see another chance comin' the way o' this one.' Betsy took the restless hands between her own. 'Think well afore you goes tossin' it aside. You trusted me with the reasons of yer comin' to this town, trusted to tell me of yer sister, now I asks you trusts Betsy Fletcher one more time an' listen to what her says. This could well be the one an' only opportoonity you ever gets so tek it... tek it an' find that wench.'

'It would be taking advantage.' Alyssa shook her head a second time. 'It would be a lie to say I could stay when I could not.'

'A lie be what yer meks it, same as truth be what yer meks it.' Betsy rose from her chair drawing Alyssa from the one she sat on. 'But the *Dolphin*'ll slip 'er moorings an' be 'alfway to the Sugar Islands if yer keeps mawdlin' over which to tell; so come yer along an' speak to the reverend, could be he'll sort yer mind for yer.'

Betsy had insisted. She had thrown a shawl about her shoulders and with a terse 'come yer on' and no backward glance had marched from the Mission Hall. Her plump figure thrust through the busy dockside streets until they came to a large house set beside a high-steepled church, and it was in that house, in a room smelling of beeswax and books, she had related her misgivings to a white-haired priest, his elbows on a wide desk, his chin resting on the fingers of his hands as he had listened.

Then there had been silence. A silence so thick and heavy it had felt like a living thing clutching at her, sucking her deep into itself, closing off her sight, her hearing, stifling breath until her lungs were ready to burst.

Placing her bundle of clothing on the narrow bunk set against the wall of the tiny cabin, Alyssa let the memory wash over her.

'Well now, there is a problem that is after being no problem at all.' The priest had spoken at last, his lilting accent gentle against the rumble of carts making their way to and from the quay. 'It's meself not making all things clear to Betsy. It isn't the helping with the teaching is being wanted, though to be sure that is ever welcome; no, 'tis a woman being close to hand is needed.'

He had eased back in the chair which had seemed too big for his frame, the wings of it spread from each shoulder giving him the appearance of a large bird ready to lift in flight. Standing in the dimly lit cabin Alyssa saw in her mind the smiling eyes become grave as the priest had switched his glance from Betsy to herself.

'You see,' the hands resting now on the desk had touched a pile of papers, the fingers idly rifling the corners, 'Mister Rawley, who is going out there to take charge of the school, is concerned for his wife, she is carrying their first child. He worries sickness may be brought on by the rolling of the ship on the water and his mind would be after being eased were there another woman aboard to care for her should this happen. It is himself and not the church is after offering free passage should you be willing to be companion to his wife during the voyage.'

There had been no more discussion, no time to visit Mr Rawley and his wife in order to speak with them regarding what might be expected of her; only time enough to rush back to the Mission Hall collect her bundle of clothing, then to kiss goodbye the woman who had helped her.

Betsy's face had been flushed from hurrying through the streets. Round and pink it had

224

glowed like a summer moon caught in the gleams of a setting sun and though she had smiled her eyes reflected the caution contained in the words spoken so quietly they were a whisper.

'*Tek heed for yerself, wench...*'

In the close confines of the cabin Alyssa heard them echo in her mind.

'*...long voyages has men ache for the company of a woman an' not every seaman be a gentleman so keep you close to that there Mistress Rawley and 'er man.*'

No sooner was it said than Betsy's own husband was walking her back to the docks, his long stride having her skip to stay level with him. Then in the shadow of a sleek-hulled ship he had left her.

She had glanced at the prow, intricately carved into a large sea creature. Poised as though about to leap into the water lapping below it, the grey-painted body gleamed silver in the morning sun. Captivated by the beauty of it she had stood gazing until a man had shouted to her the gang-plank was about to be raised so if this were the vessel she hoped to sail in then she should come aboard now.

Only then in that last swift glance along the body of the ship had she noticed the name. Bold and white against black-painted timbers it proclaimed its name: *Dolphin*.

Strange! Alyssa smiled to herself. Strange the ship she now was passenger on should be the very vessel the man who had taken her to the Mission Hall had thought her to be travelling aboard.

'*The ways of the world be strange...*'

The words were so clearly heard that Alyssa started, her glance seeking the speaker. But the words were only in her head, words her father had spoken to an enquiring child.

'*...the ways of the world be strange, and only heaven be privy to them all.*'

Untying her bundle Alyssa stared at the meagre contents, that last thought playing on in her mind. Heaven knew all things, so her father had said, but his daughter would never again call upon its knowledge!

20

'You wished to see me.' Cain Lindell glanced at two men being shown into the study of Deepmoor House. 'You will please be brief. I have an appointment within the hour.'

'I believe you to be both a liar and a thief ... is that brief enough for you?' He had not meant to open a conversation quite so bluntly. Paul Tarn controlled the stew of anger he had felt since reading the letter he had received a few days before. The letter he had shown to the man who accompanied him to Deepmoor.

'What the hell ... are you out of your mind!' Dark eyes glittering, Cain Lindell rose to his feet, one kick of his heel sending the chair he had been seated in crashing to the floor.

'Not out of my mind,' Paul answered, determination to hold on to his temper keeping his words clipped and tight. 'But I think you must have been when you stole another man's identity.'

'Stole? Are you saying I am a thief?'

'I have said it already and am perfectly willing to repeat it in court.'

'And answer to that court for false accusation!'

'If it so be!' Paul watched the hand reach for a bell-pull, a hand which shook slightly. 'But first perhaps you should hear what else will be said in that courtroom, what lies behind my accusation.'

His hand hovering beside the bell-pull which would summon a servant, Cain Lindell met the eyes of the younger of his callers. The man was perfectly serious.

'I fear you are making a mistake.' He tried to prevent the frisson of alarm causing his hand to shake having the same effect on his voice.

'Are you Cain Lindell, nephew of the late Laban Marshall and inheritor of his estate?'

What was this? Were either of these men what he had feared on a previous occasion, a relative of Marshall come to stake claim to the fortune that man had left behind? If so that relative would find out just how hard a struggle he was making for himself. Fortified by the thought Lindell dropped his hand from the tapestried cord.

'That is my name and my good fortune,' he replied, the look he rested on the man who posed the question one of sheer animosity. 'Might I be accorded the privilege of knowing from where comes the idea I am not Cain Lindell?'

'Certainly.' Paul met the animosity with indifference. 'It comes from Laura Tarn; I trust you know her.'

Moving to stand before the fireplace, Cain Lindell laughed smoothly before answering. 'I do

227

not know a Laura Tarn; it is as I tell you, gentlemen, you are making a mistake.'

Watching the man, hearing his laugh, Paul's anger threatened to breach the dam of his throat. Forced to swallow hard, he took a moment. This man was so sure of himself. But then so had Laura been sure, and Joseph Richardson; he had been certain of the name Lindell for the grooms at Bancroft stables had heard it pass often enough between their master and his friend.

Lindell had not shown by the flicker of an eyelid that he knew Laura, had not given the merest sign of recognition of the name Tarn when the servant had spoken it on conducting them into the study; but was that due to a superb self-control or was this man truly who he claimed to be? There was only one way of being sure.

'You do not know Laura?' Paul went on. 'I find it somewhat inconceivable a man would not recognise the name of his fiancée, the woman he had asked to be his wife. She saw you at Bancroft Hall and was distressed you had not called to see her.'

Fiancée! Christ, he had not taken that into consideration! Lindell's nerves jolted then a steady coldness settled along them. There was no fiancée. This was Bancroft's doing, he had a hand in this, he had hatched some plot to relieve himself of repaying his gambling debts; but Bancroft would find it did not do to try double-crossing Cain Lindell. Glancing pointedly at an oak-cased mantel clock he snapped, 'I asked you to be brief, now—'

'I believe you do not know Laura Tarn because you are not who you claim to be, you are not Cain Lindell.'

228

Calmly stated, the interruption rippled the ice holding Lindell's nerve. Had Bancroft taken things further than paying some woman to claim a promised marriage, had he told Tarn and this other man the real story? Oh, Bancroft knew it all right; he had never claimed to know, but a man suffering a fever is not master of his words and things he would keep secret were often revealed, and he had been ill, a bout of fever which had kept him at Bancroft's house on the plantation. It was after that occasion that the man had acquired a smugness about him, an air of superiority, like a spider watching a fly. Well, this spider would get caught in its own web. Anger held tight he looked directly at Paul. 'I do not know what allegation Bancroft has made but while you are asking questions you might ask him some. Ask him about the girl he raped, ask about the girl he shipped off to foreign parts. Ask about the girl with red-gold hair!'

Sitting with his sister in the gentle warmth of a garden filled with flowers, Paul related the events that had taken place at Deepmoor House, of his accusation directed at Cain Lindell.

'He tried bluffing but it soon became obvious he had no knowledge of the real Cain Lindell, the names of parents or sister and the only document he could produce was a letter of introduction to the owner of a plantation Lindell had thought to buy on the island of Jamaica. He could see we knew he was lying and that was when he decided to tell us everything.'

Taking Laura's hand he looked at her, the rays

229

of evening sun touching her face lending colour to its paleness.

'The man you had hoped to marry had been taken ill shortly after the boat docked. Island fever, so the doctor had said, brought on by some parasite finding its way into the bloodstream. With no hospital or nursing staff the patient was left to recover in the hotel bedroom. But he did not recover. Edward Farnell – that is the name of the man you saw riding to Bancroft Hall – went to Lindell's room next morning to see if he required breakfast, and found Lindell dead. Seizing the opportunity, he went through the dead man's possessions and having read that letter of introduction, Farnell realised that Lindell was as much a stranger to Jamaica as was he himself. No one knew him therefore no one could dispute should he claim to be Cain Lindell. The opportunity was too good to miss so he exchanged everything of his with that of Lindell, clothes, baggage, papers; anything and everything that would identify him as the other man. And the deception worked. He took over the Spindrift coal mine, assumed ownership of Deepmoor and its properties, he became master of it all...'

'I can understand people in that country being deceived,' Laura said quietly, 'but here in England, in Buckinghamshire!'

'He never dared go to Buckinghamshire. So far as Lindell's family knew, he was dead. Farnell posed as an old friend of Lindell's and was given a certificate stating date and cause of death and signed by the doctor who had attended Lindell. This he posted to the family.' Paul stared out

230

across the garden, still not believing the audacity of the man he had confronted.

'But his Aunt Marshall?' Laura frowned.

He also had wondered how that woman could have been deceived. 'She had never seen him,' Paul answered. 'Samuel Marshall had prevented his sister's marriage so when she came of an age she defied him, marrying and going to live with her husband in Buckinghamshire. Brother and sister had no contact with each other from that day except one letter telling Marshall of the birth of his sister's son. Mistress Marshall confessed this when she was asked to join us in the study at Deepmoor. She also spoke of the letter sent to Lindell advising him of his uncle's death and of his being the inheritor of Marshall's estate, a letter vouchsafed by Lindell's mother as being forwarded on to her son unopened after he had left for London; so you see, his family knew nothing of that inheritance and Farnell gambled on their never finding out. They would not, had you not seen him riding up to Bancroft Hall.'

Somewhere in the garden a playful breeze snatched the perfume of Jasmine flowers, brushing it past Paul. That was the perfume she had worn!

'...*ask about the girl with the red-gold hair.*'

Alyssa Maybury had red-gold hair. Was she the girl, had she been raped by Bancroft who then had her sent out of the country? Memories which the scent of flowers had fluttering like petals hardened suddenly, sitting like lead in his stomach.

'...*ask him about the girl he raped.*'

Like any other thorn in Marlow Bancroft's side,

231

Alyssa Maybury had had to be removed; but simply sending her abroad risked the possibility of her turning up to threaten at some future date. That was not the type of venture Bancroft indulged in. The heaviness rolled solid and painful into his chest and throat. Alyssa Maybury was likely removed not just from the country but from life.

'So what will happen to Mister Farnell now?'

Laura's quiet words hung in the air as Paul struggled to clear his mind of a young woman with hair flaming like a deep summer sunset, of eyes violet and deep and a rare smile which intensified the beauty of a face he could not forget. But he had to forget! After all, the girl he had brought from the heath was nothing to him. He swallowed hard, urging his senses to the moment. 'The man who went with me to Deepmoor was an Inspector of Her Majesty's Constabulary. He took Farnell into custody.'

'Will he go to prison?'

'Yes.' Paul nodded. 'As the Inspector told him, stealing a purse, taking an item of property is serious enough, but robbing a man of everything, of stealing his very name, is akin to murder. That is the way the court will probably see it and if so, Farnell will likely be imprisoned for the rest of his life.'

Beside him Laura shivered. 'Oh Paul, how dreadful.'

It was no more than the swine deserved! Conscious of his sister's finer feelings Paul let the exclamation lie in his mind, saying instead, 'Mistress Marshall now has no fear of being turned from her own home and her lawyers will ensure all of her late husband's property is returned to her.'

'But the Lindell family, they will not have the happiness, the blessing of a son returned to them.'

'No.' The single word left to rest on the warm silence, Paul retreated into his own private world.

The Lindells would not know the happiness of seeing their son again ... and neither would he have the pleasure of seeing Alyssa Maybury.

'No, Mister Tarn; I'm sorry I can be of no assistance to you. I really do not know of any Alyssa Maybury. I must profess it strikes me as strange your coming here to enquire of her whereabouts.' Marlow Bancroft's look was steady but beneath the calm appearance his nerves flickered. How had this man come to know of his connection with that girl, who could have–? The thought snapped off, breaking away before the next. Lindell! Of course ... it could be no one else!

'I have it on reliable authority she came here to Bancroft Hall,' Paul Tarn answered, dislike of the man staring blandly back at him adding to the difficulty of controlling the cold anger inside. 'My sister was concerned for the girl, she hoped perhaps she had found employment in your household.'

His sister was concerned ... so he had not called about the question of rape. Marlow Bancroft felt the breath ease in his chest. 'I leave the hiring of internal domestics to my housekeeper and butler respectively. The hiring of a new maid would not call for my personal attention.'

Personal attention! If what the man Farnell

confessed was indeed the truth, then Marlow Bancroft had given that in full measure.

'Of course.' He nodded, controlling the urge to punch the supercilious smile from that face. 'However, I could hardly question either of those members of your staff before requesting your permission.'

'Well, you have that.' Marlow reached for the bell-pull hanging beside the fireplace. 'Ask what you will; if the girl is here then your sister need have no further worries as to her welfare for she will be well taken care of.'

Watching the other man, seeing the disdain curve his lips, Paul felt dislike turn to contempt. The man had a reputation as a gambler and a womaniser, his marriage having had no effect upon either; he would not have cared tuppence for any girl he raped.

'My sister will be pleased to hear it,' he said, the reply carrying no smile. 'But if Miss Maybury is not employed in this house then your house-keeper will most probably remember her having called here; she would remember a girl with red-gold hair.'

Red-gold hair! Marlow's nerves jerked. How many women in these parts had hair of that colour, he had encountered only–

The thought broke as the summons of the bell brought a manservant into the room.

'Ask what you must.' Nodding to Paul, Marlow turned sideways on to the ornate fireplace, one foot resting on the stone but beneath the non-chalant stance every pulse pounded. Had that bitch of a girl spoken to the staff? Had she told

234

any of them what had happened? Told them she had been raped by him and very nearly raped a second time by Lindell?

'Will that be all, sir?'

The servant looked at Marlow who, lost in these thoughts, took a few seconds to answer and when he did it was to Paul. 'Well, Tarn, have you asked all your questions?'

'Thank you.' Paul acknowledged the servant who had replied readily and, he felt, honestly to all he had been asked.

'So.' He turned fully to face his visitor as the door closed behind the departing manservant, his stare openly hostile. 'You have asked what you came to ask, now you can leave!'

'Not all of what I came to ask.' Paul returned the stare, his own equally hostile. 'There is one other thing.'

'Then bloody well ask it somewhere else!'

Not even glancing at the porcelain figure the angry swipe of Marlow Bancroft's hand had sent crashing into the marble hearth Paul answered, 'I have.'

'You have,' Marlow forced through gritted teeth. 'Yet still you bother me. You had best leave my house, Tarn, before I kick you out of it!'

'Like your friend Lindell kicked Alyssa Maybury out of hers, kicked out the girl you raped!'

21

'Like your friend Lindell kicked Alyssa Maybury out of hers, kicked out the girl you raped!'

The words Paul Tarn had spat at him burned like acid in Marlow Bancroft's mind. Lindell had been a fool to speak of that. No one could prove the truth of it, no one would dare accuse the owner of Bancroft Hall ... but Tarn would accuse. Tarn would dig and dig, but should he find the girl it would still afford him nothing, for what was the word of a common slut when placed against that of a Bancroft! But confessing the rape of Alyssa Maybury was not the root of Marlow's anger; it was the rest of what Tarn had been told.

He had thought that to be the ace in his hand! He thumped a rage-filled fist into his palm. He had thought that the threat to divulge what he had learned at the plantation house, the delirium-invoked mumblings of Lindell lying sick with malaria, the rambling which had told him of one man stealing the identity of another, to be the way of cancelling every last one of those debts and now–

'Damn you, Lindell!' He swore loudly. 'Damn you for a bloody fool!'

What if Marshall's lawyer claimed the money Lindell had loaned was money belonging to the Marshall estate? What if he claimed that the notes stood?

But that was only part of his worries. The foot he had rested on the marble hearth kicked savagely at the heavy brass fire-irons. He should have done for the man, seen the bastard dead weeks ago, got rid of him before he got even a chance to sing his little song, but he hadn't and now the man who called himself Cain Lindell was in the custody of the magistrate.

But maybe things were not as black as Tarn had painted them. Marlow drew a long breath, trying to steady his racing thoughts. Maybe Lindell hadn't said all of what Tarn claimed; perhaps that had been a trap, Tarn's way of trying to get Marlow Bancroft to incriminate himself.

The fellow would have to do better than that. A contemptuous smile hovered on Marlow's lips. Tarn was a bumpkin, a jumped-up nobody, he need have no more concern of that man. Lindell, however, was different; he would fight with every sly trick he could dream up, and now he was in gaol. Marlow's smile slid from his face. For Lindell the game was up and thinking that he would not reveal every last detail of their relationship would be like thinking day would not follow night. No! Marlow felt the rawness of fear touch his throat. Lindell wasn't a fellow to remain silent, he would not protect another man while he rotted in gaol.

'We have reason to believe you can provide us with information concerning an assault upon a young woman.'

How long before he heard those words being addressed to him, how long before an Inspector of Constabulary paid a visit to Bancroft Hall?

He could lie, of course he could lie ... but well enough and consistently enough to fool the law? They might not be satisfied with his answers and if not...?

Christ! One hand swept savagely along the length of the mantelshelf sending the remainder of the group of delicate porcelain figurines smashing to the floor scattering fragments across highly polished parquet.

If not, the law would return and when it did it might not be just to enquire about the assault on a woman but maybe of the rest. No ... not maybe! Marlow's eyes glittered with a cold rage. The law would have learned the rest, Cain Lindell would have taken care they did!

There was no way out! Staring into the wide greyness of the empty fireplace a feeling of staring into his own grave brought a ripple of ice to his spine. No way out unless ... yes! He straightened, standing a moment his brain spinning to a new thread, then, one hand snatching abruptly at the tapestried cord which would again summon a manservant, he relaxed. There was his answer. He would return to Jamaica, the law would not trouble him there.

It was arranged. Marlow Bancroft would not be interviewed by any bloody Inspector of Constabulary! The last of the dowry Felicia had brought to their marriage had long gone, also the money from his mother's jewellery. Sums hardly worth considering, yet both could have settled some of his debts. Debts! Marlow smiled to himself. Marshall's lawyers and the Bank could whistle for their money, and it would have to be a very loud whistle to be heard where he was going.

Passage had been booked for three days hence, now all that was left to do was ensure nothing remained which might incriminate him. His father had revealed nothing of the business of Richardson's wife and child during his lifetime but his threats to do so had become more regular in his last years, hoping by that way to have his son behave in a more respectable fashion ... respectable meaning abandoning all that afforded that son the pleasure of living; having him settle to marriage and business.

'A marriage like yours, Father! God or the devil save me from that.'

One of those deities already had. His soft laugh one of sheer triumph, Marlow glanced about the room which had been his father's bedroom. He had to make certain. His father had not exposed those murders during his lifetime but who could say he had not left the means of doing so after his death?

Throwing back heavy velvet curtains he blinked in the sudden flood of light crashing in through high windows. If there were something to be found he would find it.

The chest! He crossed the room, the tread of his footsteps swallowed by thick Turkish carpet. Too obvious? But his father would have thought that the very reason it was safe, supposing its conspicuousness would prevent its being searched. But deviousness and Marlow Bancroft had long been bedfellows. The inner smile the thought aroused rimming his mouth he snatched open each

239

drawer, flinging contents to the floor, then with the last another short bark of laughter broke when removing layers of personal linen to reveal a sheaf of papers.

Lifting them free of their hiding place he waved them above his head, the victor with the spoils. 'Good try, Father!' He laughed again, sheer scorn thickening the already guttural sound. 'But not good enough, you ought to have known I would find these once I bothered to try.'

'And why are you trying now?'

Startled by the quiet voice Marlow whipped about, his glance fastening on the figure who stood inside the room beside the closed door.

'Why?' Equilibrium making a swift recovery, he smiled acidly. 'To make quite sure nothing remains unaccounted for.'

'Would that be nothing that might pertain to Bancroft business and estate ... or to you?'

'Are they not the same? I am after all the master of Bancroft, am I not?'

'Indeed.' Sunlight reached across the room, gilding a spidersweb of cream lace overlying mauve silk. The figure it adorned made no move, other than a short nod of the head.

'And as master I do as pleases me.'

'As you have always done.' The reply was quiet. 'But I ask again, why search this room now?'

The hand holding the papers lowering to his side Marlow's eyes glittered warningly; he had no liking for being questioned and even less liking for the questioner. 'That is nothing to do with you!'

'Like my money, my personal possessions had nothing to do with me?'

'As master–'

'No, Marlow!' Scalpel-sharp it cut across the intended reprimand. 'Not as master, not to use in benefiting the estate but as a thief to benefit yourself. You robbed Bancroft and you robbed me simply to indulge a life of gambling.'

'You have my thanks for your contribution.' Marlow smiled contemptuously.

'Did you thank her for hers, thank her before you killed her? You did kill her didn't you, Marlow? Her death was no accident.'

Between them motes danced in the beams of sunlight, danced to the music of silence.

'How very deductive!' The answer came slowly, cynical self-assurance glistening in the grey ice of Marlow's eyes. 'And of course you are correct; it was no accident. I planned the whole thing, but not as thoroughly as I might...'

Striding across the room he pushed the figure roughly aside, wrenched open the door then looked back.

'I should have had you accompany her, that way I would have been rid of you too, Mother!'

She could never have hoped things would turn out as they had. Sitting in the tiny space which was her cabin, Alyssa thanked the fates that had brought her to Bristol and to Betsy Fletcher. Without the help of that woman it might well have been impossible to procure a passage to Jamaica, for there could not be many sea captains willing to take a passenger unable to pay for her voyage.

Overhead the shouts of sailors mingled with the sounds of creaking timbers and the ringing notes

241

of a bell struck several times but none of this intruded into Alyssa's mind.

So many people had been generous in their kindness, so many had gone out of their way to help her. Her body swaying with the motion of the waves lifting then lowering the ship, Alyssa looked back over the events of the past.

Joseph Richardson. Soft with memory her eyes stared into the muted half-light of the cabin. Joseph ... he had been so like her father; level headed, practical in his advice and yes, she could say it now, Joseph Richardson had been as gentle and loving as her own father. If only she could have told him where she was going. She caught her lower lip between her teeth, a gesture of guilt as much as regret. She ought to have taken the time to tell him, not leave without a word. But then would Joseph not have tried to prevent it?

'... *it be naught but madness; a young wench travellin' overseas on 'er own be invitin' trouble.*'

Words Joseph would likely have spoken sounded clear in Alyssa's mind.

Perhaps it was madness, maybe it was inviting trouble, but weighed against the needs of a sister she loved, a sister whose life might be threatened, those troubles were inconsequential.

And returning home to England ... was that also inconsequential? Returning home! She had not thought of that, given no heed to how, to the fact she had not money enough to purchase tickets; but that did not matter, the only concern was Thea.

Twined in the thin cotton of her skirts, Alyssa's fingers tightened. How big was the country of

Jamaica? Would she find Thea? But that was not a thought she would allow. Rising to her feet, swaying from the increasing roll of the ship, she thrust the thought away. She would find her sister, somehow make a home where she could care for her and if it were that that home had to be in a foreign land away from everything she had known, then so be it.

Hidden by the closing darkness of the cabin Alyssa's mouth trembled. She loved Thea; despite a childhood which had seen one little girl excluded from a mother's affections while the other was cherished, despite the tear-filled hours of longing for that mother's arms to hold her, to hear a whispered word of tenderness, she loved Thea: but it would be a lie to think not returning home would be no cause of regret, that never seeing Joseph again, of not seeing Laura, would not be a constant heartache.

But was that the all of her unhappiness, the only cause of a weight so heavy her very soul felt crushed?

'*Admit it, 'Lyssa...*'

Caught within sounds coming from the deck, the words Thea had flung at her in the room they had shared in the house at Booth Street echoed fresh in Alyssa's ears.

'*...admit it and give the devil his freedom!*'

Admit it!

The moment of realisation gave life to words which slipped into the darkening cabin and that acknowledgement rising unchallenged in her mind brought a deep flush to her cheeks, as Alyssa recognised a deeper truth.

Not seeing Joseph or Laura, yes that would for ever be a sadness. But never again to meet with Paul Tarn, not to hear that deep rich voice or see the quick smile light those damson-dark eyes ... that would be desolation!

'How fortunate I was here, you might have suffered an injury. The sea is no respecter of persons, Miss Maybury, it is ready to have you fall at any moment. You must try always to keep a handhold.'

A heavier roll of the ship had toppled Alyssa from her feet pitching her forward.

'Thank you...' Pushing free of the grasp holding her, Alyssa was swept by an unaccountable feeling of dislike. 'I ... I will try to remember.'

'Forgive my touching you.' Lower than necessary, slightly harsh in its delivery, the apology was accompanied by a smile. 'But given the circumstance I could not have avoided it except by allowing you to fall headlong into the corridor and that would not have been the action of a gentleman.'

'Of course, thank you.'

Flustered as much by the feeling coursing inside her as by the threatened accident, Alyssa made a play of smoothing her skirts.

'You should have the lantern lit. Will you allow me or would you prefer I send the cabin boy?'

She would prefer the latter. Alyssa glanced at the man who had so suddenly appeared in her cabin. She would much prefer it, but to say so would be rudeness.

'Having the lantern lit would be most welcome.' She forced a thin smile, watching as her words, taken to mean he should light it, resulted in his withdrawing a matchbox from his pocket.

'There...'

He turned from the lantern and in its soft glow Alyssa saw the pale eyes of the man who had spoken with her on the dockside, then taken her to the Mission Hall.

'There,' he smiled, the light from the match still held between his fingers reflecting on his wide forehead. 'Now may I introduce myself, my name is Sanford Rawley.'

Alone once more Alyssa stared at the door closing off her cabin from a narrow corridor. Sanford Rawley. The name the priest at the rectory had spoken... the name of the man who had paid for her passage. It beat like a drum in her brain. Why had he not introduced himself when she had first come aboard? Why wait until they were well out at sea? The questions had hammered their demand but the strength of them quailed before the ones now seeping into her mind. How had Sanford Rawley entered her cabin? Had he knocked? She had heard no tap... had her door been open? She was certain it had not. Yet he had entered.

Breath held in her throat, Alyssa stared at the closed door.

Did his entering, given no assistance on her part, and so seemingly effortlessly on his own, mean he had a key? And even more frightening, did he believe that his paying her fare to Jamaica granted him the right to use it?

22

'He's gone, skipped the country!'

Paul Tarn looked at the man who had been his friend for many years. 'Left England! But I spoke with him less than a week since.'

'That you might 'ave,' Joseph Richardson replied, 'but he be gone right enough, no doubt off to that plantation o' his and that be the opinion come down from them workin' in the house. Seems that followin' your callin' there he was like a cat with its tail on fire, orderin' everything packed and off in less time than it teks to tell.'

'And his mother?'

Laying aside the last of the plants he had repotted Joseph shook his head, his voice clement as moments previously it had been scathing. 'Lady Amelia ... now there's a woman has my sympathy. A child should be a blessing but the one born to her has been naught but a no-good all of his life, and now to go off and leave her to face the music... Well, I tell you, Paul, if he were 'ere now I would be hard put not to give him the hiding he's long deserved, consequence of law or not.'

Joseph was not alone in that particular temptation! Paul followed the other man into the small low-beamed cottage that was Hall End, the heat of anger burning along his veins. The man who had masqueraded as Cain Lindell had told of more than stories of gambling, so much more that Bancroft would pay for their doing with the scaffold should he be brought back to England ... and he would be brought back. By God, he would!

'Lady Amelia...' Joseph resumed, his offer of a glass of elderberry wine accepted, '...if talk comin' from the Hall is to be believed then the woman be out of a home.'

Rolling a sip of wine over his tongue Paul appreciated both the flavour and the unmistakable potency. Joseph Richardson had many skills and not least of those was the making of wine.

'This talk...' he allowed the dark red liquid to slide its fire past his throat, 'do you really think it true, the gossip from the Hall, I mean?'

Sipping from his own glass, Joseph swallowed before answering. 'There be near as much known to folk as serves as there, as be to them as pays their wages. Don't much tek place in Bancroft Hall as the staff there don't come to know of. Let me answer this way. That toe-rag of a master provides enough for them servants to talk on so there be no need of 'em to go inventin' stories.'

Maybe not. Paul watched the myriad points of ruby light dancing in his glass. But to say Lady Amelia Bancroft was to leave her home, surely that was without any real foundation?

'Were the day followin' Bancroft's departure,' Joseph went on. 'The Constabulary paid a visit to the Hall, wanted to speak with the master, but that bird had flown so it were with his mother the speaking was done; it couldn't be known below stairs what that talk were about for a uniformed man were stationed outside the door of the sitting room, but it were told how after the police left Lady Amelia closed herself into her own private sitting room and remained there alone. Alone that is, until yet one more visitor called, that one leaving Amelia Bancroft in tears.'

'A second visit by the Constabulary?'

'No, Paul.' Joseph answered quietly. 'For Amelia Bancroft it was far worse than that. I got the news from Jevons – he be butler up at that house and his ear gets pressed to doors it shouldn't – well, according to what he tells he heard, Bancroft had mortgaged the Hall and its properties to the Bank and seeing the date of settlement were long past due then the Bank were foreclosing, though their representative had added that the Directors were in agreement Lady Amelia be afforded a three-month period of grace in which to settle her affairs.'

'How could Bancroft do such a thing ... leave his mother that way!'

Staring into his own glass Joseph Richardson watched the ghosts of many years flit in and out of its carmine depths; a young boy pulling the wings from a beautiful butterfly and laughing as he threw it aside, a slightly older boy bringing a leather whip across the shoulders of a stable hand, a young man tearing away the dress of a terrified girl, a grown man whose eyes had failed to conceal a truth, had belied a satisfaction and not a grief as he had stood beside a grave, a man who had grown in cruelty and deception. Twisting the glass he swirled away the face it seemed to conjure, the face of Marlow Bancroft.

'How could he leave his mother to face his

248

debts,' Joseph answered, 'that be brand enough to mark any man a swine, but who knows what other vileness the master of Bancroft be responsible for?'

He could tell of at least one. Paul drank again, the strength of the wine gaining nothing over that of the repugnance rising inside him. Bancroft was responsible for having Alyssa Maybury sent out of the country, had likely had her murdered and that, if none other of his despicable actions, would be answered for.

She had fretted over nothing, had let her imagination play tricks. Alyssa slowly unfastened the buttons of her cotton blouse. Sanford Rawley had come to her cabin only to introduce himself and to enquire after the comfort of her quarters. There had been nothing untoward in that, it was only her own silly fears and mistrust that had her seeing what was not really there.

She had felt guilty and embarrassed during dinner, guilty for her suspicion and embarrassed at what Sanford Rawley must think of her for he would have seen the fear in her eyes, and guessed the reason for it.

The blouse removed, she washed it in the bowl of water she had sponged her face in, then hung it across the back of the one chair the cramped cabin would allow. It was not the ideal way of laundering her clothes but with no change of outer garment she had no other choice. She had seen the looks of the others assembled for dinner, looks which had taken in her patched skirts, cheap blouse and worn-through boots. Removing her bloomers, seeing the small scarlet patch staining the crotch, Alyssa shuddered as memory brought the face it so often brought; a man, his hard eyes burning with lust, his hands grabbing, clawing at breasts torn free of their covering, a man who knocked her to the ground then laughed as he cruelly raped her.

Thrusting the bloomers into the bowl Alyssa scrubbed at them as she had scrubbed her body following that nightmare, scrubbed while hot tears ran down her face. Would she ever be able to forget? Would the horror of that day never leave her?

That was a question any woman who had suffered the same degradation could answer. Underwear draped over the seat of the chair Alyssa pulled her one nightgown over her head. That memory might fade with the years but it would never die, it would forever lie in the shadows, lie in the silence of the heart.

'Why, Father?' Haunted with the misery of years, the words whispering on lips still trembling, Alyssa called to the one person whose love had supported her unhappy childhood. 'Why is life so cruel?' But no words of comfort rose in her mind, no loving reply to soothe the ache of her soul, only an emptiness. That was how her life had been since the death of her father and brothers, an emptiness, a vacuum of love. Why had her mother not seen? Why had Thea not cared?

Young, fun loving, caught in the excitement of life, Thea had gone her own way. Alyssa crossed thick strands of hair one over another. Thea had refused to allow any fact of life to take happiness from her ... but then Thea had had their mother's love, a love she had returned with–

A tap so soft as to be almost noiseless stopped the rest of the thought. Fingers suddenly rigid gripped tightly to the unfinished plait. Breath caught in the same vice which held her mind, Alyssa stared at the cabin door, the door now swinging slowly open.

'I regret to have to inform you...'

Amelia read the letter again though every dot and comma, every syllable was printed indelibly in her brain.

'I regret to have to inform you...'

Crushing the page of heavily embossed notepaper she held it to her chest.

She would not be returning to her beloved Abbey, there was no place for her at Whitchurch.

Heaven was taking its revenge! The solitary sheet of paper still gripped in her hand she crossed to the window which looked out over the gardens. Heaven was punishing her for the deed she had not done. But then how could a mother betray her own son? Yet how could a woman close her eyes to those actions which trailed so much unhappiness in their wake? That was what she had done, even after Saul's telling her of their son being responsible for the death of Joseph Richardson's wife and child, and for the violation of a young girl on that same stretch of heath. Even then she had closed her eyes, closed them even though she knew that Marlow's behaviour grew worse with time.

But she had not known just how despicable her son had become, what a lecher of a man he had grown into ... not until she had read Felicia's diary.

Her stare fastened on flowers sight did not show

251

her, Amelia saw only the delicate, petite figure of her daughter-in-law, her pretty hyacinth eyes dark with ... what? Disappointment in her marriage? Hadn't she, Amelia, thought that? And who would know better the discontent, the heart-burning regret of a marriage made only for money.

But Felicia had known more than dissatisfaction, that had not been the cause of the revulsion which had showed beneath the darkness of those eyes whenever Marlow was present; that cause had been fear and it had not proved groundless.

She had found that whip where it had fallen.

Her mind recalling the scene, Amelia seemed to look again upon the turned-over carriage, the horse whinnying its pain as it lay with its legs broken, at the woman in a crumpled green velvet costume, her neck twisted, her lovely eyes still open wide though they would never again see.

Yes, she had found that whip, its bloodstained leather telling its own story, the bleeding slashes on the animal's flank corroborating a truth which had sprung immediately to mind, a truth admitted later when she had accused her son of killing his wife.

Yes, he had insisted Felicia take a drive in the carriage, yes, he had whipped the horse causing it to bolt until the vehicle overturned, yes, he wanted her dead.

There had been no contrition, no repentance in the confession, nothing but recusance, an obdurate coldness of heart which, used as she was to her son's indifference, had brought new fear to her own. She had thought that money had brought Marlow to kill his wife, thought him wanting rid of Felicia so he might marry yet more money; but realistic as that was it had not proved the sole purpose ... that had shown itself in the pages of her diary. Oh, Marlow had searched diligently, no doubt afraid the girl might have left some word of incrimination regarding himself, but his search had proved fruitless for the diary, whose existence he possibly suspected, had been removed, taken by a mother-in-law while the seemingly distraught husband carried the body of his wife into his own bedroom. The diary she had given to the Inspector of Constabulary, a diary which would do what she had failed to do ... reveal Marlow Bancroft for the monster he was.

She had hidden the truth, concealed his wickedness in order to prevent any slur upon her family name, to protect her beloved childhood home, a home which now refused shelter to its daughter.

Heaven was taking its revenge! The thought recurring, Amelia turned from the window, the crumpled letter dropping from her hand. She and her husband had sinned, he by killing to shield his son from being discovered a murderer, she by allowing it to continue for so long. Now she would sin once more.

Had she foreseen this, known in her heart that one day this would happen? Reaching her bedroom Amelia glanced about. Here in this room, in this home set on a hill overlooking a smoke-blackened town, she had re-created a tiny version of her longed-for Whitchurch; but though Bancroft Hall had held an elegance of furniture, of fine paintings and all the trappings of wealth it had not known the smallest atom of real love: not between husband and wife, not between mother and son. A tragedy of life created out of her own blindness ... out of longing for something she could never have. But now the longing and the charade were finished.

The shadow of a smile touching her lips she went to sit at her small writing table.

'Joseph Richardson.'

The heading written in a flowing hand stared up from the crested sheet. Amelia paused then laid down the pen. What good would it do? Where was the wisdom in the opening of old wounds?

Reaching to her neck she removed the gold necklace she had kept hidden from her son's voracious grasp. This had been a gift from Saul, a gift of thanks for her giving him a son. But the joy had soon died, and the pride in his son? That too had withered. So much unhappiness and it was her fault; if only she had loved Saul as she had loved Whitchurch, then perhaps ... but it was too late for perhaps.

Laying the necklace beside the notepaper she touched a finger to the central peardrop pendant of white diamonds surrounding a perfect ruby at its centre. Matched on either side by smaller though equally perfect drops, it glistened in the stream of sunlight.

'I will not ask forgiveness,' she murmured, the gleam of jewels catching the afternoon sun matching the shimmer of tears come to her eyes. 'I am guilty of much but I will not add that of hypocrisy. Lord who reads the heart of man, You know the reason of my refusal to reveal to Joseph

Richardson the truth of his loss; if that refusal is accountable as yet one more sin then let it be added to all of those I am called to answer for.'

23

She had watched the handle turn, watched the door slowly open. Huddled into the tiny bunk, afraid to sleep, Alyssa pressed her knuckles to her mouth to stifle the sobs of fear and dejection coming from deep inside.

He had walked in smiling, smiling as he asked was there anything he could do to add to her comfort. That smile ... she shuddered, her wide eyes fixed to the cabin door... She had seen its like before on the faces of two men, one who had raped her and another whose intention it had been to do the same and tonight it had been spread across the face of Sanford Rawley.

She had thought on his first entering her cabin he had come on behalf of his wife, that she was ailing, for the quiet dark-haired woman who had sat beside him during the meal in the ship's dining room had looked decidedly pale, pale and nervous. That was understandable given her condition; well advanced in pregnancy she must be fearful at the prospect of perhaps giving birth at sea, of her child being born without benefit of doctor or midwife. But the more she had seen of Grace Rawley the more she had become convinced the woman laboured under a different fear.

255

Did that fear stem from the same man her own fears stemmed from? Was that timidity, that reluctance to speak natural to the woman's nature, or was it more to do with a husband's dominance? It was not a disservice posing that question. Alyssa felt the sting of pain biting yet at her wrists. Sanford Rawley had not owned his true self in taking her to that Mission Hall or of offering free passage aboard the *Dolphin*. His kindness had been no more than a pretence, a veil hiding the real reason; was his seemingly devoted attention to his wife also a lie? Was it a show of deception aimed at fooling any with whom they came into contact?

Grace Rawley had requested to leave the table immediately after dinner, her solicitous husband replying to the anxious captain that his wife was simply tired, and to Alyssa's offer to take her to their cabin had smiled saying he would take his wife himself, but would call upon her assistance should it prove necessary.

And he had called.

Overhead the bell marking the hours rang several times, the sound drifting quickly into the night. How long before daybreak? How long before she could go on deck? There, in sight of the ship's crew she would be safe.

But night followed day, and night could bring Sanford Rawley again to her cabin. A trickle cold as the water of the sea rippled along her spine.

'Is there anything I can do?'

Although alive only in her mind the question had her nerves jolt like it was being spoken again.

'No!' It had come quickly, a verbal push to send

him away. Instead he had stepped further into the cabin, his back against the closed door.

'Come now, I'm sure there is something ... something will make the voyage more enjoyable for both of us.' Like butter in the sun the smile had thinned and spread but the pale eyes had remained hard ice chips glittering in the light of the lantern.

'No...' Nerves had her choke the words. 'No ... thank you, there is nothing I want.'

She had hoped he would leave then, prayed he would leave, but he had merely stepped closer.

'No need to pretend when we are alone.'

'Mister Rawley, I assure you I do not pretend.'

Colourless eyes borrowing from the lantern swinging from its beam had become pallid yellow, the oily smile draining from his mouth as he had grabbed her wrists, drawing her so close she had felt the pulsing throb of flesh against the thin cotton of her nightgown.

Shadows cast by the swing of the lantern swayed and lurched seeming to Alyssa's frightened mind a macabre imitation of the struggle which had taken place.

She had cried out but swift as a striking serpent his mouth had closed over hers, stifling the sound, one hand moving as quickly to cover her lips when his head lifted.

'I like to hear a woman gasp,' he had laughed softly, the grate of it harsh in the quiet of the cabin. 'It adds to a man's pleasure, but while aboard ship you should declare your own less loudly.'

A man's pleasure!

It had rung in her brain. Sanford Rawley thought to pleasure himself with her!

Perhaps it had been sheer terror, or perhaps past experience, she did not know which but something had her become still in his arms. He had laughed again, a breathy exultant laugh, his hand pulling away from her mouth to squeeze her breast, his face once more lowering to her own. Eyes closed she had waited, waited until his warm breath brushed her mouth, then she had caught his lip between her teeth, biting sharply into the soft flesh.

He had drawn away and in the pool of light spilling from the lantern his eyes had gleamed like those of a wounded animal, a grimace evidencing the sting of his mouth.

'*Now!*' She had flung at him. '*Leave my cabin and don't come here again!*'

The hand had descended slowly, the stare he had played over bloodied fingers equally slow; then his glance had come to her face, those pallid eyes glowing with venom.

'*A cabin I have paid for...*'

It had been the hiss of a viper, a sibilant murmur, its quietness detracting nothing from its threat. Strained against every sound of creaking timber, each strike of the bell calling the change of watch, Alyssa's mind could not close out the memory of those words, of the virulent malice of those glittering ice-cold eyes.

'*...a provision which would afford a man the comfort he needs, the sort of comfort a pregnant wife cannot give...*'

Blood dripping from his lip had been wiped by the back of his hand, smearing a scarlet streak into mousy-brown sideburns, but it had not halted the rest of that menacing snarl.

'*...comfort and pleasure I have paid for, Miss Maybury ... and believe me I shall avail myself of it ... as often as pleases me.*'

'*...as often as pleases me.*'

Knuckles pressing painfully hard against her mouth, Alyssa's heart drummed the threat in her brain. He would come again, the look in his eyes had vowed that even more clearly than his words; but how could she prevent it? The Rawleys and herself were the only passengers aboard, she could not hurt that woman by asking her assistance. The captain...?

A sudden tingling of nerves cutting away the thought, breath settling a barrier in her throat, Alyssa listened to the sounds brushing the stillness; the groan of timbers, canvas slapping, the whine of wind ... the quiet footsteps coming to her door.

'What do you think to this?'

Handing a rectangular box to Paul Tarn, Joseph watched the expression of surprise spread across the other man's face. It matched that which must have crossed his own when the package had been delivered to Hall End.

'It's beautiful,' Paul glanced again at the contents of the box, 'but why show it to me?'

'So you can vouch to the way I come by it.'

Vouch? Surprise becoming bewilderment Paul looked at the man sitting in his study. Joseph Richardson was no thief, he would not have stolen that necklace, that much he would stake his own life on, yet asking another person to vouch implied he had not purchased the thing. Not bought therefore no receipt! Where was this leading?

'Before you asks anything more I would ask you read this.' Joseph took the box exchanging it for a sheet of paper.

'A letter!' Reluctant to read another man's correspondence Paul hesitated.

'That's what it be.' Joseph nodded pressing the paper into Paul's hand.

'But a letter is a private concern.'

'Not that sort ain't, not when it comes with such as that necklace. I want you to read it, Paul, I want you to know I be telling no lies.'

It would not need the reading of a letter to convince him of that; in the years of their friendship he had never once known this man to lie. Unfolding the paper Paul glanced at the weather-browned face, surprise again registering on his own.

'Ar,' Joseph repeated his nod, 'it be from there.'

Why write to a man who every day was present on your property, why not simply speak with him? Bewilderment deepening, Paul unfolded the paper.

Mr Richardson.

Every mark of the pen firm yet elegant, the flowing script sat neatly beneath an embossed heading.

Your years of service at Bancroft have proved exemplary. Though we have never communed I know you to be a man in whom I can trust, therefore I

260

would request one final service. I ask you sell this pendant and use the proceeds in the way you will come to know I would have it used.
  Amelia Halford-De-Thaine-Bancroft.

'Lady Bancroft!' Perplexity marked deeper, Paul handed back the letter. 'What does she mean, "the way she would have it used"?'
  'Blessed if I know.' The paper refolded Joseph returned it to his pocket.
  'But why send the necklace to you, why not give it to her son?'
  'Why not to her son!' Joseph's voice took on an acid note. 'Why not give it to Marlow? That be easy to answer, it be because his mother knowed he would sell it then use the money as he has used that from everything else sold from Bancroft Hall, to further his own pleasures.'
  'That's as maybe, but should word of your having that necklace become known to Marlow he is certain to think the worst, and knowing him I wouldn't bet a brass farthing against his claiming you stole it.'
  'Seems Amelia Bancroft had much the same reasoning.' Joseph smiled briefly. 'That most likely be why this were with the necklace; I might never have found it tucked as it were in a drawer that box don't appear to have: it were surprise causing me to drop it when I seen what was inside had this come to light.'
  Taking a paper folded smaller than the first, Paul saw the same elegant copperplate script.

'To whom it may concern.'
261

He read quickly.

I, Amelia Halford-De-Thaine-Bancroft, of Bancroft Hall in the County of Staffordshire, do hereby give into the charge of Joseph Richardson a gold necklace set with diamonds and rubies. It is my wish, and with my full authority, he sell the piece.
Signed
Amelia Harford-De-Thaine-Bancroft.
In the presence of Alfred Jevons.

The last was less expertly written, nevertheless each letter of the signature was legible.

'Jevons,' Paul handed back the paper, 'he also knows of this?'

Returning the letter of authorisation to the box, Joseph slipped it back into his pocket. 'Most like seeing his name be added and it be him delivered the package to Hall End, but I doubt he would tell of it. Like the rest of the staff along of that house, Alfred Jevons harbours no love for Marlow Bancroft and it be certain he holds no respect for the man, not after what he has done across his mother.'

Joseph reminded Paul that Jevons had overheard the painful conversation between Lady Amelia and the Bank's representative.

'There must be much more we know not of,' Joseph added quietly. 'But naught escapes the Lord's sight and naught His retribution. It be my reckoning Marlow Bancroft will answer for his wrongdoings.'

Rising to shake the hand offered to him, Paul

262

held the next thought to himself. If heaven had justice then Bancroft would rot in hell, and if that same heaven allowed then it would be Paul Tarn would send him there.

24

His back pressed against the rail of the ship, Sanford Rawley showed a pleasantly smiling face to any member of the crew who might be watching, but standing next to him, her own face turned to the sea, Alyssa Maybury's every nerve jangled. He had not returned to her cabin last evening, the footsteps she had heard had paused on the other side of her door then moments later had moved away. But fear of what might yet happen had kept sleep from her, and though now almost exhausted she was too afraid to return to her cabin.

'Do not labour under any misapprehension, Miss Maybury,' softly spoken the breeze carried the words to Alyssa, 'our little difference of last evening does not mean I shall not call upon you again.'

She could speak to someone, ask protection against this man ... but who? Not his wife, that poor woman seemed to be carrying all the worries her small frame would stand; but to say nothing would be to leave the way open for him to follow his vile intentions.

'My wife will retire early tonight...'

He nodded, returning the greeting of the ship's

captain, then as the other man moved on turned to face the sea. 'You would do well to forget consulting the captain or any other member of the crew, they know why you are on board. As I told you last evening a man requires his comforts and it causes no lifted eyebrow when he provides that comfort for himself. You see, my dear, they know what you are ... a whore.'

'That is a lie!' Weariness vanishing in the face of anger Alyssa flung the retort.

'Is it?' he laughed sneeringly. 'That is not what anyone aboard this vessel thinks.'

Did they think that? Light wind filling the sails failed to hold the colour from Alyssa's cheeks. Did each of the men aboard this ship hold that opinion, did they all think of her as Paul Tarn had thought ... that she was a prostitute?

'As I was saying...'

Catching at her wrist he prevented the move Alyssa hoped would take her from his side, the sneer more apparent as he went on. '...My wife will retire early this evening and you, my dear, will do the same. I own to being one who likes to take his pleasure then follow it with a good night's sleep.'

There was no mistaking his meaning. Pulling her wrist free, Alyssa stumbled across the deck, only the opposite rail preventing her from falling into the sea. He had made it perfectly clear, his generosity in paying her passage had been no act of charity ... Sanford Rawley had bought himself a mistress.

'Lady Amelia dead?' Laura Tarn looked disbelievingly at her brother. 'But I saw her on Sunday, she was at Evensong, she looked as she always did; Paul, are you sure?'

'News come down from the house this morning.' It was Joseph who answered. 'I thought like you, Amelia Bancroft had no illness so how could her be dead, but then Jevons told me. After giving the mistress confirmation of my receiving that package she rang for her maid who helped her undress as usual. Then it seems her said her would require nothing more and that her were not to be disturbed until morning. Knowing the woman's temper should her orders not be obeyed to the letter then o'course that be what were done. Nobody went to her bedroom until next morning when the maid took breakfast at the usual time, that were when her found the mistress dead.'

'But how...? I mean what caused her death, does anyone know?'

Sat beside his sister, Paul Tarn's eyes echoed her questions. 'Jevons said he went to the room himself then ordered it closed until the doctor arrived, but it had needed no doctor to tell him the cause of Amelia Bancroft's death, for the bottle beside her bed told that ... that bottle had held poison. Seems the mistress had committed suicide.'

'Suicide!' Laura gasped, her hand reaching to her mouth. 'How dreadful ... but why would she do such a thing?'

'Nobody holds any idea,' Joseph answered catching Paul's quick glance, one which held understanding and gratitude. There would be time later should Laura need to be told all of what the man Edward Farnell had confessed.

'But her son, I understand he is at present abroad, he must be notified.'

'Of course, and he will be.' Paul answered his sister, 'But that may take some time even should the staff along of the Hall know exactly where he is to be found, which of course they may not.' Then returning his glance to Joseph he asked, 'Did Lady Bancroft leave any message?'

A shake of the head added to the reply, 'Jevons reckons not. There was ink and pen together with a sheet of paper on the writing table but no word had been written. But then I reckons Amelia Bancroft already to have written, if not her reasons for takin' her own life, then certainly what her wanted to follow on her death. It be in the letter her sent to me, that be the meaning of them words, "use the proceeds in the way you will come to know I would have it used".'

'I see ... yes, you are right.' Paul nodded. 'Lady Bancroft had decided upon ending her life and so she entrusted that necklace to you with the knowledge you would realise she wished the proceeds of its sale to pay for her burial.'

'That be the way I looks at it and that be what I shall do.'

'But Marlow...?' Laura began but Joseph checked her sharply.

'Marlow Bancroft can do what he likes once he be back in Wednesbury and if it be he brings Joseph Richardson afore the Justice then that be his prerogative, but I don't intend for Amelia Bancroft to lie in no mortuary awaitin' of his return.'

Rising from her own chair as Joseph rose from his, Laura touched a hand to his arm, dropping it

266

quickly as he looked to where it rested on his sleeve.

'I...' She stumbled on the word colour rising swiftly to her cheeks. 'I would like to help if you would permit.'

Paul Tarn had accompanied him to the jewellery quarter in Birmingham, that tight-packed warren of buildings close as peas in a pod but without the orderliness. Every shape, every size, some tall, some low, they huddled one into the other, each black with the grime of smoke. Not so different from Wednesbury. Walking back from Lyndon, Joseph glanced to where the spire of the Parish Church of St Bartholomew rose black against the crushed-strawberry sky of evening. Those folk he had seen in Birmingham lived much the same life as the folk of this town, crammed into houses part of which must serve as workshops. A life of hard work and drudgery while the fruits of their labours went to adorn the wealthy. But where the folk of Wednesbury worked in coal and steel the folk of that jewellery quarter worked in gold and precious gems and they had advised Paul and himself of the true value of that necklace.

The rubies were Burmese, the best in the world. Flawless, they alone were worth a considerable sum but combined as they were with perfectly matched, equally flawless white diamonds all set in heavy gold, it was deemed what to Joseph had seemed one incredible sum. But incredible as it had sounded, the advice given by those craftsmen had proved invaluable in the selling of it. Paul had made it quite clear to the buyer that its worth was

267

known and after a spate of haggling the necklace had changed hands for very little less.

Two hundred and thirty pounds! Joseph still could not comprehend a few coloured stones and an ounce or two of gold being worth such an amount, but the owner of that jewellery shop had paid it, and what was more had appeared well satisfied with his purchase.

It was more than a funeral would cost. He and Paul had agreed. And what was left? Joseph glanced again at the spire. Amelia Bancroft had made no reference to that, but Joseph Richardson had thought on it. Whatever remained from the cost of laying the mistress of Bancroft Hall to her rest would not find its way into the pocket of her son.

'My dear, do you think perhaps you should retire?' Sanford Rawley looked from his wife to the captain seated at the head of the table. 'You will be good enough to excuse my wife, she is finding the voyage very wearying.'

Hidden in her lap, Alyssa's fingers tightened together, the coldness of despair numbing her senses. He had said his wife would retire early, now he was ensuring she did so.

Eyes averted, she listened to the timid woman's response. Of course she had agreed to the suggestion, would she dare do otherwise.

'My wife tells me you also are finding the voyage tiring, Miss Maybury, should you too feel the need to retire then I am sure the captain will understand.'

How could the captain understand, he did not

know the sword Sanford Rawley held over her head. He thought, as they all must, that she had come on this voyage solely as that man's mistress and the only way of disillusioning them would bring pain and embarrassment to a gentle woman who had done her no hurt. That she could not do.

'I shall regret the loss of your company, ladies, but of course your comfort is paramount.' The captain smiled.

Comfort! Half risen from her chair the word punched against Alyssa's brain, bringing her stumbling against the table.

'Are you unwell, Miss Maybury?' The captain rose signalling a figure from the shadows.

Her answer trembling on the sudden concerned hush, Alyssa attempted a smile. 'No, I ... I am not unwell, I have not been sleeping as soundly as I might.'

Helping his wife from the table Sanford Rawley glanced at the girl now thanking the figure holding her elbow. She would not sleep soundly again tonight!

'Is your cabin unsuitable?' Grace Rawley's eyes gleamed a different question, dark circles beneath testifying to her own unhappiness.

Did she know? Was she aware of her husband's 'needs'? Had he sought a particular 'comfort' other than on this voyage? Natural sympathy underlay Alyssa's reply.

'My cabin is quite adequate, it is simply the strangeness, the sounds, the–'

'Ah!' The captain nodded. 'The roll of the ship, darkness below deck, creaking timbers, they all combine to arouse fear on a first voyage, especially so for a woman. It is not an uncommon occurrence.'

Not an uncommon occurrence. Alyssa followed the figure the captain had instructed see her to her cabin. Nor, seemingly, was it uncommon for a man to have both wife and mistress accompany him.

How had this happened to her! A sob of despair catching in her throat she dropped to the bunk. 'Why, Father?' An unconscious whisper behind fingers covering her face called to the love which had sustained her childhood. 'Why? I wanted only to help Thea. I wanted only to bring her home.'

Somewhere beyond the shadowed gloom of the tiny cabin the sounds of a bell ringing several times joined with the song of the wind. How long had she been sitting, how long before morning released her? The thought barely registered, Alyssa stiffened, a tap at her door acting like a razor on her nerves. Sanford Rawley!

'Father...!' Born of instinct the whisper remained on her lips. There was no father to protect her, nothing to prevent Sanford Rawley doing just as he had threatened.

If she did not answer, if she pretended sleep then maybe he would go away. The hope, flimsy as butterfly wings trembling in her chest, died with the second tap. He would not go away ... he would not forgo what he saw to be his due, his legitimate purchase.

Why not cry out? She stared to where the cabin door was lost among shadow. Why not scream, why not cry out? Tell the whole ship of the man's deceit, his disregard of a pregnant wife, the lust which had him force himself upon a girl he had asked join them on the pretext she be there should that wife need a woman's assistance? Questions flew in her mind, each followed by the same answer ... Grace Rawley!

'Miss Maybury...'

Barely louder than whispers of the heart the soft call brushed the darkness beyond the reach of the lantern. He had not called her name on that previous visit but simply walked in. Was this some new torment designed to add to her suffering? Did announcing his arrival, of knowing the misery and wretchedness it aroused, add another dimension to his amusement; did it bring him yet another source of odious gratification?

'Miss Maybury ... do you be awake?'

There was something different! The voice was quiet yet somehow not the same, the words 'do you be...', she had not heard their use on Sanford Rawley's tongue. Another deceit, this time devised to have any who might overhear believe a member of the crew to be tapping at her door? Taut as stretched wires, Alyssa's nerves hovered on the edge of breaking point.

'It be me, Miss, Sutton.'

Sutton, the young crew member who brought her a pot of tea to the deck! Relief trembling in every part of her Alyssa called permission to enter.

'I 'pologises if what I done be wrong...'

Just within the circle of dim yellow light a gangly figure stood, his hands twitching awkwardly, eyes downcast.

'...but you see I d'ain't think as things be right.'

271

She didn't care what he thought, what the reason for his coming, she cared only that he was here.

'I 'eard it...' he glanced upward, the look in his eyes defensive. '...I weren't eavesdroppin' honest I weren't, I were on my way to the stores, the cook wanted flour for usin' next mornin' and said it wouldn't wait ... it were as I passed your door I 'eard 'im, that Mister Rawley, I 'eard 'im sayin' about comfort a pregnant wife couldn't give, then ... then I 'eard you cry out an' Rawley he come from this cabin a' holdin' of his mouth. He didn't see me, I dived smart like, lyin' against the bulkhead 'til he were gone. Then this mornin' I seen a cut to his lip and knowed it were no result o' shavin', and at dinner you looked so pale an' scared so ... so I begged a word with the captain. He be a fair man, Miss, reckons on a man bein' due what he's paid for, but when it 'pears that bargain be one sided then the captain he teks another view...'

Alyssa listened in silence to the words tumbling after each other.

'...well 'earing what I 'eard, an' thinkin' what I thought I told it all to the captain; seemed first off he would cuff me for not goin' straight on past your cabin then he said for me to bring my pallet an' sleep outside of your door an' if questioned I was to say the captain 'ad ordered me stationed there every night until we docked, that way I would be on 'and should Missis Rawley reach 'er time.' He smiled shyly. 'You knows, Miss, 'ot water an' the like.'

The cabin boy was to sleep outside her door, he

272

was to be there until the ship docked! For several seconds relief held Alyssa in its heady grasp, then looking at the earnest face, at the lad she realised could be little more than fourteen years of age, relief fell like a stone.

'No.' She shook her head. 'I could not ask you to do that; your duties, your sleep...'

'Don't pay that no mind, Miss.' The earlier defensiveness gave way to assurance. 'Cabin boy don't be called on at night, 'e don't 'ave to stand watch or nothin' an' a pallet in the corridor don't be all that different to a pallet on the floor of the crew's quarters; 'sides,' he grinned, the suddenness of it catching the lantern gleam, 'I'd sooner spend the rest o' me life sleepin' on the ground than go tell the captain I were mistook... I don't 'ave to do that do I, Miss?'

No, he did not have to. Release from tension bringing warm tears, Alyssa smiled through them towards the firmly closed door. Thanks to a young lad she could sleep.

'Thank you.' Bathed, her clothing washed and set to dry over the chair, Alyssa murmured the heartfelt words her eyes closing in longed-for rest. 'Thank you, Mister Sutton.'

But it was not the cabin boy smiled back. In the unconsciousness of sleep Alyssa watched the arms of her father spread wide, his face wreathed with love; but behind him another younger man, handsome face dark with contempt, damson-ripe eyes glittering disgust, turned his back to her.

25

'It be a sight, don't it, Miss.'

Stood on a jetty reaching into crystal-clear water, Alyssa stared at the scene taking place around her. Could where she stood now be a part of that same world? The words Sutton had spoken had referred to a sky filled with glorious colour. Gold and crimson, magenta and pearl slashed through with turquoise, it had reached from horizon to horizon, a great canopy en-folding a sea of glittering aquamarine, a fantasia of colour singing its music to the soul.

Escorted by Sutton she had caught her breath that first evening, afraid that to breathe would shatter what seemed could only be a dream. But its beauty had been real, the spectacle of sunset even more glorious as the journey brought them to what Sutton proudly informed her was the Caribbean.

But where was that beauty now? Her bundle of belongings tied in a shawl the heat of the day made unnecessary, Alyssa glanced over to a group of buildings edging pale smooth sands, a line of low-backed carts drawn alongside.

It was much the same as she had seen in Bristol. Warehouses, great bundles of goods being off-loaded from ships their sails furled, only here the tall black needles of their masts pricked an incredibly blue sky. The same and yet so very different. That other port? She searched her mind for the thread she could not quite grasp, then a faint breeze carried it to her. The smell! At Bristol it had been scents of spices and fruit and the acrid odour of burning pitch, but here ... here the air was heavy with sweetness, like a thousand honey-combs all stripped of honey at the same time, but this had not the pleasantness of honeycomb she had seen at Lyndon, this was overpowering, a cloying syrupy thickness coating the lips, tasting on the tongue, and beneath it ... something else...

A loud shout drawing her attention, Alyssa glanced towards a low-fronted building from which a column of half-clothed figures emerged. Bent under the weight of sacks each the size of a man they staggered across the sand to where a bevy of boats bobbed lazily in the calm shallows waiting to ferry the sacks to sea-going vessels stood off in deeper water.

There were so many figures! She stared as if she was seeing for the first time. Line after line, processions of men all carrying cargo for ships waiting like so many vultures, the same figures running back to fetch yet more. It was watching them pass, faces beaded with moisture, dusky arms and torsos glittering as though caught in a shower of rain, she recognised that something else ... the stench of human perspiration.

Those men – her glance followed the trotting figures dressed in ragged calf-length breeches of rough homespun cloth – they were the same as the few she had seen at Bristol docks, but here each one had skin the colour of ebony.

'You must be feeling very pleased with yourself!'

Close to her elbow the quiet voice caught Alyssa in mid-thought yet her senses reacted with lightning speed.

She thought she had seen the last of him! Every nerve sounding alarm she turned about.

'Yes, you managed that very nicely.' Sanford Rawley's mouth was a line of anger. 'But you are no longer aboard ship, Miss Maybury, you no longer have your little watchdog to stand guard. You took advantage of my generosity...'

'I did not...'

The snarl ripped through objection, pale eyes gleaming menace.

'...you took my offer of passage knowing well the price to be paid...'

'No ... that isn't true, I...'

Alyssa tried again but as before her attempt at answer was destroyed with a virulence that struck like a blow.

'...but there is nothing free in this world, neither is Sanford Rawley a philanthropist. You may think you have got away with robbing me of my due but in that you are wrong; I will have remuneration of one sort or another and it will be no light reparation on your part. This is a small island, it has no employment for a European woman, no means by which you can earn enough money to get you back to England. Oh, you will not starve. Not right away ... there are those among the plantation owners will welcome a white woman to their bed, but their payment consists of food and board; but then, Miss Maybury, familiarity breeds

276

boredom and with that comes the need for change: when that happens you will find yourself here on this dock giving yourself to any disease-ridden scum who will throw you a slice of bread.'

There had been no objection to his organising the burial. Hat in hand, head bowed, Joseph Richardson stood before a headstone of grey marble. Amelia Bancroft had been born to all the comforts of life. Daughter of landed gentry, wife of a wealthy industrialist, mother of a son grown to healthy manhood, she had a life thousands of women could not even dream of, yet it was a life she herself had ended. For what reason had been the question asked by the authorities, but the finding of a crumpled letter bearing the crest of Whitchurch Abbey and signed Harford-De-Thaine, a cold brief letter informing her she could be given no home there, and the bottle beside her bed, a bottle the doctor confirmed had contained tincture of Aconite – put those facts together with information no doubt supplied by the Bank stating the Hall and its estates were no longer Bancroft property and the answer to the official enquiry had been 'suicide due to disturbance of the mind'.

Yet had all the story been told? Joseph let his thoughts play undisturbed. Had there been more to Amelia Bancroft's death than had been revealed ... matters known now only to her son? Marlow Bancroft! That man was unworthy to be called 'son'!

Turning away, his glance travelled across the churchyard a slight frown creasing his brow. A woman ... a woman standing beside the grave of

277

David! Alyssa? No, not Alyssa. The touch of a smile replacing the frown he walked to where Laura Tarn was placing a small vase of flowers against a small stone cross.

His shadow falling across the small patch had her lift her head then rise quickly to her feet, an embarrassed apology accompanying the colour come to stain her cheeks. 'Joseph, I ... I know I have no right ... Alyssa told me of the boy and I ... I thought that with her not being able to visit his resting place she would not mind my doing so.'

She had done this for Alyssa. Joseph glanced at the flowers. Lemon-yellow dianthus interspersed with taller stems of blue Bellflower they glowed against a depth of green foliage.

'I am sorry ... I should not have taken advantage...'

'No, Laura, you've taken no advantage, this be a kindness.' Relieved he had not thought her forward, Laura looked again at the flowers. 'The colours, I thought he would like the brightness,' then turning again to Joseph added, 'I know he could not see them in life but heaven restores all things to us.'

Heaven restores all things! Beneath his own smile Joseph's heart twisted. Heaven had not restored his family to him, it had only given yet more heartache. Gruffness catching in his throat he said, 'Alyssa would thank you were her here but I thanks you in her stead.'

Acquiescing to insistence he walk her home to Lyndon, Laura's mind played back the words Joseph had spoken beside the child's grave. There had been a depth of feeling in them, an emotion

278

she recognised in herself; loneliness? Yes and more ... despair was what she had heard, despair for yet another loss to his life, another love taken from him. Joseph Richardson was in love with Alyssa Maybury.

Alyssa watched the carriage drive the Rawleys out of sight, his snarled threat hanging over her like a cloud.

'No employment for a European woman...'

But there had to be something, someone who would give her work, and if not...?

'...giving yourself to any disease-ridden scum who will throw you a slice of bread.'

He had said it with so much venom, so much malice, but worse, he had said it with so much conviction.

'...Remember...'

A whisper, a touch of breath it brushed her mind.

'...things don't always be what they seems...'

Her father's words. Trembling against the tears they threatened to bring, Alyssa searched for their relevance. Then with realisation she smiled. In childhood her father's practical way had guided when things had seemed too difficult to bear, now his words were guiding her again.

'...things don't always be what they seems...'

Of course ... she was not alone! Thea was on this island, Thea would no doubt have money enough to get them both home to England.

The letter given her by the maid had mentioned a plantation. Nerves steadied, Alyssa's brain functioned logically. The maid had worked at

Bancroft Hall; perhaps the plantation belonged to that family, probably someone here on this wharf would tell her how to get there.

But whom to ask? She watched the stream of bodies fetching and carrying from boat to wharf. They were obviously from the island; they may not even speak English.

Unsure of what to do she stood, the full force of the sun beating down on her uncovered head. Maybe no one would be able to understand, no one she might ask if they had seen her sister, but then standing in one spot would not find Thea.

Turning to retrace her steps to the water's edge she hesitated, a loud shout from somewhere behind claiming her attention. She had not caught all of what had been shouted but the few words she had heard were spoken in English.

Dizzy with relief she spun quickly, just in time to see a tall fully clothed figure disappear into a warehouse. She could ask there.

'Bancroft you say!'

Skin leathered by exposure to the sun, blue eyes glinting coldly, the man she had enquired of ran a slow glance over Alyssa.

'Bancroft, eh!' He gave a half-laugh. 'I wonder he didn't bring you along of himself, not like him to chance a girl coming out here by herself, no that's not Bancroft's style at all, might lose him money and in your case that could prove a hefty sum to lose.'

Uncomfortable beneath what was a blatantly criticising look Alyssa wanted to walk away but knew it might prove difficult finding another person to answer her in words she could understand.

A deep breath fighting a wave of nausea she answered, 'Mister Bancroft did not pay my passage here.'

'Now there's another surprise.' Bleached by the sun an almost blond lock of hair falling over the forehead was pushed impatiently back. 'They say you learn something new every day.'

The look he gave her, the manner in which he spoke, it was so discourteous, almost insulting! Heat floating in waves beneath the roof of the low building, stifling throbbing heat which seemed to burn up the air, scorching every vestige of breeze, had moisture trickling along Alyssa's spine. What was wrong with the man ... had he forgotten how to be civil ... had he ever known how to answer a question politely? Her head beginning to throb Alyssa's usual patience snapped.

'So I have heard,' she retorted sharply, 'so maybe I could be instructed as to whether there is a Bancroft plantation on this island, and if so, how I might reach it! But if that is something you have not yet learned then I will enquire of someone else!'

'You do that...!'

So much a snarl it had Alyssa take an involuntary step backward.

'...might just be you will find a man who will answer, but me ... I have no time for Bancroft and none for the women he trades in. You want Marlow Bancroft's place then you find it for yourself ... though this much I will tell you... Take care who you ask, there are some wouldn't mind putting one over on Bancroft ... snatch his latest import from under his nose.'

'Wait...!'

The call followed after the man who swung away, his whole posture that of contempt and in the oppressive somnolent heat his muttered words drifted to Alyssa.

'Two of a kind ... trust Bancroft to cover his back!'

He was in love with Alyssa Maybury!

In the sitting room of Lyndon House Laura Tarn poured tea into china cups.

She had heard it so clearly in his voice, in his words, the pathos and yearning, the loss of hope. None of them were strangers to Laura Tarn, they walked beside her each hour of her every day.

'Have you given any thought to what you might do in the meantime? After all, it could be quite a while before the business of Bancroft Hall is settled and then time again before the place is sold.'

Paul's words drifted almost unheard over Laura's head, her own thoughts dominant in her mind. She and Joseph Richardson shared the same despair, felt the same heartbreak and she could not help him.

'I've given no thought to that.'

At the fringe of Laura's conscious hearing the conversation went.

'Then it is time you did.' Paul took the cup, his glance holding to the man now accepting his. 'Look, Joseph, you have been a silent partner long enough, won't you take your place now?'

'I never wanted–'

'I know,' Paul interrupted. 'You never wanted

to be a partner in the steel business, but you must understand. The money you loaned to help finance the first factory, I could never count that a gift so with your refusing to accept repayment I had no choice but to name you as equal partner. It has been that way ever since; now I am asking you to work with me.'

For a moment it seemed Joseph would not answer then quietly he said, 'I thought to leave Wednesbury.'

A thunderclap it crashed on Laura's brain. Joseph was leaving Wednesbury! Was it to look for Alyssa Maybury? But then why else would he leave?

'Joseph.' Paul was speaking again. 'I would not ask if there were one other man I trusted as I trust you, but there is not and for that reason I ask you stay on in Wednesbury, take care of my sister until I return.'

'Take care o' Laura, that don't need no answer, but return!' Joseph's frown was quizzical. 'Return from where?'

'Jamaica,' Paul said. 'I am going to Jamaica.'

'Sugar press!' Joseph shook his head. 'I didn't know you had dealings with sugar.'

'*We* had dealings with sugar ... partners, Joseph, remember.'

'*We* had dealings with sugar.' Joseph smiled. It was going to take some getting used to.

'It is a new venture.' Interest lighting his eyes, Paul spoke quickly of a request made for the construction of a press by which sugar cane could be crushed more firmly therefore extracting every

283

last drop of juice. 'You see,' he finished, 'this press could lead to orders for several more. There are, I am told, several plantations out there, that is the reason I want to take the machinery to Jamaica myself ... see the thing set up properly. But that could take several months and though Laura is perfectly capable of running the business in my absence I would feel happier knowing you were there should need arise.'

'You must now allow Paul to keep you here in Wednesbury.' Laura had listened without interruption or question, but now walking with Joseph from the house she said what she felt she must. 'It was selfish of him to ask, I ... I wouldn't want you to stay.'

There had been a quick pain in those blue eyes, a nuance of the same flitting across his face. Laura shifted her glance to the fields spreading out to meet the sky. Lyndon House was centuries old, an ancient manor built by a Norman knight, the land surrounding it a gift of William the Conqueror. How much happiness had it seen, and sadness...? Yes it must have witnessed that also, she would not have it witness more on her account.

She could tell him the pain she saw there in his eyes, that he could not completely erase from his face, would end with time but that would be to lie for she knew that when love was deep and true the pain of losing the one to whom the heart was given never healed. It would always be there as her pain was always in her heart.

'You miss her very much, don't you?'

She had not intended to voice the thought, but softly as it slipped from her lips, Joseph heard.

She had spoken out of turn. Joseph had long been a friend but to speak as she had! Laura felt the colour flood into her face.

'Yes.' Standing beside her, the touch of evening sun gilding the faint streaks of silver at his temples, Joseph Richardson drew a long breath. 'Yes, I miss her.'

Caution and embarrassment losing any hold it had, Laura looked at him. 'Then you must go, you must try to find Alyssa.'

'Alyssa?' Joseph turned to her with a look of complete bewilderment.

'You must find her, end the unhappiness.'

'End the unhappiness.' Joseph's half-laugh bruised the quiet air. 'Finding Alyssa Maybury would not do that.'

'But you love her.'

'I don't deny it, yes I love Alyssa Maybury but not in the way you seem to think, I love that girl as I might a sister or daughter, but not in any other way.'

He loved ... but was not *in* love. Yet she had seen it in his eyes, heard it in his voice; but she had allowed her mind to lead her the wrong way... It was the old pain Joseph suffered from, that of losing his wife and child.

'I'm sorry, Joseph.' She returned her glance to the expanse of fields of wheat, golden heads crowned with the embrace of approaching sunset. 'I should have known Ruth...'

'Ruth!' He took the word from her. 'Ruth was my life, losing her took that from me. I was like a man dead until Alyssa Maybury...'

'But you said...'

285

'Listen to me, Laura, listen for I might never again have the courage. It were Alyssa brought me from the darkness, the grave I had dug for myself. Her allowing my help with the child and with her mother gave life back to me. It made me see where I had been blind, showed me what I had let my life become. I was afraid to love again, I had closed my heart to it, refused to accept what every day became more plain. I did love again but that love was not for Alyssa Maybury, it was for you. But seeing your unhappiness, knowing it were your feelings for Cain Lindell...'

'No ... no, Joseph.' The face lifted to his wore a look of radiance, the gentle eyes bright with tears. 'The feelings I had for Cain Lindell were those of youth, of infatuation. I grieved for his death, for the pain it brought to his family, but the love I imagined myself to have ... it was not real, the shadows of my heart do not stem from love lost with Cain Lindell but one I thought never to realise ... it is you, Joseph. You are the man I have loved these many years and it is you I will always love.'

'Laura... Oh, my love...!'

Caught in his arms, his mouth against hers, it was left to the breeze to whisper across the sun-blessed fields.

26

The man she had spoken with had hardly been anxious to help, the look he had given her had been openly scathing and the manner in which he had replied to her perfectly ordinary enquiry had been positively rude; and what had he meant by those words she had heard him mutter as he stalked away ... 'trust Bancroft to cover his back?'

He had been downright churlish! At home in Darlaston a man speaking to a woman as he had ... but this was not home, this was a foreign country and she was alone. Beneath the surface of resentment, Alyssa felt the pull of tears then pushed them away. She would not let one man's rudeness deter her, there had to be someone else spoke English! Yet despite his treatment of her, of her own determination she stared in the direction the man had gone hoping he would return, would speak with her; it would not matter how ungraciously so long as he directed her to the Bancroft plantation.

The sweetness which pervaded the air out there on the wharf was stronger in this building. Trapped by the low roof it seemed to hang over everything to circle and re-circle, an invisible cloud leaving traces of itself on the mouth, settling thickly in the throat, a honeyed sugary taste too sweet to be pleasant. Alyssa's stomach churned while behind her eyes the throb of a

287

headache increased.

Leaving the warehouse she breathed deeply but the attempt to rid her throat and lips of the sickly coating, to give some relief to lungs which felt ready to burst, brought little relief.

There had to be someone ... she could not stand here for ever... Those smaller boats ferrying cargo ... one of them had to belong to the *Dolphin*, those men would answer in her own language.

Allowing no time for a change of mind she ran to the line of boats asking at each one, becoming ever more desperate at successive shrug or shake of head indicating failure to understand while some answered abruptly they had no knowledge of any such plantation or where it could be found.

Were they being deliberately obtuse, purpose-fully unhelpful? But that was unfair. Standing at the fringe of the gently lapping water Alyssa tried to keep a logical mind. The boatmen she had asked, they most likely worked only ship to shore so would have no knowledge of who or what was further inland.

Neither did she!

Striking like a stone hitting against glass the thought shattered the last of Alyssa's persever-ance. No one was willing or able to help, she did not even know in which direction she should go. The bundle fell from fingers suddenly devoid of strength and tears blurred white sand with brilliant turquoise sea, its fringe of swaying palm trees melting into one dark line.

'Father.' Unheard even by her own mind the strangled word slipped between dry lips.

Laura and Joseph! How could he have been so blind? Standing on the deck of the clipper ship Paul Tarn smiled at the horizon. All the years since Cain Lindell's failure to return to marry her he had thought the shadows of unhappiness haunting his sister's gentle eyes to stem from that lost love. But it had not been the love lost from Lindell's seeming desertion but from that she held for Joseph Richardson. If she had only spoken of it ... if the friendship he and Joseph had shared for so long had led the man to confide ... but both had kept their secret. It had been so much a waste of life ... but then was not pride so often harmful, did its pernicious effect not destroy friendships? Only when it was allowed to ... as it had been in his last conversation with Alyssa Maybury! But had it been pride or had it been jealousy had him virtually accuse her of being Joseph's mistress? Which had kept him from immediately apologising?

'Taking a breath of air?'

A shadow of resentment at being disturbed flicking his mind Paul nodded to the man come to stand beside him. Thoughts were his only contact with Alyssa Maybury, imagination the only way he could speak with her, hear her voice, see the face he did not want to forget. *He did not want to forget!* His glance on the shimmering water Paul lived again the moment he had first admitted that to himself, admitted he was in love with Alyssa Maybury.

'Different to the weather in England.'

Drawn reluctantly from his reverie, Paul glanced at the man now running a finger between a high starched collar and an obviously over-warm neck.

'Very.' Unwilling to appear boorish Paul forced a smile. 'What would you say to an exchange system, a little of our rain for a little of this sunshine?'

'Reckon there be folk back home would welcome that but meself, I finds this weather altogether too warm. Mebbe's a few days, but they would have to be holiday, heat like this don't make for working in, it drains a man's concentration, makes it easy for him to lose track of what he's about.'

Easy to lose track! Paul's inner smile was painful. He had already learned just how easy.

'You reckon on being in Jamaica for a couple of months you say, but I want only to get what I be sent for.'

Which would not be easy should his quarry get wind of a Police Inspector out from England. Paul's mental return was instant yet silent. They had talked privately together on several occasions during the voyage, he telling the Inspector of his transporting a machine for the crushing of sugar cane, the Inspector, though not referring specifically to his own reasons for sailing so far across the world, had made no attempt to give denial to what he must know was in the mind of the man he had accompanied to Deepmoor House, the man who had accused Edward Farnell of stealing Cain Lindell's identity; the thought of his being sent to arrest Marlow Bancroft.

But would Bancroft prove to be in Jamaica ... or would he be wise enough to have gone elsewhere knowing that island would be the first place anyone wanting to find him would look? But Jamaica was thousands of miles away from England and in Bancroft's opinion also thousands of miles from its justice, therefore a safe enough refuge in which to hide from his debtors; but that which Farnell had confessed in those minutes at Deepmoor, that he had stated Bancroft was an accomplice in, that could find no hiding place.

'Captain says we make land tomorrow.' The Inspector broke the silence. 'Best get a good night's sleep.'

Once more alone Paul stared out over an endless stretch of ocean turned to molten bronze beneath a setting sun. A good night's sleep, one undisturbed by memories, by regrets. That might be a long time in the coming.

'Be here soon, Missy.'

It drifted somewhere in a warm peace.

'Not much long to great house.'

There it was again, a voice within her dark warm haven.

'Not much mile, Missy.'

Missy. Alyssa smiled. Mark always called her Missy. In a moment he would scoop her into his arms, swing her high in the air laughing at her pretended squeals of fright. Mark, her brother who teased...

'You be awake, Missy...'

She would not answer, she would tease Mark until he caught her up. Alyssa laughed softly.

'See, Missy, bamboo.'

Bamboo! What kind of word was that? Had Mark found something new to show her or was he teasing again?

'Bamboo, it cover sky.'

Floating in her warm peaceful world Alyssa struggled to hold herself there, tried not to relinquish its comfort but already it was slipping away.

'Mark!' Husky with sleep she called to her brother then vision clearing felt the familiar sharp sting of loss. It was not Mark calling to her, Mark would never call to her again. But someone had spoken. Still only partly awake she listened. Wheels... she was in some vehicle! Eyelids stubbornly closed she felt the steady jolt of wheels rolling over ruts of packed earth, heard the rhythm of an animal's hooves, the buzz of insects all combining together, joining in a bid to soothe, to return her to that dark peace.

But she must not go there. Moving the fingers of one hand, feeling the touch of rough wood, Alyssa's nerves tingled. She had been standing on the wharf, she had stared at the tree line and then ... but she did not know 'then', memory ended in darkness. So what had happened, who was she with, who had taken her from the beach, where was she being taken?

Questions swamping her brain Alyssa opened her eyes.

'Be fine cool.' Sitting on the driving seat of a cart, a smiling brown face turned to look at her, a man pointed upward. 'Bamboo make fine cool.'

Blinking away the last remnants of sleep Alyssa glanced in the direction indicated by a strong-looking hand then caught her breath. The cart was passing beneath an arch of greenery freckled with golden spots of sunlight. Caught by the beauty of it she could only stare. Each side of a narrow track a multitude of slender plants grew high, their whip-like branches twining overhead, forming an avenue cooled by a canopy of green feathery leaves.

'Bamboo.' The man flicked a long whip above the back of an ambling bullock, his smile breaking again.

Alyssa's glance followed the line of supple ribbed stems bending and swaying with the slightest breeze. Bamboo, a nice enough name but not adequate for so graceful a plant.

'Come great house soon.'

Cast by interlacing branches shadow danced over the trackway, a medley of softly flickering movement, an hypnotic play of light and shade forming a gentle gauze that closed the mind from reality.

Alyssa clung to thoughts becoming more difficult to hold.

'Where are you taking me? Who placed me in this cart?'

Beneath a length of sacking draped over the tall supports of the cart to provide shade, Alyssa put her questions but the man simply smiled and pointed with the whip.

'Not much mile, Missy, come great house soon.'

Great house ... where, whose house? Again and again as the cart rumbled on Alyssa asked but the only response was a nod. Did the man not understand ... or had he been instructed to say no more than he had? A frisson of alarm rubbing her nerves Alyssa wrestled with the idea of jumping from the wagon. And then what? She stared at the density of vegetation. Could be there was no house within miles ... maybe no one at all she could ask help from.

'Missy, here great house.' Flashing white teeth a vivid contrast to the rich deep mahogany of his skin, the man smiled then jumped from the cart, his strong hands lifting her easily to the ground.

There was no house here, nothing but fields of tall growing plants. Why had he lifted her from the cart? Turning to ask, Alyssa's heart sank. The cart was already trundling into the distance, already becoming lost among the profusion of vegetation. He couldn't leave her here! He couldn't leave her alone! Desperation making her voice shrill Alyssa called after the disappearing cart but the sudden squawk of birds flapping up from the ground proved her only answer.

But that was not all her cries had produced. Relief sweeping through her Alyssa looked at the group of figures which had emerged from between tall thick stalks. Women... oh, thank goodness!

'Can you tell me...'

The question was cut in half by strangled gasps the faces of the women contorting with fear. Why were they so afraid? Confused by their reaction Alyssa tried again, 'Can you tell me...?' But the women were gone, running from her, their terrified cries carrying back from the masking greenery.

'Come back ... please I only want to ask...'

It was no use. Alyssa watched the ripple of disturbed plants settle into place. The women were gone.

Near to setting the sun cast an orange glow over

what could only be wide acres of crops, the same crops which had marked much of the way from the wharf. Alyssa glanced again at the fields some inner hope they might part and show the women who had fled from her but the only movement was the ripple of breeze, the only sound the rustle of dry yellowing leaves.

'Hello!' Loud on the heavy silence her call spread across the land but the slight wind brought no reply. Perhaps if she waited. Those women knew she was here, they must tell someone and that someone come to help.

But they had been more than simply taken aback, more than initially frightened, those women had been terrified. But for what reason, surely they must have seen a white woman before? But what if they told no one the cause of their fright, told no one she was here? Alarm which while on that cart had brushed her nerves now became definite fear. She had no food and worse no water and soon it would be night!

Trying hard to withstand rising panic Alyssa glanced at the sky. Orange and scarlet was giving way to the purple of evening but there was no relief from the heat. It pressed down from the very air, beat up from the ground. She tried to swallow, to slake her parched throat, to ease a tongue which seemed suddenly to fill her mouth. Without water how far could she walk! Trickles of perspiration wet on her cheeks, the throb returning to her head, she sucked at air which only scorched her lungs, burned in her eyes, an all-encompassing mind-drowning heat.

The bundle held in one hand of a sudden

becoming an enormous weight dropped to the ground. She could not breathe ... her throat was closed! Her lips parting in a soundless cry, her head spinning, her body strangely weightless, Alyssa was helpless against a force dragging her down, drawing her into a furnace of blinding white heat.

27

'They are not all men carrying bales to those boats, some of them are women, doesn't that seem unusual to you?'

'How could it?' Inspector Richard Morgan's smile flashed briefly. 'This is my first visit to Jamaica, I am not familiar with what is or what is not usual.'

From the comfortable lounge of a hotel situated in the curve of a bay Paul Tarn watched the play of colours: rose-gold, garnet and aquamarine they filled the whole sky, touched the ocean tipping the crests of amethyst waves rippling onto almost white sands along which tall palm trees etched a dark outline. The whole scene was breathtaking. A memory of Eden? It was beautiful enough. Yet the wharf where he had disembarked had shown a very different picture. Men dressed in rags jumping to the crack of an overseer's whip, men running despite the heat of tropical sun, women too carrying bales ... people treated like slaves. The last image arousing afresh the disgust he had felt when on that wharf, he turned to the man who had travelled out from England aboard the same ship. Meeting the policeman who had been with him when confronting Farnell, learning of his going to Jamaica, had been a little surprising but his company then, as now, had been welcome.

'What Farnell said that day at Deepmoor, about Bancroft, I mean,' Paul changed the subject, 'could there be any truth in it or do you think it simply a way of shifting blame?'

Tarn had heard it all, he had agreed to testify in court to having been present when Farnell had confessed his crimes, that confession citing Marlow Bancroft as a knowing and willing accomplice, therefore there could be little harm in discussion. Satisfied by the thought, yet ever the policeman, Morgan answered.

'What I think or don't think is not the issue. It was a confession given and signed in the presence of witnesses and stated again in court. Due to that the judge ordered Bancroft be brought back to England.'

'And you were sent to bring him back.'

'As you see.' Morgan shrugged.

Ordering them both a refreshing drink of lime juice touched with ginger and sugar Paul returned to the view. Was the rest of the island as beautiful or was Long Bay one on its own?

'Do you go inland tomorrow?' Morgan broke the companionable silence.

'Yes, it's a matter of just a few miles so I am told but with heavy machinery and not knowing the state of the roads it could be anybody's guess how long it will take to reach Mandeville.'

'Judging by the bullock carts on that dock I hope you ain't pre-booked a passage home.'

'Might make it around Christmas.' Paul joined the other man's laughter.

'This place be warmer than England but I prefer home especially at Christmas.'

Home! Paul watched the kaleidoscope column of sky and sea. Rose-gold giving way to scarlet and copper, amethyst water to purple. Lyndon at Christmas! Trees and fields silver-white with frost, apple logs blazing in every fireplace hugging the rooms with warmth, Laura trying to hide the sadness as presents were exchanged. Thank God there would be no more sadness for Laura nor for Joseph, they had found each other ... and Paul Tarn? How long before his heart smiled again?

'Reckon Bancroft won't be so pleased to see England. It's not a good Christmas that one will be havin', not if Richard Morgan be any judge.'

Drawn from his thoughts Paul drank a little of his lime and ginger before saying, 'You are certain of his being here in Jamaica?'

Lips pursed the policeman pondered the question, his glance on the darkening horizon. 'Certain as can be,' he answered quietly, 'his mother ... God rest her ... seemed to think his plantation would be the place he would bolt to ... but here or not we'll find out in due course.'

'his plantation would be the place he would bolt to...'

Words returning as the Inspector retired for the night became pushed aside by others.

'...ask about the girl he raped, the girl with red-gold hair.'

Fingers turning white from the pressure with

which they held the drinking glass, Paul stared out across the bay.

It had not taken as long as he had expected. Paul watched the steam-operated machine crush long stalks of cane, squeezing out every last drop of juice which then fed into a container of heated water and lime juice to be cleaned and filtered.

The workers had been nervous at first, afraid to touch the 'monster' which breathed steam but the plantation owner had reassured them it was no live beast waiting to devour them.

'This is going to increase output as well as remove the burden of having to mangle every piece of cane by hand, the men will welcome that.' Standing beside Paul a man dressed in white cotton shirt and brown leather boots topping tan trousers watched the continuous procession of canes feeding into the machine's shredder. 'I must say you have the whole thing well designed, feeding cane juice from heated wash to clarifier, then filter and evaporator before taking the syrup on into the vacuum pan and from there to the centrifuge, all by a system of connected tubes. This a far better method than having great open vats of boiling juice and it keeps the finished product free of any insect deciding to take itself a warm bath. I think, Mister Tarn, you will be supplying machines like this one to every sugar plantation on the island … except perhaps for Beau-Ideal.'

'Beau-Ideal?'

'Don't let the name fool you!' The planter frowned. 'Oh yes, it once was all the name might imply, a beautiful location set at the toe of the Blue

Mountains, a river running right through keeping the soil moist and ideal for the growing of sugar cane, Morant Bay some half mile away ... yes the place had all it needed until Bancroft bought it.'

'Bancroft!'

'Yes.' Turning from watching the newly installed machine its buyer looked at Paul. 'Bancroft ... do you know him? Sorry if he is a friend of yours but I stand by what I've said, Beau-Ideal was one of the most prolific producers of sugar anywhere on the island until Bancroft took over, now ... well, I won't tell you what the place is now'

'Bancroft is no friend of mine, but I do intend to call upon him.'

'Then you'll see for yourself.'

It was abrupt, like each word was acid in the mouth. Had Bancroft and this man had a falling out?

Accepting the offer of a cool drink Paul followed his host, his glance roving over a two-storey white stone built mansion set around by a wide white-painted veranda, shuttered windows open to the scents of hibiscus and oleander, of citrus and pine. Set against a background of lush green tropical forest rimmed around by soft grey-violet mountains, their tops brushing a brilliant blue sky, its grace and beauty merited the name by which the estate workers called it, it was indeed 'great house'.

Seated in low bamboo chairs drinks served by a smiling houseboy, immaculate in spotless cotton jacket and trousers, Paul broached the subject uppermost in his mind. 'Bancroft's plantation. Does it produce much sugar?'

'Not nearly as much as it should!' The reply was caustic. 'It used to give at least one hogshead – that is sixteen hundred weight – to an acre, giving between three and four hundred hogshead per year, now the yield is more like eight a year; but then Bancroft doesn't need to grow sugar cane – his money comes from the sale of a very different crop!'

Meaning? His drink finished Paul rose to leave, the enquiry kept to himself.

Having accompanied Paul to a carriage that would return him to Long Bay much more comfortably and a deal speedier than the bullock cart he had come by, the planter shook hands, then as Paul seated himself said in an almost apologetic tone, 'When you get back have yourself a trip along to Yallans. Ask at the warehouse there about a new delivery sent along the coast to Beau-Ideal. Find out for yourself how Bancroft makes his money.'

Farnell had been a fool. Had he remained here in Jamaica he would never have been suspected, never have been found out in his lies. Now he was in police custody. But not Marlow Bancroft. Marlow laughed, the brandy he tossed into his throat turning the sound into a gurgle. Bancroft would never be arrested. He swallowed the alcohol, savouring the bite as it passed his throat. Even if some here knew, still no one would dare to speak of it. Bancroft revenge was widely known across this island. Even so, Farnell had made things awkward ... there could not be the frequent trips to England. 'Damn the man and his stupidity!' Sending his glass crashing to the floor, Marlow swore angrily. The trade from England had been lucrative and now... 'Damn!' He swore again bringing a fist hard down, the bamboo table it struck rocked precariously. But he wasn't finished yet; the cargo he had brought this time was worth a deal of money and he would get every last penny. And when that batch was sold what then? Where and how to get the next? But you set no foot on a bridge until you got to it! Filling another glass he drank deeply. He had not reached there yet ... and in a few days' time he would set that bridge back even further.

'You is havin' visitor, Massa.'

Marlow held brandy on his tongue but the savour he tasted was satisfaction of making the expected visitor wait. Let him know who was the premier player in the game, who it was held the whip hand. Although the fingers of that hand were somewhat loosened thanks to Farnell, that situation would be redressed. Even so. Marlow swallowed then turned to face the servant awaiting instruction. Best not to keep a buyer waiting too long.

'Salaam.' The tall man who had been shown into a sitting room cooled by doors opened onto a wide veranda offered a slight bow while the fingertips of one hand touched heart, lips and brow.

'Afternoon.' Conveying every trace of the thoughts so recently in his mind, Marlow's reply was curt to the point of dismissive. 'Tea!' He flung the order to the waiting manservant. 'And bring another decanter.'

Beneath his flowing, vividly white robe the visitor's hand tightened over the handle of a gem-encrusted dagger. To drink alcohol in the presence of Yusuf-el-Abdullah was more than a discourtesy; more than disrespect it was an insult, an affront to Allah! One day, Inshallah, this ignorant dog of an Englishman would pay the price of dishonour.

Tea brought, the servant dismissed, and his glass replenished, Marlow dropped to a chair. He had no liking for the man sitting opposite him nor any time for the bargaining which Yusuf-el-Abdullah seemed to think compulsory. He, Bancroft, had the price of the consignment firmly in mind and that would be non-negotiable. The man might wriggle and squirm but maggots of his sort were easily trodden on!

'I must inspect the goods first.'

That was Abdullah's first gambit. Marlow smiled into his glass. There would be no other. Raising his glance he looked coldly at the other man. 'The sugar is of the quality expected, the crop is pure as always ... but if the price is too high there are others who will happily take the cargo.'

Another insult! Beneath the white burnous headcover partly shadowing his face, Yusuf-el-Abdullah's eyes glittered resentment. How he would relish driving the blade into the throat of this pig but at least for now he must deny himself that pleasure. Rising to his feet, no smile softening his hawk-like features, he replied. 'Shukran ... thank you ... but once given the word of el-Abdullah is not broken.' Then with Marlow's glance fastening on the canvas bag withdrawn

303

from beneath his robe added mentally, neither is a vow made before Allah; I vow, should the grace of the Almighty permit, then Yusuf-el-Abdullah will take the life of this infidel.

'Mother!'

Lost in her own dark world, Alyssa cried her childhood pain.

'Mother, love me ... love me like you love Thea...'

Standing beneath a great golden moon a man dressed in ragged cotton pants glanced fearfully towards a line of trees. The woman would be heard ... he would be whipped! Shoulders glistening brown-gold in the moonlight hunched, his body wincing as if already feeling the slash of leather.

'Mother, hold me ... hold me like Thea...'

Partly drowned by the constant drone of insects among night-hidden crops the soft cry had the man look sharply over his shoulder. He could not keep her here, it was too risky; but her cries ... first he must silence her cries.

Glancing carefully in each direction he checked for signs of movement, head cocked listening for sounds other than cicadas. Deep draughts held in the nostrils examining the scents of the air ... all would tell of white man coming.

Satisfied no one was approaching, his movements silent as a wraith, he slipped into a windowless wooden shack. Using no means of light he crossed to a corner of the small room then dropped to his knees and dug into the packed earth floor, muttering beneath his breath when his fingers closed over a small pot.

Again finding his way without use of torch, he recrossed the room. Reaching to a shelf crudely nailed to the wooden wall he took a cup and a jug. A little of the contents of the pot mixed with water from the jug he carried it to where Alyssa lay. She must drink it, he would make her drink it. But not too much. Lifting Alyssa's head he trickled the liquid into her mouth. The woman must only sleep. The Obeah would take his life if the woman died.

Jug, cup and pot returned each to its place, he stepped from the shack, listening and watching as before.

The moon was almost directly overhead. Soon it would be time.

28

Her mother was calling.

As if trudging through thick mud Alyssa's brain struggled to lift her from the depths of sleep. Time to get up... Sounds beyond sleep urged her to wake. Time for school, they would be late...

'Thea.' Cracked lips moving in the darkness felt no sting of blistered skin. 'Thea, get up...'

Unseen, unheard by the young woman lying on a bed of dried palm leaves, a figure moved silently among shadows cast by a fire of burning branches, a figure coming to stand beside the makeshift bed.

'Thea...' Still locked in her dream world Alyssa

called to a younger girl, whose bare feet danced in a pool of fallen leaves, her red-gold hair freed from ribbons streaming in the breeze, lifting about her head like flames. 'Thea, no...'

Taking a burning stick, the light of it shining on Alyssa's face, a man watched her brow crease, the dried lips move, the soft cries become those of fear.

'No, Thea, you can't ... you can't...'

Behind closed eyelids the dancing girl had become a young woman, a woman holding a baby over the rim of a black pit while Alyssa ran towards her.

'Thea, stop!' Head twisting and turning in the throes of nightmare, Alyssa's cries echoed on the stillness as the child was dropped.

'No...!' The cry Alyssa did not know she had made followed her mental image of the falling child, then as she looked the pit became a lake, its dark waters silvered by a high moon. On its surface floated a mass of rags, rags which swirled with the lap of breeze-tossed waves, rags which swirled and parted to show a pale staring face. 'Mother...!' Her mouth opening to the scream Alyssa did not feel the touch of a small animal-skin flask against her lips, did not taste the bitter liquid running over her tongue; locked in mental agony she stared at the face of her drowned mother.

'I intend to go there today.' Paul Tarn's answer brooked no argument.

'You are certain the woman you speak of was here?'

'The man I spoke with at Yallans was definite, a

306

young woman with deep red-gold hair; he had her put on a cart that would pass the Bancroft place.'

Richard Morgan's brow furrowed. 'He had her sent?'

The meal finished, Paul ordered coffee asking it be served on the hotel's wide veranda.

'He hadn't wanted to,' Paul answered, as the Inspector settled into one of the deep bamboo chairs. 'Said he'd wanted nothing to do with Bancroft or the women he – and here is the worrying part – nothing to do with the women he trades in.'

Thanking the waiter who brought their coffee, Richard Morgan stirred sugar into his cup before asking quietly, 'Was that all was said?'

Taking his own cup, Paul shook his head. 'That man had a real dislike of Bancroft and didn't care who knew it. He seemed to think as I am coming to think.'

'Oh, and just what *do* you think?'

'I'll tell you what I think,' Paul returned, his mouth tight with sudden anger. 'I think Bancroft is in the business of white slaving and so sure I'm proved right I'll wring the neck of that swine myself!'

'White slaving!' The Inspector's brow creased a little deeper. 'That is a very serious accusation; did your man at Yallans have any proof of such activity?'

'He said nothing specific, but then he wouldn't be expected to, I was, after all, a perfect stranger he was speaking with.'

Helping himself to more coffee, Morgan waited a moment before answering. 'This fellow said nothing specific yet you are of the opinion

Bancroft is engaged in slaving?'

'Talk with him yourself, ask him why he referred to a young Englishwoman as Bancroft's latest *import*.'

Adding cream to his cup Inspector Richard Morgan stared thoughtfully at the pale circles blending into the dark brown of the coffee. An unfortunate turn of phrase ... or a deliberate use of words? He would indeed be visiting the warehouse at Yallans Bay but for now...

Setting his cup aside he leaned deeper into the chair his gaze going out over the brilliant blue sky, a relaxed, nonchalant movement designed for the benefit of any who might be watching. 'Mister Tarn.' Purposefully slow, as though already half given to sleep, he spoke quietly. 'What I am about to say requires your solemn oath you will not speak of it to anyone. Do I have that oath? Then I can tell you,' he went on, assured of Paul's given promise, 'the accusations made by Edward Farnell were supported by Lady Bancroft.'

'Bancroft's own mother! She knew about–!'

'Quietly please, Mister Tarn, there could be ears other than ours listening.' Eyelids drooping deceptively he continued the charade of a businessman snoozing away the hot hours of the afternoon, but the cautionary note showed Paul that the Inspector was wide awake. 'Lady Bancroft did not know until she found the diaries belonging to her late daughter-in-law.'

'His wife also knew!' Paul could not keep the incredulity from his reply. 'Lord, this thing gets worse and worse.'

Exhaling deeply, the very picture of a man

replete after a good meal, the Inspector watched the bay from beneath half-closed eyelids.

'Bancroft's wife knew,' he yawned, 'but she was no accomplice. The diaries speak repeatedly of her husband's ill treatment of her, of a beating she was given after questioning the quite often sudden disappearances of young girls he and Farnell brought out on each visit to England. Then it seemed she overheard a conversation between Bancroft and a man she described as *"very foreign, dressed in a flowing white robe, a white headcloth bound about the brow with a thick black cord"*. They were discussing the price of a new cargo. Bancroft – the diary says – became angry, his voice carrying clearly through opened windows. *"The offer is not high enough."* This and the following sentence was heavily underlined. *"Four girls, each not yet seventeen, I can sell them for three times the amount you want to pay."* It was after this that Felicia Bancroft feigned pregnancy in order to return to England.'

'Poor woman!' Paul breathed with new anger. 'She must have gone through hell – but so will Bancroft when I catch up with him.'

Not entirely free of regret, Richard Morgan's answer was muffled by another pretended yawn. 'You cannot be allowed to catch up with him, that is for the law to do.'

'But what if the swine gets wind of who you are? What if he decides to leave the island?'

Beyond the hotel the waters of Long Bay gleamed an incredible blue, a soft breeze teasing ripples capped with gold.

'He would get no further than a certain trading

vessel bound for the Orient, a vessel that was stopped before leaving territorial waters. You see, Mister Tarn, like yourself I had my suspicions about women being used to load cargo, especially when later that same day I saw them being ferried out to a waiting ship from which they did not return. I spoke of this and of Felicia Bancroft's diaries during my meeting with the Governor in Kingston. I had to present official papers stating my reason for coming to Jamaica and was told by him that he had received word to that effect in the diplomatic bag. He offered every assistance, including having that ship stopped and searched.'

'You mean the captain stopped voluntarily?'

A small smile touching his mouth, Richard Morgan rolled his head slightly to bring Paul's face into view. 'Not quite,' he chuckled, 'but you see, Mister Tarn, no sensible captain would argue with a gun boat of Her Majesty's Navy.'

'You promised us some entertainment, Bancroft, I don't bloody well count a few hands of cards to be entertainment!'

Marlow Bancroft watched the flurry of playing cards stream across the baize-topped table. His guest was impatient, but then he was meant to be.

'Stakes too high for your purse?' He glanced across the table. 'You can always pull out. I'm sure we will all understand.'

'I've got money enough!' An already flushed face turned a deeper shade of red. 'I could see you out, Bancroft, have no fears on that score.'

'I'm happy to hear it.'

310

The snide reply adding a quick temper the reply bounced back. 'I bet you bloody well are! And don't think I don't know you'll tek me ... tek each man here ... for every last penny, we ain't all fools, Bancroft!'

No? Marlow's smile never reached his mouth. Then what was he doing here ... what were any of them doing here?

Collecting cards the man had thrown down, Marlow took time arranging them into an orderly pack, a move intended to add to his guests' irritation, then: 'You must surely have known the expense – this after all is by no means a first visit – yet still you came. I wonder why?'

'You know bloody well why!' The aggrieved reply snapped back.

Calm as the other man was agitated, Marlow placed the neatened cards at the centre of the table. 'Indeed I do. It is only here you can enjoy the kind of entertainment you prefer, only here you can indulge in those particular pleasures; however, gentlemen, the proposed entertainment is easily called off should you so wish.'

Sitting around the table the three others remained silent, choosing not to meet the look Marlow played over each in turn.

'I take it then you would rather we continue ... but might I suggest a small divertissement...?'

'No doubt a bloody costly one!'

Secure in the knowledge that his guests were not about to abandon their much-anticipated evening, Marlow answered urbanely, 'Quite the reverse. What I propose is we play one more hand of cards but not for money; instead the winner

311

will get to choose, will he be the star performer in the game I have arranged?'

It whet already drooling appetites. Marlow passed the pack of cards to his flushed associate. Whichever way the cards fell there would be only one winner; Marlow Bancroft would take the real prize, the prize of several hundred pounds.

Mother and Father, she could hear them talking in the living room. Eyes closed, Alyssa lay still. Soon Father and the others would set out for the colliery and in a while Mother would come to wake Thea and herself. Thea would be cuddled and kissed awake while she would be given just a call. Warm tears squeezed beneath tight-shut eyelids, if her mother would kiss and cuddle her. 'Only once, Mother, just once, let me feel loved like Thea...'

A voice pitched higher than a moment since halted the thought. Father was angry ... but he never got angry ... yet Mother was crying... Mother was crying! Eyes suddenly wide open, Alyssa made to rise. What was wrong with her legs, why did they feel so heavy, why couldn't she move?

'Father!' Turning her head towards the door, the cry died on her lips. This was not the bedroom she shared with Thea...!

Memory terrifyingly clear flooded her brain, sweeping away the half-dreams. Women had run screaming from her, they had left her in the middle of nowhere ... the heat, the thirst, the darkness. Then there had been a man, he had stood beside her ... or had that been an hallucination, a last hope of a mind falling into unconsciousness?

But she was not unconscious now. Mists completely cleared from her brain, Alyssa tried again to move then froze at sight of the figure coming towards her.

Highlighted by the flames of a small fire, it pranced, its movements accompanied by a drone of words she could not understand. Closer it came and closer until it stood over her. Throat locked with fear, Alyssa stared at a face showing clearly now, but it was a face carved from wood, a mask set about with an abundance of feathers and small bones. Through slits cut into the mask a pair of eyes glittered, the flickering flames of the fire revealing a body daubed with patterns of grey-white streaks which seemed to slither like snakes along an arm as it was raised above the feathered headdress – and glinting in the hand, a dagger!

No! Alyssa felt the cry she could not make. Her petrified stare followed the movements of the gleaming blade scything the air as the figure began to prance again. All around her it moved, first bending then straightening, the knife slashing and slicing within inches of every part of her body and all the time came the low chanting of strange words.

This man, for rocked as her mind was with fear, Alyssa knew this was what the dancing figure had to be, he must have found her where those women had left her, had rescued her only to kill her, as part of some unspeakable heathen ritual.

Then he was still. Terror refusing to release its grip, Alyssa stared at the figure which seemed somehow to have become part of the fire, the

313

light of it glancing from feathers, from glistening skin. Then he was bending over her, the closeness filling her nostrils with a pungent odour of leaves and herbs.

'Lemanja.' The word spilled on a breath. 'Lemanja,' he smiled again, the dagger touching her breast.

They would be at Bancroft's place by early evening. Paul Tarn watched the sprinkling diamonds of sunlight sparkle on sapphire waters. Richard Morgan had tried to prevent his coming to Morant but had relented at his insistence that by being a British citizen on British soil, and moreover one not accused or suspected of any wrongdoing, he had the right to go anywhere he wished. Morgan had realised that, short of having him placed under arrest, there was little else but to have Paul travel with him and so had provided him a place in the launch the Governor had placed at the Inspector's disposal along with several members of the island's militia. The Governor had taken Morgan's report very seriously. The explanation had been given over a lunch of fresh lobster. The Act of Emancipation granting freedom from slavery had been passed in 1834, and as a result, in no part of the British Empire, would the buying and selling of one man by another be tolerated. As for white slaving, the selling of women and sometimes boys into sexual slavery, that carried promise of the direst penalty of law.

So why, given what he suspected, given the evidence of those diaries, why had Morgan not arrested Bancroft sooner?

314

Cracking a lobster claw and scooping out the juicy flesh, the Inspector had savoured the last of his meal before answering.

'Hearsay.' He had dabbed his mouth with a pristine table napkin. *'Any competent lawyer would claim what we had heard was simply hearsay, that Farnell's claims were no more than a man out to save his own neck; as for the diaries, who was to say they had in truth been written by Felicia Bancroft? They might as easily have been written by anyone. No, Mister Tarn, evidence was what was needed, irrefutable evidence, and that we have, the evidence of four young English girls taken by a British gunboat from a ship owned by one Yusuf-el-Abdullah. Knowing his arrest could lead to an international incident very probably not welcomed by the British Government, Abdullah freely admitted to having bought his "cargo" from Marlow Bancroft and as a gesture of goodwill handed the captain a document of sale signed by Bancroft.'*

'Hadn't that been a risky thing to do, signing a paper showing the sale of women?'

Sitting in the launch, the touch of breeze tempering the heat of the sun, Paul remembered Morgan's smile on hearing the question.

'Cunning is as cunning does,' Morgan had answered. *'As I see it, Bancroft wanted money, Yusuf wanted a receipt. One went with the other or no deal. Abdullah was aware of the possibilities of being caught – a receipt would prove he had not kidnapped those girls.'*

'But he was still taking them against their will.'

Sipping at coffee into which he had stirred several spoonfuls of sugar, the Inspector had mulled on the question before saying quietly,

315

'The will of a woman is not always respected in our own country, Mister Tarn. Who is to say the same is not so in the country of Yusuf-el-Abdullah?'

Who indeed! Paul's gaze travelled across crystal-clear waters to a palm-fringed bay, the words spat by Edward Farnell burning in his mind:

Ask about the girl he raped...

How much had *her* will been respected!

29

The knife had not been thrust into her. Senses numb with fear, still Alyssa realised there was no pain of open wounds; she had not been cut. Nerves quivering, she lay perfectly still. The man who had cavorted around her had obviously brought her here for no other reason than to use her in some horrific rites, otherwise he would have taken her to where there were people who could speak to her in her own language.

So why had he not finished what he had begun?

A few yards away in the semidarkness, fresh fuel, fed to the fire had it blaze, the flames lighting what Alyssa saw was a small room and huddled at one side was a woman.

A woman! A first reaction to scream for help faded as the woman touched her forehead to the ground. Alyssa narrowed her eyes the better to penetrate shadows rimming the edge of firelight. What was the woman doing?

'Lemanja ... Lemanja...' Almost as though replying to a spoken question the woman straightened then touched her forehead to the ground several times, with each move calling the word in a quiet trembling voice. The woman was afraid! Alyssa's hopes of rescue died. She was as afraid as Alyssa was herself. The word she used was the same the man had spoken when holding a dagger against her breast.

But this woman was not being threatened with a dagger.

From the open doorway a puff of breeze tugged at flames, lifting them high, and in the brilliance Alyssa saw clearly. The woman was praying, praying to a figure set in a niche decorated with ferns and flowers. But where was the man?

Sensation returning slowly to her limbs, Alyssa pushed up on to her elbows. He was gone ... he was gone! But even as relief flooded warmly in her veins, the man stepped from the wall of black shadow. Enhanced by the glow he moved soundlessly to stand beside the fire and as he did so Alyssa saw the mask had been exchanged for a larger one, its eye-slits painted to look enormous, the nose and lips of exaggerated thickness and where feathers had adorned was now a small platform and stood on it a carved figurine. The face was a small replica of the mask covering the man's face but the figure was that of a woman. Naked except for waistband, wide collar and long shoulder touching earrings. Black hair drawn from an exceptionally wide forehead forming a tall cone shape topped with an elaborate array of feathers, it held in one hand the effigy of a woman while in the other what appeared to be a stalk of maize. Balanced on the head, merged with shadow, it seemed almost part of the living figure.

As though caught in a trance, unable to take her eyes from the scene, Alyssa felt her nerves jolt when from beyond the shack a bird called, its strident cry ripping the pulsing silence. Disturbed by the sound the kneeling woman rose and turned, a cry of fear loud in her throat as she saw the figure. The play of light touching patterns of grey-white stippled over the entire effigy giving the appearance of movement.

'Lemanja...' the woman gasped, falling at the man's feet her hands pressed to her face. 'Lemanja, Mamma Spirit, Lemanja, a big Spirit, Mamma no hurt ... no hurt.'

For a moment the man did not move, then, painted snakes gliding across his shoulders and chest, he raised one arm. Lifted above his head an object glittered in his hand before becoming lost in shadow. But she had glimpsed it. Sickness catching at her throat, Alyssa's eyes shut tight. She had seen the knife.

The woman had been able to move. Thought filtered slowly past the horror holding Alyssa's brain. Why then had she not tried to escape, why kneel there waiting for the knife to fall?

Compelling, demanding an answer, Alyssa reluctantly opened her eyes. The woman still knelt but now the blade flashed just inches from her head.

...no hurt ... no hurt...

The words shone like a beacon in Alyssa's mind. English! Nerves which had been frozen with fear

318

suddenly throbbed. The woman had spoken in English and the man ... he must also have an understanding of it. Realisation building hope, Alyssa tried to call out but the words remained trapped in a throat parched and swollen from thirst.

Please, please look this way ... please help me! Every fibre of her being projected the thought. At the edge of the fire, lit by flame, she saw the knife set aside and the woman rise to her feet.

Don't go ... please don't leave me here.

It seemed the unspoken plea had reached its goal, for the woman's head turned. Holding her breath Alyssa stared at the face, its mahogany skin bronzed by reflected flames shining like brown gold, but no response gleamed in the black eyes.

Please ... you have to help me! Alyssa's eyes shouted their entreaty but already the face was turned from her. The woman removing a bead necklace from her neck giving it to the man who examined it by the light from the fire before draping it about the carved figurine balanced on his head.

Was the necklace the price of that woman's life? Was it payment? Fixed to the scene being played out before her, Alyssa watched the pair. Would the man let the woman go free? And she herself, Alyssa, did she have something he would take in exchange for her freedom? The coins ... the few coins in her pocket, maybe...! Trying to reach for them she fell back, her strength not returned enough to support her on one elbow.

The man was moving again, sliding in and out of the light, grey-painted patterns silvered by the glow slithering and sliding over a glistening body which seemed to have become part of the dancing flames. Round and round the woman he danced, a singing chant barely audible above the crackle of burning wood until, a harsh cry ripping from his throat, he jerked to a stop, his body taut and rigid. With the stillness came silence, a deep unearthly smothering of all sound.

It could have been a painting on canvas. The fire burned without sound ... the two figures stood motionless, even the flames no longer flickered and danced.

It was then it came.

Barely brushing the silence, hardly a touch on the deathlike stillness, yet unmistakable, a sound circled the room.

New fear adding to the stricture in her throat, Alyssa's nerves tightened. They must hear it also, yet seemingly locked in trance neither the man nor woman moved.

A rustle of breeze disturbing dried leaves? An animal burrowing among the tall grass? Ears honed to the sound, Alyssa listened.

It was nearer now, a sibilant breath sighing among the shadow. No ... no... More than a breath ... a word.

'Damballah.'

Beyond the rim of firelight something seemed to slither, a gliding pricking the stillness.

'Damballah.'

It flicked the darkness.

'Damballah.'

It kissed the shadows:

'Damballah!'

Loud and harsh it rang on the silence and like a puppet answering the pull of strings the man stretched a hand towards the woman, a hand which held a carved snake.

'Damballah.' He spoke tonelessly, the words seeming to come from outside himself. 'Damballah, Seeker of Vengeance ... drum sing, Damballah come.'

The woman accepted the object, the tension broke and flames pluming upwards showed her turning away into the swallowing darkness.

No ... please...! Alyssa's silent cry followed the disappearing figure then froze in her mind as the man, knife once more in hand, moved slowly towards her.

A few minutes only! Flanked by the militia, Paul walked alongside the Police Inspector. The man had not wanted to grant what was asked, arguing that should Bancroft get wind of what was happening he would probably make a run for it. And go where? Paul had counter-argued. Even should he evade the soldiers, wasn't the harbour blockaded by a gunboat? And as for hiding out in the dense forests skirting the distant mountains, Marlow Bancroft was too fond of life's comforts to stick that for any length of time. The reasoning or the heat? Paul was not certain which had eventually overcome the policeman's objection, resulting in the agreement that Paul would be given five minutes to speak alone with Bancroft. It would be enough! Lips set tight Paul's mind reverberated with his self-made promise. It would be enough time for Bancroft to answer a question or choke to death on the refusal!

'I would have expected to see a few more people than we have,' Inspector Richard Morgan commented. 'But then with dusk it's too dark to work the fields.'

That he could understand. Paul walked on without answer. Sharp-bladed scythes were not things to be using in half-light and with the day's work over people would want to be in their homes. Would Bancroft be home? The question had not occurred before and now that it had Paul felt a momentary uncertainty. Both he and Morgan had enquired after Bancroft's place; had someone informed him of their asking questions? Had the man already skipped the island?

'Bancroft is more of a fool than I took him for!' Coming to a standstill, Richard Morgan stared at the house. Tinted rose by the lowering sun, it stood proud against a backdrop of green guarded by violet-crowned mountains, a cascade of jewel-bright colours of sunset gleaming off tall un-shuttered windows. 'Yes.' Morgan nodded slowly. 'The man is an absolute fool risking the loss of this along with Bancroft Hall. He should have been made work hard for a few years then he would have appreciated just what it was his father passed on to him.'

Would he? Paul mused, his own glance taking in the beautiful 'great house'. Work of any kind was anathema to the likes of Marlow Bancroft; he would only work hard at avoiding work.

'Remember, Mister Tarn, five minutes, then I come in.'

The house was as gracious inside as out.

322

Having stepped from the veranda into a wide room, Paul's glance took in brocaded sofas, wide armchairs, gleaming walnut tables and cabinets filled with porcelain. So there was still a little wealth left. Given the gossip that had come from Bancroft Hall, the tales of Marlow selling everything of any value, it was surprising this house was not stripped of its contents – but servants? It was strangely empty of them.

Conscious of the seconds of those allotted five minutes ticking by, he crossed the room to a spacious hall off which a broad staircase wound in a half-circle.

Would Bancroft be up there, taking a nap before dinner? With nobody to ask, he would simply have to look for himself.

Reaching the head of the stairs he hesitated as a muffled sob caught his attention. Alyssa! The thought a cannon shot in his mind, he thrust back a partly opened door. It was not Alyssa ... but then could he truly have expected to find her here!

Across what he saw now was a bedroom a young woman was smoothing a pillow. Her yellow dress hung from thin shoulders and a bright blue cloth was wound about her head. A housemaid, at last someone he could ask if Bancroft was here in this house. About to put thought to word, he was forestalled by the woman's gasp as she caught sight of him. She stared through sloe-shaped eyes filled with tears that spilled over her cheeks. To Paul's surprise he saw that her eyes held more than tears; they held hate.

'Wait!' He called sharply, one hand reaching towards the obviously frightened figure, but he was pushed aside the woman darting headlong for the stairs.

What on earth had her so terrified? Paul glanced at the bed she had been smoothing, then at the rest of the room. There was no one in here yet something had made the woman afraid and tearful.

'Don't you bloody tell me no!'

Bancroft! Paul spun in the direction of the shout.

'No bloody nigger boy tells me no!'

A scream of pain followed the angry shout. Paul shot out of the bedroom into a thickly carpeted corridor interspersed with closed doors. Which one? Which one hid Bancroft?

'If 'e don't know 'ow to play with it then p'raps it should be teken off 'im.'

'Yes, Bancroft, tek it off 'im, then Pastow can show 'ow it be done, it was 'im won the card game, it be 'im gets the prize.'

Bancroft wasn't alone. Paul followed the sound of voices. He wasn't alone in kind either, judging by what was said and the coarse laughter coming after it. Flies gathered around rotten meat!

'You hear me, nigger boy, you do what I says to do or I slice off the means and have your bitch of a woman roast them; then I'll watch while you eat every last bit!'

'No, Massa ... it wrong...'

Words giving way to a scream and the crack of a whip Paul smashed a boot against a door, sending it crashing inward anger rearing at the sight meeting his eyes.

Naked, splayed across a table with her wrists and

ankles tied to the legs, a girl sobbed and standing before her a man the brown skin of his unclothed body glistening red with blood running from the lacerated weals across his back and chest.

'What in God's name!' Almost unbelieving what he looked at, Paul felt his anger turn to white-hot rage.

'You!' Bancroft had turned at the sound of crashing wood. Now he stared at Paul. 'Get out ... get off my property, or do you want me to help you leave?'

The warning was clear as the menace of the flicking whip but wrath a passion driving him, Paul had already sprinted the distance between them snatching the whip into his own hand.

'Release the woman, release her now or do you want *me* to help *you* do it.' Slowly each word matching the threat facing him a moment before, Paul flicked the tip of plaited leather bringing it to sting Bancroft's clenched fist.

'That was a mistake.' Marlow's cold grey eyes blazed black ice. 'Now we will cut your balls off and feed them to the pigs along with the rest of you.'

30

He would kill her now. He would plunge the knife into her body and kill her. Fear a drug holding her limbs in a frozen trancelike state, Alyssa stared at the man who came to stand over her, the flicker of firelight lending life to the lines painted on his body until it seemed they slithered like so many snakes along his arms and across his chest. If she could reach the few coins in her pocket, if she could show them to him, then maybe he would take them in exchange for her life, spare her as he had spared the woman.

'Lemanja...'

No more than a whisper it brushed the flame-lit silence.

'Lemanja...'

Trapped in her world of fear, Alyssa looked into eyes glittering down on her, eyes of living jet, eyes devoid of any pity or any understanding other than that of sacrifice.

'Lemanja ... great mamma spirit...'

Mesmerised by terror Alyssa watched the knife rise. Held high over the feathered head it seemed to draw the light of the flames to itself, to absorb it until the blade gleamed like a slim shaft of lightning, while around its haft grey-painted fingers coiled like miniature serpents. Then it was moving. Glittering silver, it sliced the shadows cleaving a shimmering trail through a darkness so heavy so stifling Alyssa felt the breath pressed from her lungs.

'Lemanja come.'

Louder than before the man's cry echoed on the night, then faded into silence as the hand swept down, carrying the glistening blade to Alyssa's heart.

The darkness was gone. Where the flames of a fire had leaped now only a dull red glow gleamed in a circle of charcoaled earth – and the man...?

Alyssa's glance swept the room. The man who had brandished the knife, why had he not thrust it into her? Was what she had suffered already simply a prelude, a beginning to some longer drawn-out ritual? And where was he now? Was he so certain of her drugged state he had left her alone? Senses now more alert, Alyssa stared into the greyness afforded by a shaft of pale light entering through the open doorway. Was he gone or was he just outside?

Pinpricks of pain stabbed her sluggish limbs as Alyssa forced them to move. She must take a chance. If she could escape from this place, get beyond it to the fields then surely someone would help her. Lips compressed against the sting of complaining muscle, she pushed to her feet, swaying from the sudden swirl inside her head. A moment to steady herself, just a moment and then—

'Drink!'

Eyelids which had closed against the swimming in her head flew open. Alyssa catching her breath at sight of a figure silhouetted against the stream of pallid light. He was here, the man who had danced and pranced about her, who had thrust a knife to her breast ... he was still here.

'Drink!' One stride carrying him into the room, he thrust a hollowed-out gourd at Alyssa.

She must not drink, whatever was in that shell would be laced with the drug which had kept her helpless for so long. If she had to die then so be it, but she would not swallow that drug. Determination lending strength, she struck at the hand knocking the gourd to the ground.

327

What would he do now? Alyssa stared at the doorway, empty now the man had left. Would he bring more of the drug, force her to drink? To struggle would be of little use; her strength had been sapped by heat, thirst and fear, so much so she could have no chance against him nor would she have any chance now of escape.

'Missee drink.'

The gasp turning to a sob, Alyssa's legs folded to leave her in a huddled heap on the ground.

'Missee need drink.'

It was soft, a blend of sympathy cushioning the words. It was a woman's voice! Hardly daring to believe what her brain was telling her Alyssa raised her head.

'Water clean ... no hurt.' A cloth bound about the head, bone earrings dangling from her ears a woman smiled offering a similar gourd to that dashed from the man's hand. 'Water ... no hurt,' she repeated, then lifting the gourd to her own mouth she drank from it.

She would not drink if the contents were drugged; what purpose would that serve when together the man and this woman could so easily overpower her. Reason overriding doubt, Alyssa took the container, tears of relief trickling down her cheeks as the deliciously cool water eased her parched throat.

Every drop drained, Alyssa handed the empty gourd to the waiting woman, her whispered thanks a murmur in the stillness.

Reaching a hand to Alyssa's elbow the woman urged her to her feet, saying quietly, 'Missee go now.'

Go! Alyssa stared at a face that the strengthening light showed was deep honey-brown, at the large burnt-toffee eyes that pleaded trust.

'Missee go ... *now.*'

A tug at her arm pulling her forward, Alyssa stumbled from the room blinking at the pink pearl of a dawn sky which momentarily robbed her of sight. Then as vision returned she saw the man. Stood in the centre of a small clearing the trees and bushes enclosing it draped with bits and pieces of coloured cloths beginning to flutter in the breeze of morning, he watched her. The woman had said for her to go but would he prevent it? Throat tightening, Alyssa grasped the woman's hand as coal-dark eyes remained fastened on her. Then the painted man lifted one arm.

'Lemanja, great mamma spirit ... Lemanja keep safe.'

It droned against her brain like the hum of some giant bee, droned as he pressed a small hard object into her palm, then with no further sound he disappeared into the hut.

Why had she been taken to that place if not to be offered in pagan ritual? Why had the man let her leave? Why had he given her this gift? Question upon question stumbled through Alyssa's mind, matching the stumble of her feet as she followed after the woman gliding quickly into the screening vegetation.

'Wait please.' Still weak from the ordeal of the past hours Alyssa halted. 'I ... I have to rest.'

The woman shook her turbaned head, setting the bone earrings swinging. 'Not rest ... go.'

In the haste of leaving she had not realised this woman was the same one who had been in that hut the night before, a woman who, she realised, had some understanding of the English language. Relief coursing through her, Alyssa dragged cool air into her lungs before asking could the woman take her to the Bancroft plantation.

Eyes dark as treacle flashed like warning beacons. The bone earrings banged against her neck as the woman's head swung vigorously. 'Not go,' she said, 'not go great house, massa be there.'

Master ... Marlow Bancroft? He owned the plantation mentioned in the letter given her by a maid from Bancroft Hall, the same letter which had advised she bring Thea away from Jamaica; had it also meant she must bring her away from Marlow Bancroft?

'You don't understand.' She resisted the pull of the woman's hand. 'I have to go there, I have to find my sister.'

'No.' Deep-brown eyes beamed the same warning. 'Not go, massa hurt, massa cruel.'

Was the woman saying she would be in danger going to the plantation, that she might come to harm?

'Not go Beau-Ideal!' The woman tugged again.

'Not go where?'

Alyssa's frown revealing lack of understanding, the woman answered in quick short phrases showing deep agitation. 'Beau-Ideal Bancroft great house not good place ... massa not good man ... massa hurt with whip ... must not find missee ... others say you be *duppie* ... ghost ... but Lem'll bring you to Obeah man, he know you not *duppie*.

330

He call Lemanja keep missee safe, knife cut away power of evil...' She caught at Alyssa's hand, touching a finger to the tiny wooden figurine cradled in her palm, saying reverently, 'Lemanja.'

So the man had not intended to kill her! The knife he had touched against her body had been an instrument of magic, a power called upon to counteract evil. A warm flush not entirely due to the growing heat glowed pink on Alyssa's cheeks. He had thought only to help, to protect her, while she had thought him a murderer. But what of Thea? Had the Obeah man given an amulet to her ... had she already returned home to England? There was only one way to find out. She must face Marlow Bancroft.

'Sister.' She touched her hair as the woman pulled again urging her to walk on. 'My sister, her hair is the same colour as mine. She might be at the place you call Beau-Ideal. Please, I have to go there.'

Had the woman understood? Had it been too difficult for her to grasp? Alyssa could only hope as she followed the flash of yellow dress weaving among tall ferns.

Where had she brought her? This was no house ... the woman could not have understood after all.

'Missee sister.'

'No, please try to understand.' Alyssa shook her head in frustration. 'Beau-Ideal, I need to go to Beau-Ideal, my sister...'

'Not Beau-Ideal.' Tears glistened in soft brown eyes glinting like dew on almost ripened black-berries. 'Missee sister not at Beau-Ideal, missee sister there.' Pointing to a mound of earth on

331

which was planted a replica of the carving still held in Alyssa's hand, she dropped to her knees touching her forehead to the ground.

Thea was here? Alyssa stared at the encircling forest. Did she have a house somewhere among the trees? About to put the question she hesitated as the woman lifted a small pot from in front of the carved figure, then rising to her feet, tears still sparkling she handed the pot to Alyssa.

Round like a bowl, unglazed and rough to the touch, the lid topped by a pottery version of the goddess Lemanja, Alyssa held it. What was she supposed to do? Not wishing to offend the woman whose help she still needed if she were to find Thea she tilted her head enquiringly.

'Missee look.' The woman's glance rested a fraction on the pot then lifted back to Alyssa. 'Missee look, see sister.'

Another ritual, another act of magic. The smile coming to Alyssa's lips died to be replaced by a frown as she removed the lid. There in the belly of the pot, gleaming red-gold, was a coil of hair.

Standing there beside the mound of earth Alyssa felt the world sway while the woman talked quietly of how Thea had been abused by Marlow Bancroft and his friends. How when she had fallen ill of fever he had thrown her from the house. Lemuel, the woman's husband, had taken her to the Obeah man but his magic had failed to save her. She had died and been brought to this place. The few belongings she had with her had been placed in the pot so the spirits could identify her and carry her home.

It was Thea's grave! Her sister lay beneath that black mound. She had come too late! Sickness thickening her throat Alyssa picked up the soft gleaming hair and saw the blue bead necklace it had covered. That more than the lock of hair said 'Thea'. It had been a gift from James. He had taken them both to the fair the Easter it had visited Darlaston and there had paid sixpence for two necklaces. A green one for Alyssa and he had laughed as he placed it about her neck. And a blue one for Thea, a necklace Thea had worn when she had run away from home and now it lay here in a small pot set to mark her grave. Tears falling freely, she picked up the necklace, its glass beads glinting in the sun where they fell like blue water between her fingers.

'Thea...' she sobbed, pressing the necklace to her lips. 'Oh Thea...'

'Missee come now.' Urgency definite in her tone the woman glanced to where the trees stood thick and folding as heavy green curtains. Then agitation making her movements sharp she took the pot from Alyssa, and reaching to the bottom extracted several coins which had lain beneath hair and the blue necklace.

'Spirits not need.' A brief shake of the head accompanying the words she pressed the coins into Alyssa's empty palm, then reached for the necklace still twined about the fingers of the other hand.

'No!' Her reply a sob, Alyssa caught the gleaming strand to her breast. 'This is all I have of my sister, all that is left of Thea ... I want to keep it, to keep a little of Thea with me.'

'Not take.' The earrings swung gently. 'Lemanja need … take missee Thea home.'

The earnest appeal, the eyes alight with belief, caught at Alyssa. The man who had used a knife to cut away the evil he thought surrounded her, who had given her a tiny carving believing it to provide protection, and this woman who though obviously afraid was helping her – they trusted in their religion, took comfort from it. Beads and idols! Paintings and plaster saints! Where was the difference when both could provide comfort? And where was the difference in her taking the necklace or leaving it in a pot on the ground? There was none. She did not need a string of beads to remember her sister. Thea would always be with her in her heart. That was her comfort. Despite the hurt still smarting Alyssa smiled and released the necklace. God keep you, Thea. The prayer silent in her heart, she watched the lid replaced and the pot returned to its position before the idol and the woman's reverent touching of her forehead to the ground, then as she rose and began to walk away Alyssa looked once more at the mound of dark earth, a final murmur soft on her lips. 'You will find David with our parents and brothers; love him, Thea … love your son.'

At the edge of the tiny clearing the yellow dress stood bold against deep green foliage, the blue turban bobbing like the head of some exotic bird, but it was the urgency behind the quiet call had Alyssa leave the simple grave.

They must have walked for hours leading her through a maze of uncultivated land, occasionally halting cautioning silence by touching a

334

finger to her lips. But where were they going? Alyssa sucked greedily at air too hot to soothe the ache in her lungs, feeling only the cracked dryness of her lips and throat, the pain in legs threatening to give way beneath her.

'See ... Missee go.'

The woman's words, merged with her own cry for rest, were momentarily lost to Alyssa; it was only when they were repeated that she became aware that they had cleared the trees. They were now standing on a slope of land that dropped away to a long stretch of beach fringed by a line of buildings from which men were carrying cargo to several small boats waiting to ferry it out to a ship stood off in deeper water. A port! Alyssa stared at the scene. The woman had guided her to a port!

Catching at her hand the woman touched the coins Alyssa had not realised she still clutched, then pointed again towards the sea. 'Missee go boat,' she smiled, 'missee go own place.'

'But these are yours.' Alyssa held out the several sovereigns. 'You earned them trying to help my sister ... by helping me.'

'Not good.' The blue turban bobbed vigorously. 'Lem'ull an' Sara no can have coin ... massa know, he whip Lem'ull an' Sara, he whip bad, say Lem'ull an' Sara steal. Missee keep.' She pushed away the hand holding the money. 'Missee go, not come Beau-Ideal more time.'

'I–' Beginning to protest Alyssa broke off, following the woman's suddenly terrified gaze. A tall and bronzed man, sun-bleached hair glinting in the strong light, was striding up the rise towards them.

'I won't let him hurt–' The rest died on her lips for the woman was gone, a fleeting glimpse of yellow disappearing like a sunbeam lost among the trees.

31

'You will need to cut mine off first and then those of the men come along with me.'

Sitting in a hansom driving him the final stage of his journey back to Lyndon, Paul's mind returned as it so often had to the evening he had gone with Richard Morgan and the men of the militia to Beau-Ideal.

Stood on the remnants of the splintered door the Police Inspector's face had registered disgust.

'Gentlemen.' He had glanced at each of Bancroft's associates whose brows were drawn with incomprehension at the rapid turn of events. *'Unless you, with Mister Bancroft, wish to avail yourselves of a cell in one of Her Majesty's prisons I suggest you leave now.'*

There had been no need of a second invitation. Paul smiled grimly at the memory of the undignified scramble to be first out of the house. But grim as it was even that smile faded when memory forged on.

Blood oozing from wounds criss-crossing his back and legs, dark head dropped to his chest, limbs quivering with fear, the man who had refused to obey Bancroft had whimpered, *'Not do, Massa ... be wrong.'*

How many men would have had the courage of that one, the courage to face the whip rather than rape a helpless girl? She had been only a girl. His glance on trees donning the first amber colours of early autumn, Paul saw only the face he had seen look at him as he had untied the cords holding her wrists and ankles. Scarcely more than a child, she had gazed with eyes blank with terror while he had wrapped her in a cover snatched from a bed, a girl who had sobbed out how she had been duped into coming to Jamaica by the promise of becoming lady's maid to the mistress of the house. But after witnessing scenes of cruelty and abuse she had asked to be returned home to England. It was then she had been strapped to a table, Bancroft ordering a field hand to rape her. Accused of treating his workers like slaves he had laughed they were free to leave at any time.

'Free as this young girl was free?'

'You have no evidence.' Marlow had met the question with contempt. *'Who will believe scum willing to sell their souls for a shilling?'*

Richard Morgan had shouted for a house servant to take the injured man and the girl, telling a thin woman in a yellow dress and blue headcover who came to the room to care for both. She had looked at him, Paul remembered. She had looked at him with eyes filled with a question he had not then understood.

'An English judge and jury will believe,' he had resumed as the man and girl were helped from the room. *'They will believe the several English women I have had removed from a boat belonging to*

Yusuf-el-Abdullah. They will believe the bill of sale signed by yourself and now in my possession; they will believe information given me in England that you engage in white slaving.'

'Information, pah!' Bancroft had snorted indifference. *'The word of Farnell, a man guilty of stealing another's identity ... how far do you think that will take you?'*

'Mmm.' Richard Morgan had pursed his lips. *'Maybe not quite as far as what can be added to it.'*

Bancroft had laughed aloud. *'Added by whom? Another little genie from your magic lamp?'*

Morgan had waited for the laugh to subside then as Bancroft turned his back had said quietly, *'No, Mister Bancroft, no genie and no magic lamp, just a couple of diaries and your mother.'*

'My mother!' Contempt replaced with an anger wreathing his face, Marlow had breathed the words. *'My mother told you?'*

'Only the place you might be found, the rest was in the diaries written by your wife.'

'Felicia!' The answer had snarled across the room. *'I should have killed her here in Jamaica, not waited to do it in England. As for my darling mother, I should have killed her long ago.'*

Taking a slim volume from the pocket of his coat Richard Morgan had identified himself as an Inspector of Police, stating that Bancroft was to be taken to England to face charges of white slaving and the further probable charge of murdering his wife.

But Marlow Bancroft would never stand in the dock of any court.

Paul leaned his head against the upholstery of

338

the carriage, his closed eyes seeing again the images they watched almost nightly.

Darkness had fallen with the abrupt speed of the tropics no twilight lowering the day gently into night, no lingering of a sun loath to set but simply a breath-snatching blaze of glory and then a sky of velvet black in which a million stars twinkled.

The militia had pointed out the hazard of sailing during the hours of darkness and Morgan had seen the impracticality of it, agreeing they remain at Beau-Ideal until morning. There had been no minutes alone with Bancroft, nor would the opportunity to speak privately with him occur, for he was to spend the night under guard and next day be taken to Kingston to be formally charged in the presence of the Governor. But the question gnawing inside demanded to be asked. It was after dinner and Bancroft was drinking heavily of the island's second product, rum. Potent and heady its bouquet permeated the close air of the dining room prompting the Inspector to suggest a move to the veranda.

Bancroft had sprawled into a low bamboo chair. The memory was so vivid Paul seemed to feel the soft balmy breeze feather against his brow and to smell the perfume of flowers as intoxicating as wine, but over it all the memory of the sheer rancour in the look Bancroft had thrown at him. Unveiled the malice had blazed, a ferocious devil-inspired savagery finding its equal in words snarled as from a caged animal.

'Our friend the Inspector has told us the reason of his gracious visit to Beau-Ideal but you, Tarn ... why

are you here?'

With the question, though quietly spoken, Bancroft's vengeance had become palpable, a malignity whose pulse seemed to throb in the gloom, an evil waiting for fulfilment.

'I came to ask the whereabouts of Alyssa Maybury.'

In the secrecy of his mind Paul heard again the triumph blatant in the man's reply.

'Aah!' He had looked over the rim of his glass his eyes glittering hate. *'The girl with the red-gold hair... the slut, a wanton redhead you ... your sister... were so concerned for.'*

'She came here.' Paul had mastered the urge to slam a fist into the mocking face. *'I was told so by a planter at Mandeville, it was he had her put in a cart which would pass this place so don't bother with denials.'*

'Denials?' Bancroft had smiled. *'Why would I deny it? Yes, she came but she is here no longer.'*

'Then where?'

Bancroft had heard the anxiety behind those words, his relish of it a deep flavour in his reply.

'Out there.' He had waved his glass, a dismissive gesture.

'You see, the slut had the bad manners to die while I was visiting friends.'

Alyssa Maybury was dead!

Paul stared through the window of the carriage. The sneer on Bancroft's face had been too much and the fist which had bunched at the sudden pain of hearing those words had landed a blow hurling him and the chair across the veranda. But satisfaction had been no healer, the pain had gone on … it was with him still.

The punch may have been unexpected but it had done nothing to curb Bancroft's insolent mockery. That he would not be convicted of any wrongdoing had been an obvious belief, a belief sustained by several more glasses of rum; then the sound of a drum beginning to beat somewhere in the darkness had him smash his glass irritably into the shadows.

'*A ceremony?*' Inspector Richard Morgan had turned a glance towards the sound.

'*Some might call it that.*' Bancroft had risen to his feet. '*I call it a nuisance; bloody witch doctor and his ju-ju spells. The locals believe in Obeah … witchcraft. In exchange for a gift they are given a voodoo token designed to protect them against* Duppies *… ghosts … or in some cases as a means of gaining revenge against someone who has caused them harm. The most drastic is what they call* Mbissimo Pasio *… Soul of the Flesh … with this they have the guarantee their chosen victim will die – but don't let that keep you awake … ju-ju has no effect upon white men.*'

Saying his goodnights he had taken a key from his pocket and handed it to Morgan. '*To my bedroom,*' he had sneered, '*you may wish to lock me in … or perhaps Tarn could sleep there … a dog at the feet of the master.*'

Next morning they had found Marlow Bancroft dead.

But how? Inspector Richard Morgan was baffled. He had locked that bedroom door himself, had kept the key in his own pocket, had set a guard on the veranda below the window, yet on unlocking the room next morning had found

341

the man dead in bed. A purpling weal bruised his throat and his eyes screamed terror as they stared sightlessly at a snake the morning sun glinting on wooden coils.

The house servants had been summoned and watching the girl in the yellow dress Paul felt instinctively he knew the reason for the fear she had shown on seeing him watch her bent over this same bed.

'...*the locals believe in Obeah...*'

The words of Marlow Bancroft had been stark in their illumination. The girl believed in magic. The wooden snake was a voodoo object ... she had not just smoothed a pillow, she had placed that fetish beneath it.

So Police Inspector Morgan had returned to England empty handed but he Paul Tarn had remained a while longer at Beau-Ideal. Why? To ensure the plantation continued with some semblance of order until a new owner took over. So he had told himself yet he had known there was a deeper reason. Beau-Ideal was the last place Alyssa Maybury had been and some deep-felt tie kept him there. But finally had come the realisation he must return to England.

He had gone to speak with the man Bancroft had whipped, asking could he perform the task of overseeing the plantation, saying he himself would take all responsibility for the appointment.

'*Yes, Massa, Lemu'll do.*' A straw hat twisting between his brown fingers, the man had nodded.

'*Not Massa, it is Mister Tarn, and I thank you for your help, Mister Lemuel.*'

Paul smiled to himself recalling the look of total

surprise which had crossed the man's face, a look quickly followed by one of gratitude and pride. Maybe for the first time Lemuel had been addressed with civility.

Turning back towards the house gleaming white against a curtain of green he had hesitated. Somewhere among that lushness Alyssa Maybury was buried. If he could visit the grave, make an offering of flowers...

Calling the man to return he had wondered how to make him understand; there were so few words he appeared to understand.

'Mister Lemuel.' He had paused, searching for the rest, then his hands augmenting his words he had continued. *'Woman,'* he had outlined the curved shape of a female. *'Hair,'* he had touched his own head, *'colour...'*

But how to demonstrate colour? Did Lemuel have even the faintest knowledge of what he was attempting to convey?

The sky! He had pointed upward only to see a puzzled look cross the other man's face. Then in the hedge sunlight had glinted on a beautiful plant, its scarlet trumpet-shaped blossoms streaked with gold. Repeating the process of description he lastly pointed to the flower and Lemuel had nodded.

It was no more than a mound of black earth. The roughly carved figure of a woman placed on a wooden platform, one hand holding another female effigy while the other held a stalk of maize.

'Lemanja...' Lemuel had whispered reverently, touching his forehead to the ground. Then respect

paid and again on his feet, he had pointed out a small pot set in the ground before the idol, repeatedly pointing from it to Paul indicating he should pick it up.

It had held a lock of red-gold hair.

32

Bancroft had not lied. Alyssa Maybury had died and she was buried in a plot bordering Beau-Ideal. Soon he would have to tell that to Laura and to Joseph Richardson.

The carriage driving him home to Lyndon bumped over uneven setts bringing Paul's glance once more to its dusty window. In the distance a tall black spire received the blessing of sunset. St Bartholomew's church ... and across from it Hall End Cottage.

A lurch strong as the jolt of the carriage heaved at Paul's stomach. Alyssa Maybury had been happy in that house, happy as anyone in her straits could have been; that then was the place to say a final goodbye. Leaning forward he re-directed the carriage driver.

Lemuel and Sara. How much they had both risked in helping her, taking her first to the hut of the Obeah man and from there to the port. She had tried to tell Sara she would not be hurt but the woman had fled, only her frightened whisper 'not come Beau-Ideal more time' lingering in the

344

sweltering heat. It had been a warning, a warning not to approach Marlow Bancroft. But to leave without justice for Thea! The thought had burned as she stared at the figure striding towards her.

Bathed in the gentle warmth of early evening Alyssa allowed her memory to wander.

He had reached the crest of the rise of ground, a short whip tapping a leather boot. His sharp eyes raking over her as he growled she was asking for trouble coming to the beach alone.

Trouble! Despite the pain of learning of Thea's death, of the circumstances leading up to it, despite her aching head and limbs, of the weariness induced by a long trek through what had seemed to be interminable undergrowth with every spiky bush and branch scratching at face and arms, of tall grass alive with sounds of creatures she could not see, Alyssa had almost laughed. Hadn't trouble been her constant companion since being turned from her home in Darlaston?

The face regarding her with more than mild curiosity had not proved to be that of Marlow Bancroft nor indeed of anyone she had seen before, but he had frowned at her demand to be taken back to Beau-Ideal.

'*Whatever you have against Bancroft I advise you let it go. Look down there.*' He had pointed to the beach where dark-skinned figures scurried like so many ants. '*Do you know anyone down there? Do you have relatives or friends among the plantation owners? Forgive my bluntness but the state of your clothes tells me otherwise, and without that kind of assistance I fear for your chances against Bancroft.*'

She had stood for several moments staring at

the scene below, at the hurrying figures bent beneath heavy sacks, and only then had come the full realisation of how alone she was. She had no relative in Jamaica, no friend to turn to for help except Sara and Lemuel but she could not ask them to back an accusation made against a powerful plantation owner, a man who could take away their home and their livelihood. It would cause so much pain and it would not bring Thea back. In the end logic had prevailed and she had followed her adviser to the beach where he had organised her passage home, the sovereigns Sara had given her paying the fare to England and on to Wednesbury.

Going to Jamaica had been a journey of hope, a search for love, but it had proved only one more journey of heartbreak. But then was that not how it had always been for Alyssa Maybury?

Arms held tight across her chest Alyssa hugged herself against a hurt so strong it seemed to tear her soul.

A circle of dreams! That had been her life from childhood, a circle of broken dreams while fate led her on its never-ending path. She had searched for a way to her mother's love, searched until death had snatched that mother from her as it had snatched the one source of affection she had been certain of, the lives of her father and brothers. And David? The blind little boy she had loved with all her heart, he too had been taken from her.

A circle of dreams! Alyssa swallowed the sob rising to her throat. That was all life could be for Alyssa Maybury.

He had requested the hansom drive through Wednesbury town and on past the ancient smoke-blackened church to Hall End Cottage. Joseph would not mind his coming to the house he had determined not to sell. He had guessed Joseph's reasons; it would be kept against Alyssa Maybury's return. Now Paul Tarn must tell him Alyssa Maybury would never return.

Instructing the hansom wait for him, he entered the small house and stood for a moment as his vision adjusted from the brilliance of sunset to the shadowed interior. He had known the cottage so many years, knew everything it held. He let his gaze rest on chairs and dresser. Each had known his touch, known that of Alyssa Maybury.

A sound catching his attention Paul felt the quick surge of guilt. He had asked no permission to come here ... supposing Joseph had let the cottage for a term? He must apologise for his thoughtlessness and leave.

About to do so he paused, his senses flicking at another hush of sound.

Had he heard a sound or had it been a trick of the mind? Undecided he paused, then the need for apology rose strongly and he stepped into the scullery. This room too was empty. If he had indeed heard a sound it could not have come from here, so from a bedroom? But he would not go upstairs, he would return to the hansom. If anyone called after him he could apologise from the carriage.

As he half turned back towards the small living

room a fresh sound had him halt. It had not come from a bedroom but from the garden. Whoever was out there did not know of his presence, he could leave as he had come and only himself to know. But that was not his bringing up. He had trespassed on another person's privacy and for that he must give his apology. The decision reached, he walked from the scullery.

Bathed in the soft glow of an autumn sunset Alyssa felt the swell of unhappiness spilling into her throat. Paul Tarn, the man whose image came with sleep, the man she had not wanted to fall in love with. The man it had taken her so long to realise she had fallen in love with. But as with her mother that was a love she would never know returned. So often since leaving Wednesbury and on the long voyage home he had filled her thoughts; she had only to close her eyes to hear his voice in her mind, to hear it as it seemed she heard it now but then her eyes opened and her heart knew one more broken dream.

'Alyssa.' It brushed the gentle evening, a caress touching her soul. Why? She choked on a sob. Why was fate so much against her it not only robbed her of love but tormented her with the shadow of it?

Standing in the scullery doorway of Hall End Cottage Paul Tarn fought to control the swirl of the world around him. What he saw there in the garden, the gleams of sunset sparkling on red-gold hair ... Alyssa Maybury! But it was not Alyssa, how could it be, hadn't he seen...? Angry at himself, he grabbed at his rocking senses forcing a logic he did not truly want. The girl he looked at now was not real, she was a figment of imagination brought on by memories this house held. What he saw was an unreality, the product of a tired brain. Yet it seemed so real! Of all the times he had conjured her in his mind none had proved as real as this. 'Alyssa.' Logic failing in the face of desire, the name slipped from his lips and at its whisper the figure turned and across the quiet sunblessed space he saw the glint of tears reflect in deep violet eyes ... her eyes! Alyssa Maybury's eyes!

'Please ... please no more...' Crying against the pain of longing sweeping through her, Alyssa covered her face with her hands.

If this was fantasy he wanted to hold on to it, to keep the woman he loved with him if only a moment longer. Not caring he spoke only to himself, needing to say the words which for so long had lain silent in his heart. Paul Tarn murmured to the phantom, to the woman who would forever be a part of him, 'Alyssa.' Gentle as the evening air it lay on the silence. 'Alyssa, my love.'

Had the illusion answered, or was it no more than exhaustion had him see those lips move, had him hear his name come from them?

'Mister Tarn ... Paul...'

A broken sob it got no further, one stride taking him to where Alyssa was standing.

'Alyssa!' Enfolding her in his arms he held her close. 'Alyssa, my love, don't ever leave me again.'

His love! Her lips beneath his, Alyssa felt the hot tide of happiness sweep through her. Paul Tarn loved her.

Minutes later, still holding her as though afraid she might yet vanish into thin air, Paul posed the question. 'How ... I mean, Bancroft said you were dead ... I saw your grave ... the lock of hair.'

There would be time for explanation. Alyssa smiled as his mouth took her own. Time to tell him it was Thea's grave, a lock of Thea's hair he had seen. Looking into his eyes as he released her from his kiss, seeing a replica of what she had held so long in her own heart, Alyssa knew the circle had at last broken. Fate might lead her where it would but the love she shared with Paul Tarn could never be snatched from her. It was deep in her soul, a love that would live as long as she did.

The publishers hope that this book has given you enjoyable reading. Large Print Books are especially designed to be as easy to see and hold as possible. If you wish a complete list of our books please ask at your local library or write directly to:

Magna Large Print Books
Magna House, Long Preston,
Skipton, North Yorkshire.
BD23 4ND

This Large Print Book for the partially sighted, who cannot read normal print, is published under the auspices of

THE ULVERSCROFT FOUNDATION

May 2/2013